JENNY WILL EAT YOU NOW

AF814854

JENNY WILL EAT YOU NOW

GILLIAN DANIELS

solstice

London · New York · Amsterdam/Antwerp · Sydney/Melbourne · Toronto · New Delhi

First published in the United States by Gallery Books,
an imprint of Simon & Schuster, LLC, 2026
1230 Avenue of the Americas
New York, NY 10020

First published in Great Britain by Solstice Books,
an imprint of Simon & Schuster UK Ltd, 2026

Copyright © Gillian Daniels, 2026

The right of Gillian Daniels to be identified as author
of this work has been asserted in accordance with
the Copyright, Designs and Patents Act, 1988.

1 3 5 7 9 10 8 6 4 2

Simon & Schuster UK Ltd, 7th Floor,
199 Bishopsgate, London EC2M 3TY

For more than 100 years, Simon & Schuster has championed authors and the stories they create. By respecting the copyright of an author's intellectual property, you enable Simon & Schuster and the author to continue publishing exceptional books for years to come. We thank you for supporting the author's copyright by purchasing an authorised edition of this book.

No amount of this book may be reproduced or stored in any format, nor may it be uploaded to any website, database, language-learning model, or other repository, retrieval, or artificial intelligence system without express permission. All rights reserved. Enquiries may be directed to Simon & Schuster UK Ltd, 7th Floor, 199 Bishopsgate, London EC2M 3TY or RightsMailbox@simonandschuster.co.uk

Simon & Schuster Australia, Sydney
Simon & Schuster India, New Delhi

www.simonandschuster.co.uk
www.simonandschuster.com.au
www.simonandschuster.co.in

The authorised representative in the EEA is Simon & Schuster Netherlands BV, Herculesplein 96, 3584 AA Utrecht, Netherlands. info@simonandschuster.nl

Simon & Schuster strongly believes in freedom of expression and stands against censorship in all its forms. For more information, visit BooksBelong.com

A CIP catalogue record for this book is available from the British Library

Paperback ISBN: 978-1-3985-6322-3
eBook ISBN: 978-1-3985-6323-0
Audio ISBN: 978-1-3985-6324-7

This book is a work of fiction. Names, characters, places and incidents are either a product of the author's imagination or are used fictitiously. Any resemblance to actual people living or dead, events or locales is entirely coincidental.

Interior design by Julia Jacintho

Printed and Bound in the UK using 100% Renewable Electricity
at CPI Group (UK) Ltd

FSC www.fsc.org
MIX
Paper | Supporting responsible forestry
FSC® C013604

When I told my parents I had written a monster romance, my mom took my dad's hand and said, "Aw! Just like us!"

Thank you, Mom and Dad, for your love, support, and good humor.

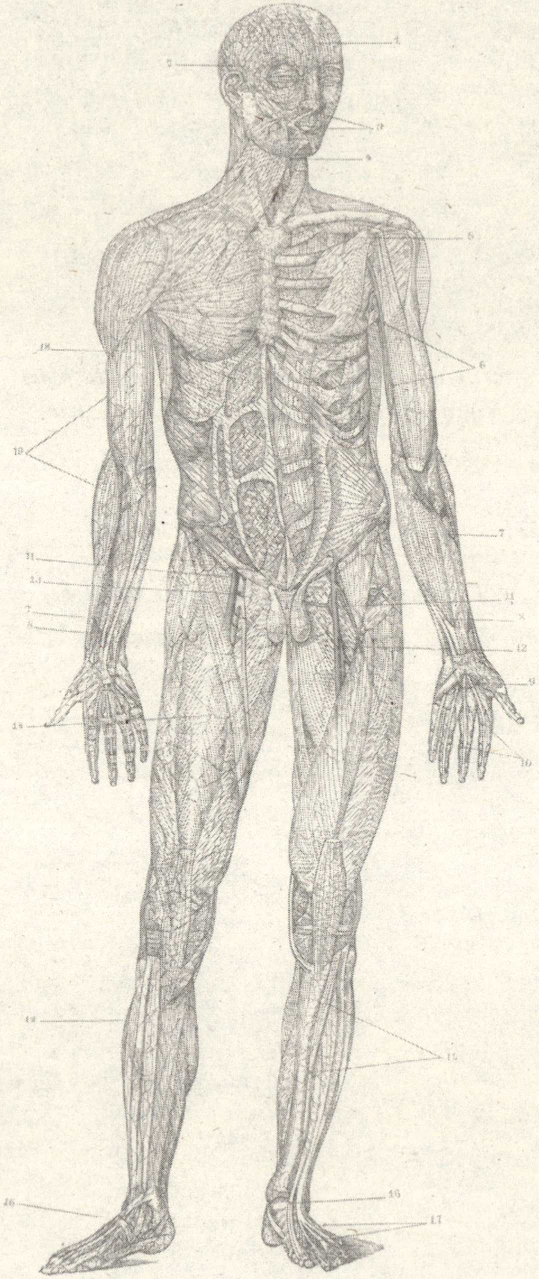

PROLOGUE

Humans refuse to eat their dead. It's baffling. Their kin, mates, and progeny bury the remains and hunt for something new to devour. It can't be real, Jenny and her sisters once insisted! Those bipedal land mammals—convinced nothing as smart as they strolls the earth and swims its seas—can't be that wasteful, they said.

Mother said it was their honor to nourish one another. When two brood mates tore each other apart in their toddler squabbles, Jenny and her sisters hissed their regrets and sang their goodbyes, and then they feasted. How awful for humans to destroy perfectly good protein! They treat their dead like waste. They throw one another away.

She didn't believe it until they threw her sisters away. Over the millennia, Jenny has seen humans beat in their skulls with stones and hammers, push spears into their pale green bellies and out through their backs. It happened when her sisters dared to hunt on land in the daylight, bold and shining, but they were also hunted when they were quiet, shy, and fed on only vermin. It didn't matter the cause. They looked and acted too uncanny to be human, and so were of course deemed dangerous. Real humans were happy to pull Jenny's sisters out of the water, slice them open, and throw them back. She remembers fishermen who hooted like their ape cousins when they did it.

Poor things. Humans are pathetic. They are worthy of her pity—or what there is of it in her small, annoyed heart. No one deserves to go uneaten when they pass. How sad men are!

Or maybe they don't eat their own because they don't think they taste very good. Jenny disagrees. Humans are ever so succulent. She pitied her sisters who contented themselves with fish. It's only when Jenny eats humans that she feels whole, skin flushed, heart and stomach pleased and sated.

She thanks the slumbering beasts of the deep and all those who weave between the stars that she is so much better, more sublime than humans. How dreadful it must be to pass one's time as a rotting sack of flesh! And what do you have to look forward to? Only the inevitable softening of the brain and descent into death. She has watched for all her years as people around her have decayed, eventually swept away into the sea or, at least, the devouring ocean currents of time.

Not her, though. Jenny is forever.

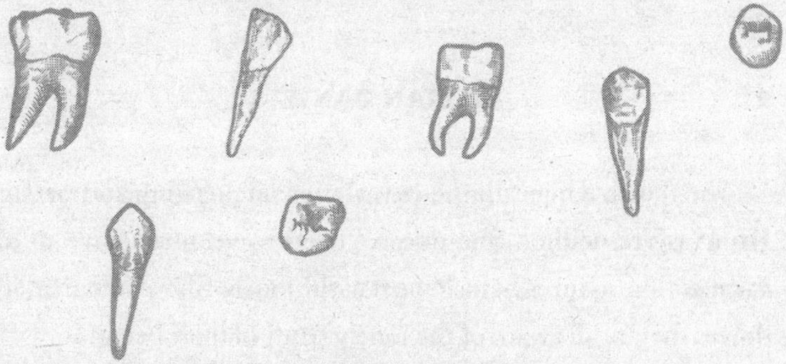

Chapter One

TEETH

The waters of Nettlewood Station are shallow, just the runoff, rain, and refuse that come down from the grates. They slop over tracks no train has traveled in years. With her beautiful, slick webbed fingers, Jenny traces the broken wall tiles. The letters of Nettlewood Station rot with age, like the humans who placed them there. Jenny has watched every cobbled street, every paved road, every building rising like a broken tooth be reclaimed and flattened by storms and fire and man. She can speak some of the languages that trip out over their tongues, because she listens to them all the time, nattering and squabbling and laughing with each other. Here in Boston, they used to sing sea shanties that lulled her to sleep. It didn't matter if they were in English, French, Irish, or dialects of Arabic. She has stayed because of that.

Also, there are so many rodents here. They burrow in nooks and crannies of foundations older than most port towns. The creatures may not be as filling as humans, but she can survive on them.

She remains beneath the city, always unchanging and perfect. Humans are neither. She doesn't need to venture above to tell them so, she assures herself most assiduously. She's certain, deep down, they're all aware of the lonely truth of their being.

And surely, humans have not forgotten that there is a creature who devours the flesh of children beneath their feet. Certainly not in Massachusetts, with the whiff of Puritanism still in the air. Everyone knows that if you come near the edge of stagnant water, of hot, muggy swamp or grim bog, of a particularly dingy stream draining into a murky grate, you might be snatched.

Well, everyone over one hundred years ago knew.

She seldom eats anymore, save for the stray rats who break into the disused station for a swim. Maybe a squirrel or pigeon that has met its demise beneath an automobile above. One day, perhaps, a young child will slip down below the street and make its way to her maw, but it hasn't happened yet. The Bostonians under which she lives are a loud, haughty people, but they keep their children close. And their cats and dogs.

Young men and women are a different matter, however. One—a tall, comely boy with a rosy complexion and blue, terrified eyes—crept along the walkway of the station a few months ago. He strayed just too close to the edge. Jenny needed only to reach up, wrap her green fingers around a delicate ankle, and pull the wailing youth downward. The lovely man hit his head on the tracks. His mouth opened to release bubbles like strings of pearls, and a halo of blood radiated from his brow. He had a particularly beautiful aquiline nose. Jenny thought it was so lovely, she snapped it off his face to eat first. He tasted a little sour, tart and delicious. And afterward, she had a time picking strings of skin and muscle from between her molars. She left the viscera to rot and the bones to float away. Men came with flashlights for weeks afterward, but Jenny hid with great success.

She sleeps above one of the soft places that make the human world more interesting, a shortcut between any body of water in the world. It branches and grows, a series of tunnels seemingly made for her alone. The gate to it, however, is closed as tightly as the ass of a turtle, except, of course, when she needs it. If she kept it open all the time, used the waterways more than she needed, she would be so exhausted, she would be comatose.

Sometimes, she thinks it would be nice to behold a face like hers, green teeth creeping over green lips. If any of her sisters still dwell in the water, she doubts it. She certainly hasn't seen them. If she were to travel to find kin who have perhaps abandoned the waves, then she would have to journey in the midst of humans. She has moved among them before and has suffered the indignity of wearing clothes and performing such habits as "manners" and "civility." No, she prefers her nakedness, uncombed hair in the cool damp of the water, nethers free to breathe as they may. She would also have to jettison her lovely, sharp teeth and the webbing between her fingers, undergoing all manner of bodily changes to blend in. And also, why leave? She's a woman who needs her rest. You thaw a bit when you're around people made of earth and years.

You, say, rent a room for a few weeks until the other members of the boardinghouse demand you leave because your manners are atrocious and too foreign. You become worked up about all sorts of things, like the burr of sobbing children and the rubber squeal of machines. You are like the horses in the streets, ungainly and confused by all the chatter around you, where it once lulled you to sleep. You are aware that there are men nearby—in open markets or theaters or outside pubs singing their beautiful songs—who can kill you the way they killed your sisters. To be around those who care for mortal matters means you might have the stink of their finitude rub off on you, their cruelties and meanness.

What is there to see that's really new? She can see enough, like rainbow splashes of oil and the wavering exhaust of automobiles. Let her eyes become scummed over as she rests. Jenny has found a place to lay her head and doze away the days.

The sedate murk of the water ripples. She wakes to the sound of intruders murmuring through her wall. Jenny's lip curls.

Those ones, the strangers, they're sniping at each other again. Much to her displeasure, the two of them have taken up residence in the closed train tunnel that runs parallel to hers. Has it been days since they arrived? Weeks? Not that she cares.

Her uncommonly perceptive ears hear a small woman—she trips and traps in what sound like well-heeled boots—and a gentleman friend, taller, smoother in voice and movement.

"Come closer, and I'm putting a knife in you," the woman says in words roughened by tobacco. You can hear the smile on her mouth. "You can't take my bottles."

"Faun, please." His vowels sit across the ocean. Not a born colonist but a new settler, here to cut and quarter the land. "Isn't the point to recycle them?"

"I am recycling them," she says.

"Oh? When? Are you getting money for them?"

"I'm using them to build a chair."

"It's been three weeks. This is like how you collect rags and say you're going to sew them into something, but I've never seen you sew. You are not building a chair. You are building something for me to trip on."

She cackles. "It can be both."

"No, because it needs to be in your area, by your column. Not mine."

"I thought this was the junk corner. It has that rag strung up there."

"That's my hammock, Faun."

He calls her "Faun," as if she is a small deer, but never has Jenny heard a deer speak with a woman's voice. Perhaps it is an endearment, like "sugar," as if she is something delicious to eat.

They are pattering ne'er-do-wells, beggars, wanderers, hobos waiting to take a train that will never come. They are disgusting, so she must hear more of what they do and how they do it. Jenny's breath runs ragged out of her mouth, as if she's listening to them make love, though if they're doing that, they have a peculiar way of going about it.

"Move your hammock if my things are bothering you," Faun says.

"You move first!"

"No, you!"

And with this, Jenny is driven to a great and terrible madness! Or, at least, she is driven to break the surface of the water. Once in the cool, stale air, she opens up the lung sacs like deflated bladders in her chest cavity, fills them, and howls. She mimics the wind at night.

For added effect, she extends her claws and scratches the wall, dragging her nails across the curving bricks. The sounds carry through.

When she wore enough clothes to go to theaters, theater taught her much. Back then, she went in stiff, starched undergarments and rouged her mouth bloody. She drank in the nickelodeons and the small stages. When it was nightfall, she went on the hunt for the drunk and half-drowned. In the day, she walked into the theaters, shabby rooms among humans with pink and brown skin, and sat across from bright red curtains over rickety floorboards. Then the curtains lifted. Actors who wore more rouge than she did walked across the stages and, by some arcane magic, made them grand. They pounded their fists and scratched and played at being lovers and mortal enemies. Sometimes, they wore wood and paper masks and pretended to be beasts. She mostly enjoyed how they tore at one another. Why, her favorite of the actors had a thin sword that he unsheathed with the enthusiasm of a man proud of his member! She clapped as he stung his fellows with it, which was great fun. She should have known, when she saw no blood bloom and pour from their prone bodies and smelled nothing of relaxed bowels, that it was called a play for being just that. They were playing. What a fool she felt at the end of the show when the actors all stood and the audience applauded! She felt alone again and hated it.

But she remembers how joyfully the people onstage playacted, so she does some of that herself now.

Leave me in peace, she thinks as she bellows.

The two in the tunnels are murmuring now, voices dropped low. This is her first time making herself known to them.

It's as close to tomb quiet as she can hope to get, because even tombs must contend with the murmuring of worms and grubs.

These grubs could do with some more silencing.

In her mind, she opens the box where she keeps language. She opens her mouth and parts her teeth. "Silence!"

What follows is a sweet, vibrating stillness.

Then the tiny woman responds. She raps her knuckles on the broken tiles of the station wall they share. "Quiet yourself!"

Jenny snarls.

The woman laughs with a voice thick with cigar smoke. Jenny can smell the burning of it, too, the perfume of paper and dried leaves. She clops away.

The man and woman resume their discussion. Now they speak, shout, and laugh at whatever volume they please, when they should be so lucky to make the acquaintance of Jenny Greenteeth and live to tell about it. If they were to wade into her water, she would eat them and use their fingerbones to pick her teeth clean.

Jenny waits, but they don't talk to her again. The emptiness that opens in her when these vagrants simply ignore her howls and scratches is a lot like hunger.

But as hungry as she might be, there's nothing for her to eat. No pigeon with a head ready to be snapped off its neck and no rat foolish enough to swim above her. Instead of eating, she returns to sleep. She wakes days later to a man and his light. Like a star, it burns through her slumber.

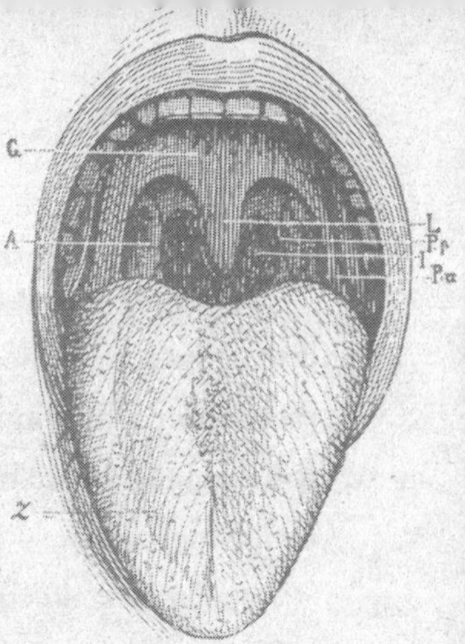

Chapter Two

TONGUE

When the star comes for her, it doesn't startle Jenny. Jenny can't possibly be startled. Of course not! She's many millennia old, wiser than any human—yet she does, indeed, jump.

A man is holding the light. Jenny can see a shadowed outline wavering in the water. He must be insane, she thinks, as he is speaking aloud to himself. She can hear his voice but the words are a fluid blur.

Slowly, her face breaches the surface. She is outside of his line of sight. This is fairly easy to accomplish, as he's completely distracted by the glow, which picks out spectacles and a full, pretty mouth. "Nettlewood Station was bricked up in 1890. Today, I'm exploring it for the revival of my—oh—wait, wait." He fumbles with the light in his hand, a star blinking twice like its distant cousins beyond the heavenly firmament. "Oh, hell."

Jenny watches him crouch down. He's far from the edge of the platform, which is unfortunate. Her very favorite place for a human to be is precariously close to the edge.

Slowly, so as not to alert him to her presence, she swims forward. She lets her body be part of the ebb and flow, matching the subtle murmuration of the water. If he stays still, if she can rise without his notice, she just has to leap up and pull him back down with her.

"Jenny Greenteeth." His voice radiates from his chest.

She stops.

"Or Ginny Greenteeth, depending where you are in England. The Penobscot and Abenaki have a Swamp Woman, a sort of ghost story. In the Baltics, they talk of rusalka, drowned women who have become angry spirits. A decade ago, I posted a video essay on sirens from Greek mythology. They're terrifying. Beautiful. Hungry for blood. To cultures near water, these women are often used to keep travelers and children from drowning. A warning story. Maybe they're worshipped like nymphs, small nature gods like satyrs! Maybe they're feared like the boogeyman. Or, well, boogeywoman. Wait. No." He stops his speech to the device. "And I could make this sound right if I had sat down to write a script first. Great. Come on, man."

Jenny is now hungry for his words. She wants him to keep talking about her. It might even work in her favor to spare his life so he may spread the gospel of her dangerous beauty, reminding humans that she is there and more than willing to devour them if given a chance.

Yet while she can live forever, she can't do so comfortably without flesh. Rats are good enough if she has nothing else, but human meat, specifically, sustains her health and humor. He smells flavorsome, too, like cinnamon and rich coffee, even with all the sweat, snot, and entrails knotted up inside him.

As he frowns into the glowing rectangle in his hand, she pulls herself up onto the platform with a splash.

He yelps and the light spins from his grasp, skids across the platform, and drops into the water.

Jenny, surprised, blunders as well. She falls back onto the watery tracks. She kicks out in the light's direction, making a churning hush of a wave with her foot. Jenny struggles to find a way to stand on the slimy tracks, slips, and falls.

Now the blue glow has sunk to the tracks themselves. It glows between slats of wood. It sits there among pennies, gum wrappers, a child's mitten, dark eyeglasses, and so much else that has sunk to meet her from the grates above.

It's flat, she sees. She crouches down beneath the water. When she takes it in her hands, it's smooth, smoother than the brick, and black as onyx, but with a sort of button carved into its center. The bright pane of glass under her fingers goes dark. She presses its strange navel to rekindle it, but the water has seemingly doused its inner light.

Jenny brings it to the surface to consider it. Droplets cling to it, the streetlight from the grate giving it an orange cast.

Above her, there's a huff of air, too slight to be a breeze. No, it's an exhale, pushed out of a pair of lungs by the man. If he looks her way, he must see watery shadows.

"Ah, fuck." The word is hollow. Sad.

In her, the urge bubbles up to surprise him, like a wildcat.

Why should she wait for him to get close, anyway? She can meet him as he ought to be in relation to her: prey. She titters to herself.

His body straightens at the sound. He walks in the direction of the voice, right beneath the grate. The streetlights color him. Jenny watches him, rigid and still. His hair is dark, mussed. He has a square face and a nose with a bump in the middle that looks like it was broken. His arms are soft rather than muscled, and he has a thick bull neck. A slight belly. There's a flush across his face that Jenny finds exquisite. His lenses catch the orange light, becoming solid lamps that hide his eyes. Momentarily, she is struck with how much those bright eyes resemble hers.

He does not know what he sees, she thinks, because he does not move. If he knew what she was, he would run. Jenny savors his lack of caution, the way he trusts this world not to bite him. She wants to keep him as he is in front of her right now, just for a moment.

He tilts his head as if he can better see the square he's lost. Or to better see her. "Damn. Is someone there?"

Jenny wonders why he has mistaken a flooded unused train station for a barricade against a river. "Damn" is also a word of condemnation, and the Christian vision of Hell brought by pale sailors and Puritans. He isn't as pale as they. She can see the olive undertone to his skin, the sort the Bostonians of years past would call "Italian" or maybe "Jewish" or "Greek."

Yes, she thinks. I am a damned thing, for it is here your little life ends.

Jenny pulls herself up onto the platform, which has transformed into a sort of stage. She is gracious enough to step into the light so he may behold her. Her body is clothed only in scum, rivulets of water, and the brush of the hideously cold air. She stands, grins, and spreads her arms out, ready to encircle him if he runs.

But he doesn't. "What?" He breaks out in a smile. She has forgotten human smiles. This one is shocked, beatific. Radiant as it is, picked out by streetlight. "No, no. Really? You?"

Jenny's heart sputters. That smile, turned on her, is strange. Wrong. She steps nearer to him.

The man squeaks. It's an indignant sound and, she thinks, very funny.

Jenny, delighted, drops onto all fours to bound up to him. The glowing thing slides from her as she goes, but she doesn't much care. It's not her treasure. He is.

He tries to scramble away, which is a very silly thing to do. The drool is thick in her mouth as she tackles and pins him. She feels the warmth of his body, smells the tartness of his sweat. His wrists are thick, but yes, there are bones beneath his flesh. They feel fragile to her. She's so much stronger than he is! She could shatter those bones, she thinks with swelling euphoria. His pulse bounces like a rabbit.

Beneath the spectacle lenses, his eyes are brown. The streetlights touch his irises with gold. He stares up at her in gaping shock.

"Please!" He twists, trying to pull himself from her grip, but she straddles his chest with all her weight. "What are you doing?"

It's amusing that he thinks she ought to answer him.

Under her silence, she feels a tremor working its way through him. She has forgotten the way men shiver, as if the ghosts inside them are pushing at the skin to get free.

Jenny wants to feel that ghost struggle more. She collapses onto him and presses her ear to his chest. Beneath it, she feels the rise and fall of his ribs, the incessant "wub-dub" of his heart.

"Oh," he says, softly. "Are you—? Are you all right?" The concern in his voice is foreign. But that's what it is.

Jenny breathes him in. Not just coffee and cinnamon, but soap. His breath smells like mint leaves and, yes, dark chocolate.

"Are you alone?" His question seems separate from his body, words spoken in a dream. Then he adds, more quietly, "Do you know where my phone is?"

Jenny wonders what the heart furiously pumping beneath her ear would look like in her hand, cooling in the hot juices freed from his body. It's like a small animal curled inside of him. She wants to tear it from his chest to listen to it better, but remembers that with humans, being what they are, it would immediately stop and he would die. When her own heart was ripped from her body by a huntress centuries ago, it grew back. It made her insides twist and wounded whatever she has instead of a soul.

A quandary, she thinks, brow pinched, as her thighs slide against his, feeling the rough texture of his trousers. She is truly hungry, but there's a snag inside of her. Some mechanism in her body won't go.

When she looks up again at his face, it is pricked in sweat. She can see, right at the corners of his eyes, tears. She opens her mouth to show him her teeth, something she doesn't intend to be a smile but a shared look of recognition. She thinks of how she was when the trains were built. It was so awful to be small and scared of humans, who often still manage to keep her off-kilter. Perhaps he feels like that now.

Jenny hesitates and stands up on her elbows and knees. She opens her mouth to ask if he really is afraid, but then his eyes widen. He frees one of his legs and kicks upward. It lands in her gut. The pain radiates from the center of her stomach. All the breath is pushed from her in a long, creaky gasp.

He clambers out from under her and scratches the bricks as he gets to his feet. His eyes are deer-wild. He turns and runs down the tunnel.

The man does not look back, and she is too rattled and breathless to move.

Jenny feels the cold grow icy in a way it was not before. Her stomach was hollow with hunger and now her chest is empty, too.

She hisses in the direction where the man has run. Rot away into the earth and air, she thinks. Gutless! Soft, stupid thing!

Jenny could chase him if she wants, she assures herself. The kick was a surprise. That's all. The years have not turned her into a soft weakling! Of course not.

She slides back into the water. The clammy damp embraces her. Compared to the cold above, the water down here is a summer's day. It holds her close and safe.

Jenny remembers the feel of his shirt beneath her hands, the way it bunched. It was soft when she crushed the fleshy sponge of her ear to his chest.

Jenny tries to sleep. Dreams are good for scrubbing away what distresses her, such as fishing nets, sharp spears, and being trapped in small, dry places with a hot and terrible fire at her heels. Though she closes her eyes, sleep refuses her.

Dawn light comes burning through the grates. She sinks down deeper, remembering the smell of his blood pumping inside his heart. She would love to run her nails along that skin—not cutting, not yet, but a sort of teasing. Would he cry? Would he fight her? Would he close his eyes and wait for her to take him, accepting that what she wanted to do, she would do with all her might?

Night comes again, and she is still awake.

She begins to suspect this is a problem. As the bright knee bone of the moon hikes up the sky, her vision is sharper and clearer than it's been for a very long time.

His hair, sticking up in all directions. She would like to card her fingers through it, as though he's a lamb who belongs to her. She would be shepherdess and wolf, both. He knew her name and said it. When she was about to eat him, he asked if she was the one who was all right.

It's confusing, so she knows she must ask for help from the only person she knows could ever help her.

She breathes deep into her lungs and lets her gills flare out. Slowly, she lets her body sink so low, she falls beneath the tracks, the tunnels, and the solid reality of it. The portal to the waterways opens and welcomes her inside.

Reality, for humans, is a unified thing, an agreement. The world, for her, has folds and divots, like a brain pried from a skull.

The water loses its dinginess. Here, in the soft place, it becomes a lovely velvet black. Then the velvet opens its dark maw into a vibrant blue light.

Jenny feels the pressure change. The waterways are something she must navigate through intuition. She has desired to swim the sewers of Paris and see the skeletons piled in the catacombs but, following only that thought, she has ended up in Istanbul, San Juan, and Rome in quick succession. Jenny doesn't tell the waterways what to do or where to open, she just follows their weaving roads. They are best used when she needs an escape from storms, gunfire, or, memorably, a flood of molasses in Boston.

When she glides to the surface this time, it's not the surface of the place she left. The train station is now the sloped walls of a water cave, a cenote where bats peep above her like baby birds. A great tree pushes out of the earth through the single opening to the sky. Its lovely, brown limbs run like raised veins along the walls.

This, the people who once lived here claimed, was the entrance to the underworld. She visits it when she feels low. From what she remembers, the Mayans were a philosophical people who wore bright clothes, drilled holes in their teeth so that they could smile with mouths full of jewels, and cut onyx stones into lenses to better appreciate the sun. Sometimes, they went down inside the cenotes to make offerings. Sometimes, the offering was human. She remembers feasting well.

The Mayans had become part of other peoples, their own ways lost to time. She has never worried about becoming lost in the same way. She has survived the millennia and so has at least one other.

"Mother," she rasps. In this dark place, she hopes her voice will pierce the veil between worlds, find the way to the realm of the otherworldly. "Some. Thing. Something happened." She clears her throat as she treads water. "Or it did not happen. I tried to kill. It was a man. But I weakened. He asked— His eyes! I was hungry and have not eaten in so long, but I did not, could not." She breathes in deep. "Mother, I would not kill him."

She waits for that voice she remembers from earliest girlhood, her existence as spawn, to rise up out of those waters and greet her. Mother's many eyes would be smiling even if her voice was thick with disappointment. Jenny had failed to hunt and feed, after all, and therefore had failed to please her.

But nothing happens. The water remains still. The bats peep above her, unstirred.

Jenny exhales and hangs her head. She's used to the silence. It doesn't diminish her love for her mother. One day, though, she would like an answer. She crouches down, sinking once more into the black. It takes time to find the gate to Nettlewood Station again.

Jenny journeys for hours, perhaps a day, maybe two. It wearies her. She swims toward broken, shimmering images of the reflected moon. Again, she slides into the velvet dark, and finds herself in an icy, gray lake under a field of stars. Jenny tries once more, and this time, she finds reservoirs dotted by geese and plastic cups. She visits hot springs with white snow monkeys huddled together and babbling brooks choked with bags. She also finds a great river beneath the bright Southeast sun, where she pushes her head above the water long enough to hear adherents of Ma Ganga praying on the steps that ascend from the shore.

Jenny hates this part of travel, the difficulty of finding her way back. She sees her home in her mind, the familiar sign for the train station that hasn't seen a train in decades. Still, finding the right path, the feel of the right kind of water molecules, is frustrating work.

Living in one place for too long makes you forget what it feels like from the outside. The thought reminds her of her weaknesses and, therefore, makes her queasy with chills. She feels sick. With difficulty, she pushes away the doubt in her abilities. She is superior to humans, she reminds herself with satisfaction.

Jenny picks at the memory of the man. She wonders how old he is. Is he young enough to still live with his father and mother? Instead of the tall, lean houses with sharp, pointed rooftops that sit above her tunnel, she thinks of him living in one of the small single-room houses of birchbark that dotted the land when she lingered near the Penobscot, who knew of Jenny as a swamp spirit, a fearsome she-monster who devoured weak men. She shudders with pleasure at the memory.

She imagines the man speaking to a wife, whose hair is long but less wild than Jenny's. Her face would be as sweet and open as his, for she can't fathom a man like that with anyone else. "The day has been awfully strange," he would tell her, looking to the horizon as he stands with her. "I was attacked by a naked green woman."

His wife would listen and nod with interest, her eyes soft as she absorbs his tale. "I see. And what did she want?"

"To eat me! She was clearly a great predator."

"Oh, husband! Were you afraid?"

Jenny imagines his brow crumpling. He would pull his wife close for strength. Perhaps he would bury his face in her hair, asking her to shield him from the hidden terrors of this unknown world.

She would respond by stroking his back with a dry, dark hand. "Be well, husband."

The picture makes Jenny furious. It's right, she feels, in what she has observed of human behavior since she rolled out of Mother's womb with her brethren into green, dark waters, before Mother left them to their own devices like a cat leaving behind her kittens, but it's also inherently wrong. It's correct he would be afraid of her, of course. It's also jarring that he would be in proximity to another woman, but yes, he would be, wouldn't he? He is attractive and has almost certainly found a wife. Maybe more than one!

As Jenny focuses on the man's face—his wide, fearful, curious brown eyes, the streetlamps when they reflected off his glasses through the gate—she at last pushes her head above familiar, oily water. She's home.

And, for the first time in many years, there are other people here. She splashes as she breaks the surface of the water above the tracks, but they are too busy yelling at each other to notice. Her sharp ears note the familiarity of their voices, the man and woman from the adjacent tunnel.

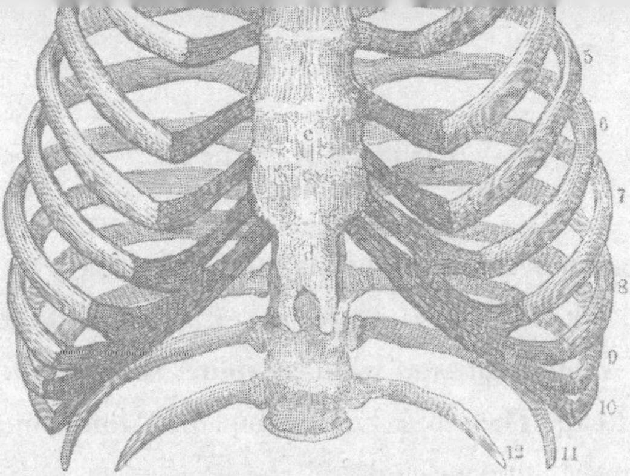

Chapter Three

RIB

They stand on a shallow strip of track. The water comes up to the man's knees. His dark brown skin is mottled in a darker brown, patches cutting over his arms and face. His black hair rises in tight coils from his scalp. "Faun, I don't have any clothes besides these."

There it is again—that accent from across the Atlantic. He points to his damp corduroy slacks, which are patched with venomous squares of green cloth. They're wet and now look awfully heavy. He holds something in his hand that puts a circle of light around them so, with their inferior human eyes, they can both see his clothes. The hem of his long green coat dips into the water.

Vagabonds! Wretches! They are no longer content to loiter in the tunnel nearby. Now they want what is hers as well, out of all the bodies of water on Earth. The insult! She bares her teeth but doesn't rise. She waits for a chance to pounce.

"Oh, honey, do you think I do?" The woman he calls Faun, with her tobacco-roughened voice, is short and stubby. The water goes up over her thighs and long skirt. She's the color of tree bark. When she grins, there are soft wrinkles at the corners of her eyes. Her hair is as white as spider silk and she wears a small knit cap. They look human, but they don't smell like it. "Who cares about your clothes?" she asks.

"I do. You really think I want what I wear to smell like this?" He waves the air in front of his nose and grimaces. Jenny thinks this is ridiculous, as everyone smells. He smells of powdered lemon, for example, and Faun smells like tea leaves and a spittoon. As he turns his head, she sees his eyes glint like pools of ink.

She shrugs. "Well, we're not in the sewers, at least."

"It's not clean down here in the train tunnels, either." He snorts. "You're the one who has to sleep near me."

Faun scowls. "It's fine. If we don't find the nexus now, then we'll wait for the sun to come up and hose off. Maybe we'll check the church's donations for some dry clothes. It will be fine, Clyde."

Scavenging for clothes doesn't seem like a particularly fine thing to Jenny. They are clearly not in possession of most things humans seem to have.

Faun brushes away her curls as she takes a sloshing step. "So, what's the nexus gonna look like? A light under the water?"

Jenny's brow knits and then smooths. What do they mean by "nexus"? Is that the name of the thing the man with spectacles was after? Or no—that was—what did he call it? A phone?

"Ah, yes," Clyde says, spreading his hands expansively. His knit gloves don't cover his fingers. "There will be a big neon sign!

It will say something like 'Interdimensional Way Station! First time? We offer a tutorial on how to travel within the web of aetheric energies!'"

Faun wrinkles her nose. "Silly of me to think you would know what it looks like, what with marching us through every tunnel in Boston."

"This place feels right." He looks down and scrubs his eyes with his hand. "You know how aetheric things are. You feel drawn to them."

"I trust you, sweetness, but we need a real battle plan here."

He huffs out a laugh. "I've never been much of a soldier, honestly. I'm no good with battle plans."

Faun clucks her tongue. "You don't need to tell me. I've seen you try to scrap and it's very sad. Remember when you came back with your nose bloody and your lips split?"

"You don't really fight, either." He sounds hurt. "You just kick people until they leave you alone."

Jenny listens to them snipe at each other. Why would two creatures agree to be in proximity at all, much less when they argue? Why not just fight until one draws blood, declares victory, and devours the other to honor such a battle? The man really must be a poor soldier, then. Perhaps the woman has taken pity on him and has agreed to travel as a sort of protector. She's short, but she doesn't appear to lack for muscle.

Clyde holds the thing producing light over his head. It's the phone that belongs to the man, the one that makes her think of electricity flowing in currents under her skin. The one that makes her feel fluttery but thick, like flowered perfumes. That phone should be hers.

She shrieks as she breaks the surface of the water. Her glorious, sleek form is clothed in shadow and shafts of lamplight from the grates. Breathing in deep, she produces a great howl and extends her claws. That's all the warning they'll get, she decides.

Neither readies to fight. The man stands there, gape-mouthed. The woman just raises a white eyebrow and steps in front of him.

"How long have you been there?" Faun drawls.

Jenny tilts her head. The woman really is brave. She masks her shock with a hiss. Did they see her fail to eat the man? No, they couldn't have. She didn't smell anyone else there. Unless, perhaps, they heard her let him go?

Jenny just points at the phone and shows her teeth.

The woman chuckles. It's soft, but there's a sort of echo as she trudges through the water. "You think you're so scary, huh? What are you, then? A bean sídhe? A specter? Maybe a river nymph who's spoiled over time?" Faun leers.

"Please stop." Clyde speaks through his teeth. He might be talking to Faun, but he's staring at Jenny.

"Know what? No." Faun laughs. "If she's so scary, she can fight me herself."

Jenny's nails are ready to rend and her teeth are well displayed in the smile she has chosen to wear. She leaps at the woman, snarling.

Faun lets out a breath and jumps. Her dirty skirts fly like a pigeon taking flight. Gray droplets geyser upward as she kicks.

Something hits the center of Jenny's chest. If Faun's foot is clad in a boot, it's a boot with a stone wedged into the sole of it.

Jenny's ribs scream. From the way the ache pulses, she suspects the woman has cracked one.

Jenny levers herself up again and now stands before them in the water. When she opens her mouth, she means to tell them exactly what she thinks of people who invade one's home, but she's still struggling against the pain. So, instead, she growls.

The woman breathes in deep and then smiles. "I knew someone would be here. I told you, Clyde."

"Great! Good job. You win," he snaps. "Now, what the fuck is it?"

Jenny barks at them and jumps at Clyde this time. So, he's not a soldier? Well! She can take advantage of that. Her claws sink into his shoulders and her teeth find purchase on his throat. The latter don't go very deep before Clyde hits the back of her head.

"Stop that," he says as if to a flea. It's far too casual to be anything but utterly insulting to Jenny. "Get off. Children bite. Puppies bite. I don't know what you are, but you don't look like either." He gives her another smack, right on the top of her head.

Jenny shuts her eyes momentarily. Then she glares and bites harder, as hard as she bites when she finds a piece of metal and wants to see if she can split it with her teeth. She has successfully bitten nails, screws, and chain-link in half. She knows that she's succeeded now when a wash of copper fluid sluices over her tongue.

Clyde's face contorts. "Crivvens. Ow." He doesn't sound as pained and terrified as a man should be. No, he sounds as if a bee has stung him. "Faun, try kicking her again."

"Off!" The woman kicks Jenny's back and arms. It's like a rain of hail, if that hail were the size of dancing feet weighted with ball bearings.

Jenny finally exhales in a squawk of pain when her split rib thrums. She releases the man and skitters away. Her spine feels jostled and hot. She crouches in a corner, turns to them in order to look over her shoulder, and hisses again.

"If you're planning to mark your territory by peeing there, please don't." Clyde gives a withering sigh. "We already had a raccoon sneaking in to do that where we are."

"That's why sleeping aboveground is better," Faun says with a note of longing. "I would take the cold at night over acrid piss."

Jenny watches as the wound she inflicted on Clyde begins to change. The holes that mark where she bit grow shallow. Then they fill up and close over, becoming mere divots. Then his dark brown skin is smooth once more.

It becomes obvious what should have been clear to her earlier. These are not normal people. Or, rather, they are not human. He may not be a soldier, but he is cloaked in something like immortality.

Clyde rubs his hand and regards Jenny with a squint. "Lady, if we have trespassed, we beg pardon."

Faun spins to look at him, water hushing in her wake. "You think that's a 'lady'?"

Clyde rolls his eyes. "She's someone, isn't she?" He addresses Jenny. "Ma'am—miss. Is this really your home?"

"Yuh-yes!" Jenny struggles for the tenuous connection between her mind and words again. She takes shaking breaths as she finds the place in her brain where she keeps the English language. "I. I am Jen. Jen-knee. Greh. Gruh—"

"Jenny," Clyde echoes. Then he clears his throat. "Jenny, do you live here?"

She hates when people interrupt her when she's trying to speak. "Jenny Greenteeth," she spits. "And you both? You! Quiet!"

Faun smirks. "How long do we need to be quiet?"

"Always! Forever. I will make you."

"Will you? How?" Faun has a haughtiness to her that Jenny intensely dislikes. It feels like her own well-tended confidence mirrored back at her.

Jenny growls. "Murder."

"Ours?" Faun cracks up. "You just tried and it didn't work."

"I hunt. You should be prey."

Faun looks around. "A hunter? Or a scavenger? This is the home of a bottom-feeder if I've ever seen one."

Jenny tastes spite in her mouth and feels truth flay her skin. She balances herself and springs.

Faun throttles her midjump with another kick.

As she feels a bruise form on her hip, this time Jenny can see Faun's legs, dense with hair. Jenny would not call herself an expert in legs, but human hair is not this thick. And the shoes, of course, are not shoes at all. Hidden under the floor-length skirt is a pair of goat hooves. They are blunted by time and dark with grit.

Jenny has to focus in order to breathe now. In and out, she reminds herself. The rib seems to be angled badly inside of her. She touches her chest, willing it to heal as quickly as the man's flesh did.

They watch her, waiting to see if she will attack again. Faun grins with small teeth like pearls, the flush of a good fight in her face. Clyde only tilts his head toward her, curious. His brows knit in concern.

"Are you . . . ?" Jenny does not have enough wind inside her to finish the question, so she lets it hang between them like a rope bridge unmoored from one side of the river.

"Do you mean, are we like you?" Clyde keeps his voice low. "I suppose we are." He blinks and his eyes are solid gray pools, free from any boundary that would define iris from pupil in the white of a man's eye. Then he blinks again, and his eyes are human once more.

Then he sneezes. "Lord. Is there mold down here? Or is it just the fact we're standing in water?"

The movement is so embarrassingly human, so informal, that Jenny feels a twist of rage, hot like the heavy, damp air of high summer. "Cowards," she says.

Faun's grin drops from her face. "Yeah? Is that what it's called when you defend yourself against a crazy woman?"

"Crazy? You are the ones who wear the wrong skins." She pulls phlegm into her mouth and spits in the space between her and these horrifying people, these creatures who are like her but lower themselves with the faces and clothes of mortals.

She did that so many times and always failed. It's disgusting to pretend to be human when you're not one of them.

Clyde frowns deeply.

Faun does not. "And whose skin should we wear, girl? Yours?"

Jenny refuses to answer. How humiliating it must be to be them, she thinks! How craven. So craven, in fact, Jenny needs to get away from them both as quickly as possible before their very pathetic presence infects her.

She turns and darts through the water.

"Hey!" The goat woman's yell edges into a bleat. "Don't run! We got some questions for you!"

Jenny tries to find anger in her for taking the phone that is rightfully hers, but no, there is none of that familiar, brittle burn of dry forest in her chest. Instead, she feels her belly and its hunger for a man whose heart hammered right against her ear.

Would they trade it with her if she could find something of value?

Jenny thinks. Her most valuable possession is this bricked-up tunnel, its gateway to her true home. She can't lift it out of the earth and give it to them and wouldn't even if she could.

Her second-most valuable possession is food. As far as she can tell, they do not spend much time hunting or foraging, and thus would likely be interested if she were to offer them something they could not get themselves. A talented hunter am I, not simply a scavenger, she thinks as she shifts her ears to a new focus. A scurrying, meaty, delicious focus.

Jenny looks up to see the rat running across the metal grate with its tiny scaled pink feet. She doesn't make a show of stalking it. She's only quick and sure. She bends down low, like a frog, and jumps.

Clyde chokes. Faun just gawks at Jenny.

Through the metal grid, she takes hold of the rat. Its fur is prickled and damp. It struggles in her hands as she drops back down. No, Jenny chides it in her mind. You came to my den. Now you are no longer your own being, but food.

And all right, perhaps that is scavenger behavior, but she's a better hunter than these human pretenders.

Rats are smart, and once they realize a creature who sometimes enjoys a bit of rat meat lurks in a certain station, they often steer clear of her. This one was not informed, she supposes. Under Faun's and Clyde's wide gazes, she curls her fist around the rat, squeezes briefly, and feels the decisive snap of its spine. It stops moving.

She holds it up for them.

"Threaten us if you want." Faun swells, trying to rise in height and failing. She has not understood the gesture. "We're not leaving until we find the nexus. If you think we'll be scared away by dead vermin, you can shove it up your ass, sweets."

Jenny frowns. First of all, the gate itself is not the nexus. It's a door that leads to the waterways. Secondly, it has become abundantly clear that Faun thinks she is still trying to get them to leave.

"The rat," Jenny says, "is not for shoving up my ass. It's for eating." She holds it out to them and explains herself as simply as she can. "I give this to you. You give me, um . . ." She reaches for the word. "The phone."

Faun is quiet for a moment. Her brow knits together. "Do you think we eat rats?"

Jenny has done something wrong. She can feel it in the rush of air in her ears. "It's what I eat."

Clyde tilts his head. "You can jump and hunt like that, but that's what you catch?"

"They are"—Jenny searches for another word, one she heard a long time ago, perhaps from a passing tourist or a fisherman in the Pacific—"economical. Like squirrels. Or birds." Jenny has the feeling of being naked in a way that she is not when she is alone.

"I see. Can you tell us when was the last time you went to the surface?" Clyde speaks slowly and with a certain amount of care.

That care, that gentleness, is deeply insulting. All it does is make Jenny feel small and remind her of her failed attempt to live in the boardinghouse. So she hisses. "Judge me not! Judge yourselves! Look at what you wear and how you wear it. Look at how you live because you dwell with mortal men in their blood stink! I care for my own flesh, and I will not be stopped from doing so."

Faun's lip curls. "Right. Got it. 'Course, 'course. And when's the last time you had a real meal?"

Jenny doesn't understand what "real meal" implies. The rat is a meal to her. Perhaps Faun means something else. She thinks of mealworms, and why yes, she has eaten those, though it's been a while. Jenny doubts she means men.

Her mind circles the man she didn't kill, like a leaf caught in a whirlpool. It's the way his pulse jumped beneath his skin, the sourness of his animal sweat. But besides the horse-wild look he wore, she's losing the memory of him.

"I want that phone." She turns to point at Clyde. She keeps her mouth small so as not to show off her teeth. "You don't want rat meat in exchange, but you say you want information about the gate?"

Clyde brightens. "The nexus? Yes! That! Where is it?"

Under your feet, Jenny thinks, though you won't be able to access it. "Phone. Then I will tell." She pitches her voice low with as much gravity as she can.

"Put down the rat," he says. "Let's go somewhere a bit drier."

"Where? Our tunnel?" says Faun.

Clyde casts his eyes upward. "I was thinking of getting real food for us. Sun's up. Zoe's should be opening in a while."

Jenny doesn't know what a "zoe's" is. With a sigh, she decides not to let the rat go to waste and peels it open with her claws. It's the color of dark rubies, fibrous and sour smelling. She devours it as quickly as she can under the watchful gaze of the vagabonds. Clyde's dark complexion develops an ashen hue.

They do not ask her about her injured ribs, Jenny notes. This may be for the best as they're already knitting back together. The rat has within it enough good meat to accelerate how she heals herself.

Faun watches with interest as Jenny removes the entrails and bones, dropping them in the water. "You're just going to leave them there, are you?"

She meets Faun's eyes. "I do as I will."

"Yeah, but that's the water where you live, ain't it?"

"All the water is the water where I live. All that ends up in my water dissolves with time, but I do not. It does not matter."

Faun sighs. "Should have guessed." She looks to Clyde. "Before Zoe's, let's hose her off. Also, we need a long coat."

"'Hose off'?" Jenny wipes the rat blood from her mouth with the back of her hand. Then she begins to pick the sinews out of her teeth. All she can think of are the hose human men used to wear under their shoes and over their legs, how they used to talk of "exposing one's calves to his best advantage," and they didn't mean cows.

"Yeah." Faun climbs the ladder to the grate. She glances down at Jenny. "You're overdue for a shower."

Jenny's unsure why she's smiling like that. She is sure she's being ridiculed. "It rains from above all the time. I get showered then."

Clyde sucks on his teeth and rubs his brow. He disapproves, she sees, but he's wise enough to keep that to himself. He follows Faun, his jacket flapping behind him.

"You've been stewing in your own juices for who the hell knows how long!" Faun shouts from above. "Now come on. Let's join this century."

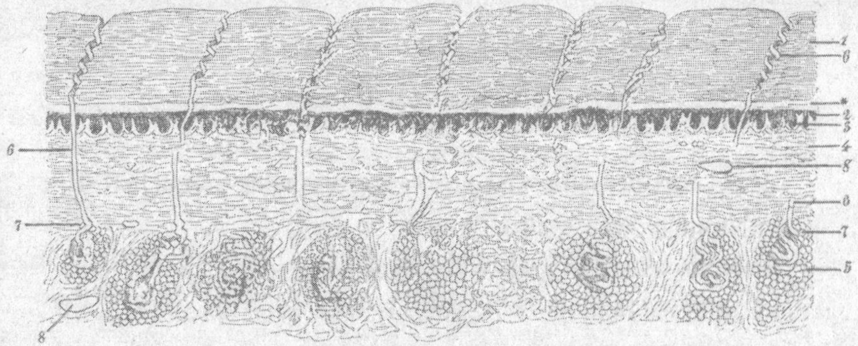

Chapter Four

SKIN

Above, the open air is sweet and the clouds are limned in pink dawn, even with the automobile exhaust all around them and its bloody taste of steel. The smoke that sat over Boston used to be thicker. Now she can better smell human life around her, the rats running free in the streets, the grease of food, the splashes of dried urine on the sidewalk, and the land beneath it that begs to be marshland again. The old waters want to return. The forest yearns to boil up over the hills.

The urge for Jenny to climb back into her tunnel is strong. She wants to keep an eye on humans, not be among them. When she longingly looks back at the grate, Faun clucks her tongue.

"Don't you dawdle," Faun says. "Joggers are going to see you. Clyde, how far is that old house?"

"A short walk." He takes off his long wool coat, which isn't as badly patched as his trousers, but is far from newly made. He holds it out to Jenny. "Put this on before we get arrested."

Jenny curls her lip and doesn't take it. She hasn't worn clothes in a very long time.

He cocks an eyebrow. "Police cars love coming 'round here. I don't want to be in a cell. Do you?"

She makes sure to show the displeasure on her face as she pulls the coat onto her body. Already, it feels too hot and heavy, filled with the smell of tobacco burned by someone else long ago. Sweat prickles along her skin.

"I'm not particularly keen on you wearing it, either," says Clyde. "That's my favorite jacket." He smiles down at her bare feet. "It doesn't cover everything, but you know what? It will do for now."

Jenny thrusts her hands deep into the pockets. Not because she's ashamed of her skin, of course—why would she be ashamed of such swamp-shining beauty?—but because she doesn't like Clyde's implication she has forgotten how to conceal herself among humans.

"Why would I want to hide my beauteous form from all who see me? I ought to be worshipped in my nakedness."

But if they hear her question, they do not answer.

Jenny also wants to see if he has somehow forgotten the phone in his pocket, but no such luck. She instead finds a book of matches with the words "Manchester-by-the-Sea" printed on the outside and a drawing of a sun with, for some unfathomable reason, black spectacles and a huge terrifying, toothy smile.

In the distance, Jenny sees a woman running. From what, she's unsure, as the woman does not look behind her at all. Instead, she moves at a moderate pace, her legs clad in a searing bright pink, her hair tied up high in a tail that flicks back and forth. Perhaps she's taking a daily constitutional. Either way, the woman does not notice them, which, to Jenny's mind, is exactly what most humans do. They ignore people who don't immediately have anything to do with them, including human-shaped things that aren't humans.

"Come on," says Faun. "The house is nearby. I remember there's a hose rolled up in the stable."

Jenny wants the only clue that will lead her to the young, beautiful man, so she follows. The sweat on her brow makes her sulky.

From behind, she notices that Faun has a wobbling gait. Perhaps that is just what happens when one walks upright with a goat's legs and inverted knees. To the untrained eye, she looks as if she's limping. Yet the way Faun shuffles about like a weak, elderly woman is deceptive. Jenny presses her chest where her ribs remain tender.

They arrive at a tall fence that loops around a great house. It's iron and painted over with a thick, uneven white paint. Dried rivulets sit on it like frozen tears. Jenny touches a claw to it and begins to pick at one such bump.

"Please stop that." Clyde sounds tired.

Faun *tsks* him. "No one will notice some minor property damage. The family hasn't lived here for a decade." Her eyes cut to Jenny and then she frowns. "We do have to get in there, however." Faun proceeds to touch a single spoke of the gate and unscrew it. She lays the stick of metal aside and then removes the next post. As she works, she pokes her pink tongue out of the corner of her mouth.

Clyde looks down the street, nervous. He scratches the back of his neck. This must be how they operate as a pair. Faun is practiced in getting into where she does not belong, and Clyde is practiced in watching for the consequences.

There's a strange sinking in Jenny's gut. She used to have sisters a long time ago who did indeed watch over her as well as laugh, tease, yell, and fight about food, their violence and love for one another all mixed together. She wasn't always alone. Jenny makes a point to look away from them for a moment, at least until she can fold the feeling deep down back into herself. Her mind is a tangle of pathways where things remain untouched.

She wishes the memory of the beautiful man into one of those dark corners, but he won't go down there. He sees her with eyes magnified by spectacles and a mouth ajar in wonder.

When Jenny looks up again, Faun has scrambled through the bars. Clyde slides in after her. Jenny doesn't know what manner of creature he is beyond the fact he isn't human and has, perhaps, an alternate shape. He smells like an aquatic thing, she thinks, like her, but used to darker depths.

They look back expectantly at her.

With as much dignity as she can muster, she pushes herself through the gate. A moment of horror fills her when it seems as if her broad hips are too wide. She suppresses an unflattering grunt and levers herself forward. Now free, Jenny stumbles. She stands and smooths the coat downward.

When she looks up, Faun grins and Clyde covers a mouth that most certainly has a smile on it.

She bestows on them her best milk-sour scowl.

Clyde clears his throat and waves his hand as if to mollify her. "Come along."

As they walk, she sees that the grass is longer than she would expect from the property of such a grand house. Jenny thinks perhaps this is evidence that the owners are not here.

Faun certainly acts as if she owns the place. She walks right up to the stables and slides open the door.

For a moment, Jenny fears the disturbed whinnying of horses, the stench of their manure, and the bite of their teeth. Instead of those great, sleek animals, she sees a sleek combustion vehicle sitting there. It's so clean, she knows no horses have been here for a long time.

Though the wool coat leaves her feeling hot and itchy, she wraps it more tightly around herself. The world moves too quickly, she thinks. She hates how queasy it makes her.

Faun pulls out a large spindle with a long, thin green tube wrapped around its center. Its end is fastened to a faucet inside the stable. She looks up at Jenny. "Want to go first?"

Jenny narrows her eyes. "First at what?"

Clyde squints at the house. "It's all right. We won't look. And no one else is here," he says, scouring the grounds once more. "Except a security guard who walks the property at noon. We've done this more than a few times, I reckon." He glances at Faun. "Mind if I have a go first, actually?"

Faun gives him the end of the green tube—a water hose, Jenny sees in dawning realization. "Go around the back, as usual. Unless you want to stay and give me a show?" She waggles her white eyebrows at him.

Clyde winces, and he won't meet Faun's eyes. He spurns her advances politely. "I'd prefer to keep my bits to myself, thanks." He begins to unwind the tube from its enormous thimble.

Faun titters. "Saving yourself for marriage, Blossom?"

His mouth firms into a small frown. "Been there, done that." He squares his shoulders, sighs, and lets the long, snaking body of the hose trail him through the stable door.

Jenny feels a flush of pride in the fact that she has never lowered herself to marrying a human. Yes, she has decided to engage in physical relations in the past. This includes a huntress in the moonlight with dark, challenging eyes and the smell of jasmine on her skin, and a formidable scarred man in a monastery who had the long braided hair of a warrior rather than a priest. She had then promptly hunted and eaten them afterward, or at least tried to—the huntress got away and wounded her grievously in the process. Giving in to something suspiciously like loneliness had been embarrassing enough; no human should be allowed to escape after having a slick-skinned lover like her in the dark, swampy night.

If she was isolated, Jenny reminded herself as ardently, as viciously as possible, then it was her wish to be. How dare anyone think otherwise?

"If you wish to clean me, dousing me in water won't do any good," Jenny proclaims to Faun. "I have submerged myself in water for centuries!"

"You mean in garbage runoff and rat juice? Yes, we can smell it very clearly, thanks."

Jenny is brought up short. She doesn't smell, as far as she knows, or at least she doesn't notice it anymore. And if she did smell, how dare Faun point it out to her? "If that's all this is about, I can get rid of that."

"With what? Are you a bog witch, too?" Faun laughs and then waggles her fingers. "You got a spell to cast?"

Jenny does not suffer fools gladly, but she thinks of the ridiculous man with his silly, lovely brown eyes and jarring broken nose. She gives a nod, shucks Clyde's coat off, and stands, naked, in front of the stable.

Faun makes a noise of protest. "What are you doing? People can see you from the street!"

"They can't." Jenny pricks her ears in that direction. "There's no one there." She admires her claws before she begins. They are sharp despite years of disuse.

She makes a shallow slice along the length of skin across her throat and begins, slowly, to peel it down her chest.

It stings. Tiny knives seem to be stabbing her as the dry, scaly pink skin beneath is revealed to the air. She feels more alive than she has in years of sleeping in the flooded train station. It's also satisfying to pull away the green epidermal layer in a single thin piece.

Faun covers her mouth.

Clyde peeks around the open door, his brow dripping. Droplets of water cling to his jaw and curls. "Are you molting?"

"Yes," Jenny says crisply. "If I am to go among humans, you are correct—I should not look like myself." She pulls the skin of her face away, first from the chin, then the jawline, cheeks, forehead, and ears. She's pink as a rat. When she looks down at the mask she has pulled away, she laughs to see the oval holes for the eyes and mouth. A surprised face, made of *O*'s. It's comical, and to her surprise, it came from her.

Clyde enters the stable once more, fully dressed. "You're pink underneath?"

"Of course not." Jenny is haughty. "It's from the rat. I ate him and now he's a part of me." As she rips the green skin from between her hair follicles, pulling out several strands as she does, Jenny can't suppress a feeling of pride. Clearly, these two vagrants can't do any such thing.

Clyde winces. "If you can always do that, why do you hide underground?"

The cold air slices the newly exposed under-skin of her face raw. She gapes at him in horror. "I'm not hiding! If anyone hides, it's them!" She points at the street, desperate. The blue, early autumn sky is slashed with orange clouds. Vehicles have begun to roar down the street, oblivious to three strangers in a house that isn't theirs. "I have a home! I have a sanctuary! They're the ones who are trapped in their awful, rotting bodies in the foul-smelling carcass of this city." If she says it firmly enough, she can convince herself.

"All right, all right." Clyde raises his hands in placation. "I only meant it might be easier to go out and get food that isn't, erm, rats."

"Better to eat rats than lower myself to eating human food," she snaps. "Humans are meant to feed me in the sense that they are my food."

Faun gives a short, harsh laugh. "So why do you want one of their toys?" She slides her hand quickly into Clyde's trouser pocket, which elicits a "Hey!" from him, and holds up the little box.

One of the drawbacks of this new skin is that Jenny's blood is now closer to the surface. She can feel its heat travel across the bridge of her nose. "That's not any of your concern. If it's just a toy, why not give it to me?" Jenny holds out her hand, which is still a lovely green, her remaining skin gripping it like a long glove.

"Fat chance." Faun cackles. "Sweets, you're telling us all there is to know about the nexus. Anyway, you seem like fun. Why wouldn't I want you to stick around?" The smile on her face is wide and genuine.

Jenny is at a loss. "Fun?"

"Clawing, biting, and eating sewer rats? You seem like you know how to have a good time. I've walked across every grimy corner of this planet since nine hundred years before the priests started to shout about the birth of some half god in Bethlehem. I drank wine with my mother and her maenad sisters as we sloshed our way through Greece. I've never been afflicted with anything like you." Faun yanks the hose nozzle out of Clyde's hands, leaving his pink palms empty. "All right. Me next, and then our new, dear friend, Jenny Greenteeth, last."

Jenny is baffled.

She busies herself with continuing to peel the extra-dermal layer away. Next is her chest, the skin over her breasts and nipples, her stomach, the dimple into her belly button, and the flesh that clings to her sex. She shucks it all down her legs like a pair of stockings. Her exposed pink dermis will flush green again in a few hours as she expends the energy from the rat, of course, but she still feels a sense of mourning as she tears away pieces of herself.

The damned phone better lead her to the man. She hopes he will taste as good as she thinks he will. She'll use his splintered finger bones to pick her teeth. That image fills her with a deep flush of satisfaction.

When Faun returns, her long skirt is damp along the edges, as if she grazed a puddle and didn't care enough to dry it. She motions toward her white curls. "Your hair. Do you want to wash it?"

Jenny sneers. "I do not, no."

"Well, the green hue and the greasiness look punk, so I gather you'll pass." Faun shrugs. "I guess you don't want to wash your teeth, too? I get you might want to keep them that, uh. Mossy green color. Because of your name."

"It's not moss," says Jenny. "And should I deign to speak to any human, I will not smile at them."

"Is there a way to make them not green?" Clyde stretches, first one arm angled behind his head with the elbow pointed upward, and then the other.

"I find myself an animal with the correct tooth shape, eat it, and then pull my own teeth out. Then I let them grow back."

He laughs. "You what?"

"I said I pull them out."

Clyde winces. "I imagine that doesn't feel too good."

Jenny peels the greenness from her back in patches, dropping them into a pile of bright summer leaves. "I don't need it to feel good. I just need it to work."

He stares at the skin on the ground, frowning. His brow smooths as he studies the pieces of herself that she discards.

She curls her lip at him in a way that she hopes is menacing. "What are you, anyway?"

"A man," says Clyde.

"I know. What else?"

"No need to worry about that." He pastes on a false little grin, eyes crinkling at the corners.

"But you are a thing like me. Strong. Long living. Am I wrong?"

"No, you're right." He scratches the back of his head. Then he looks toward the distance. From the way the wind from that direction tastes in her mouth, he's looking toward the sea, invisible but only a few miles away. Perhaps he's nostalgic for home.

Jenny wishes to press more but admitting that she's interested in this stranger causes her embarrassment. How much lower can she bring herself as she grovels for their favor?

Faun combs her fingers through her damp hair and stares off in contemplation. "Next: new clothes for Jenny and, if we're lucky, us as well. Thankfully, we no longer have to worry about makeup to cover her complexion. Isn't that nice of her? Then? Food."

Jenny eyes a starling with speckled feathers winging its way across the yard. It lands in the grass. It's beautiful with its mean little eyes. If she were to pounce on it and eat, it would unfortunately cause her skin to pucker like a plucked hen. "We could have food first."

"No," Clyde says. "Just how many rats can you stand to eat at once, anyway?"

"Twenty-three." Jenny swells with pride. "How many can you eat?"

"I don't eat rats."

Faun giggles. "Never been tempted to try?"

"No. Have you?" He raises an eyebrow.

"Not that I can remember, but I spent a lot of my formative years very drunk and stupid. Who knows what I managed to eat and keep down?"

Clyde looks ill, and Faun laughs at him.

Jenny scowls. "No. Wherever we go," she says, "I want to eat a man."

"Well, then. I envy you if you think we have the money to buy any kind of meat at all," says Clyde. "Maybe if we're lucky, we can pull sushi out of the garbage."

She refuses to admit that she doesn't know what that is.

"Faun, if you and I planned ahead, we would have found a way to store and sell antiques the way others our age do." Clyde looks glum. "Then we could stay in hotels whenever we like."

Faun waves her hand dismissively. "That takes security numbers and safety deposit boxes and not having had all your stuff burn in a fire years ago."

He looks displeased. "You seem almost happy with nothing."

"Sometimes I am. There's freedom to owning nothing except the clothes on your back. Riding the railways, sleeping under the stars, you know?"

Clyde has a wariness to him, one that makes his eyes look much older than the face in which they reside. "And getting snapped at by dogs, thrown out of parks, starving to thinness without being able to die? Oh, yes, immortality is a dream!"

"Well, if you need me to murder you, honey, you just need to ask nicely." Faun smiles wickedly.

Jenny, pink and new all over, slides Clyde's heavy coat onto her shoulders again and feels the sting of wool. She buttons it to the collar and then bends down to pick up the remnants of her molted self. In a patch of soil that must have grown flowers once, she scratches a hole and buries the green skin there.

For a moment, she remembers her kin in the swamp of their birth. Her sister with eight eyes instead of two fought against the girl with the longest teeth. They both gave each other wounds too deep to heal before their blood left their bodies in underwater clouds of viridian. She and her remaining siblings wept. Their mother said kind, loving words over their bodies. Then, all their faces wet with bog water and salty tears, they feasted.

When she stands and turns, Jenny sees Clyde and Faun watching her. It's distrustful, perhaps, the way their eyes track her. They also seem fascinated, like they've just paid a penny to enter a carnival.

She bares her teeth in a show of dominance. They, to her shock, smile back. After that, they even seem better disposed toward her.

They leave the property together the same way they came in, this time with Clyde putting the bars back in place on the gate.

As they walk, she is distracted by shops that are opening for the day. Based on the smell of acrid coffee, she knows some of what they pass are cafés, but they look alien and strange to her. Some of these shops are covered in what appears to be fake wood. Customers walk into these places, often with dogs that belong on farms yet are now on leashes as they happily pull their harried owners about. Among them are women laughing and chatting to no one as they hold their own rectangular phones, and men pushing dark, complicated-looking baby carriages with deliciously fat, chubby-cheeked infants inside. The world has both completely changed and not changed at all. As usual with humans, once you step away from them long enough, you realize just how mundane they are.

She follows Clyde and Faun to a church. Outside of it, in a procession of what she assumes to be boisterous worshippers, are people in loose, mismatched clothes. They also wear oversweet perfumes and soaps, which slide into her nose and stay there. She can smell sunbaked park benches and hunger on them, too.

One of the women is in a knit cap. She's soft, pale, wrinkled, and slumps over a shopping cart missing a wheel.

"Hello, Mags." Clyde is bright and encouraging.

"'Lo," Mags replies, and she does, indeed, seem very low. Her breath is a cloud of whiskey, as ripe as the smell when Jenny first saw men drinking it years ago. Mags stares into Clyde's face and gives him a lazy grin. Her cheeks have the hollow look of someone whose molars have been knocked out. "How's it going, hon?"

"Oh, I'm well." He sighs and looks around. "Barney here?"

Mags nods toward a tall brown man with a cloud of curly hair. He has thick legs and a pronounced limp, as if one leg is shorter than the other. When he turns and sees Clyde, a smile stretches across his face. He throws his arms open. "Bring it in, son," he says, though he looks younger than Clyde. Probably is, as he smells mortal. They embrace and pat each other on the back.

"How've you been?" Clyde asks when they part.

"Good, good. Slept in a sleeping bag on the Common last night. God, I love Boston when it's still warm, you know? I'm out of here in November. No idea how you lived in Scotland so long."

"Yeah. I get that a lot. I like rain and cold, I guess."

"Man, forget the rain. I got three years of good eyesight left." He points at one of his eyes, which is cloudy. "I'm going to try to spend at least some of that in Barbados. Or Florida. Wherever my girlfriend and I can get to first!"

"I get that." Clyde glances back at Jenny and Faun. "Any clothes left in the donation box?"

"They're gone." Barney laughs. "But I have some boots and a hoodie I grabbed from outside Goodwill."

"Thanks, man." Clyde follows him to a pile of trash bags next to the church stairs.

Jenny tries not to smell the humans too much or listen to the pulse of their guts and blood. Their bodies are less than hers, she reminds herself, beating their way toward death. Cattle, really, self-aware livestock to the likes of her. How does Clyde speak to them as if they are equals?

They are far too used to the ways of humans. Whatever food Clyde and Faun intend to ply her with, she already knows it won't be raw meat. It will be cooked, lean, and awful. It won't satisfy her.

Mags motions toward Jenny. She appears to be leaning the entirety of her weight on the shopping cart. Jenny, who has not spoken to a real live human in many years, finds herself curious. She frowns at her and moves forward, maneuvering her bare feet around a bottle someone smashed on the brick walkway.

The elderly woman, with bloodshot eyes and broken capillaries in her nose, says, "If you're gonna do meth, don't pluck your eyebrows after. Word of advice from the old to the young. If you can't die old, die beautiful." She pats Jenny on the arm with a delicate hand, small as a girl's, and pushes her cart away.

Humans have so rarely reached out to touch her like that. In her mind, Jenny thinks of the man looking her in the face. Saying her name.

Faun covers her mouth and laughs into her hand. She studies Jenny, dimples in her cheeks. "She's right. Your eyebrows are barely there now, sweets. I think you peeled them off with everything else."

Jenny shrugs. "They grow back." Like the green in her skin, she can pull out her hair as much as she likes—and sometimes has out of boredom, frustration, something to do—and it all comes back again.

Clyde returns to them with neatly folded clothes. They smell like moths, but they don't appear to have holes in them. He hands Jenny a sort of shirt and, when she begins to unbutton her coat in front of them, he panics and waves his hands until she stops. "At least let Faun and me block you from everyone else!"

"Hey, hey!" A long-faced, sallow boy brays like a donkey. He has acne across his jaw; long, beautiful lashes; and a bruised eye going purple and black. "Free show!"

Faun gives him a cheerful wave. "Go fuck yourself!"

He kisses the air. "Love it if you do that for me!"

She extends her middle finger.

He laughs.

Clyde and Faun pull her behind the church and help her dress. Faun refers to the shirt as a "hoodie." It's black, and on the front it has the face of a woman with flowers in her hair, her eyes blank without pupils. Jenny's also given a tight pair of trousers that hug her buttocks and thighs. The boots look like the kind that walk over her grate during the winter and have cotton on the inside that's far too warm for the heat of the sun.

It's more clothes than she's worn in a long time. She doesn't like them—they make her feel too heavy—but she knows a gift when she receives it. "Thank you," she murmurs, but it's at the same time a man opens the church door and begins to yell for everyone to get in line, don't shove, the beds are limited, don't fight for them. She doesn't think her companions hear her feeble gratitude. Which is for the best, she decides.

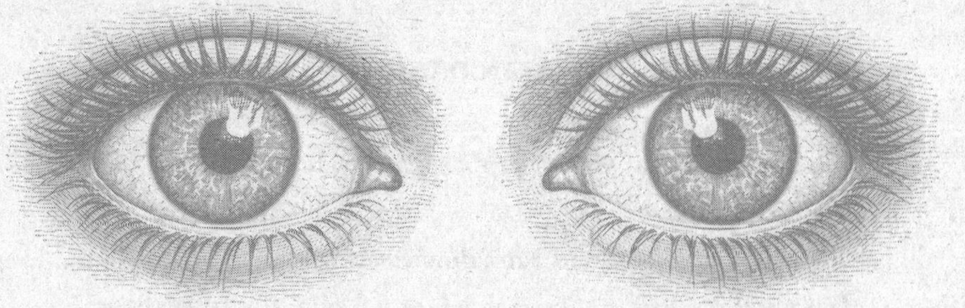

Chapter Five

EYES

Zoe's is a restaurant and it's a mile's walk away. Automobiles whir past and Clyde quizzes Jenny on what he must imagine is pertinent information for getting by among humans.

He points at traffic lights swaying in the wind over an intersection. "Do you know what those are?"

Jenny wrinkles her nose, which feels raw after her peeling. "Yes. They tell vehicles and horses to stop if they're red. Or to go if they're green. Or to speed up if they're yellow."

"Sounds right," says Faun, who shoots a grin at Clyde that makes Jenny think it's probably not as right as she thinks it is.

No matter, Jenny reasons stubbornly. "If you're asking whether I know not to launch myself in front of one, yes, I've learned as such. I've been knocked down by a car before."

Clyde's eyebrows raise. "You have? Did you break anything?"

Jenny is baffled at his concern. "Of course not. I'm strong and very fast." She watches a vehicle trundle down the block, the kind that, with a different set of wheels and treads, would look like a tank from the Great War. "I suppose they were smaller then," she admits out loud.

She follows Clyde and Faun down a set of concrete stairs to a glass-windowed shop. Above the door is a sign: ZOE'S BREAKFAST, LUNCH, AND DINNER. Another sign on the door boasts "hummus," "fresh avocado," and "milkshakes."

A small bell rings when they enter. Jenny looks up, expecting to see the bell's curve and its clapper above her head, but the sound appears to emanate from the very air.

The room smells of pork, fried eggs, burnt sugar, dark coffee. Also, and most delectably, humans.

The freckled pink waitress behind the counter looks doubtful when they come in. She's a round-faced girl with spectacles that have rhinestones at the corners. Her eyes look over Jenny, starting at her old boots and ending at her "plucked" eyebrows. "Are you lost?"

"It's fine," says a man behind her, a dark brown, muscled individual with his hair cropped tightly to his skull. He motions at the empty restaurant and looks to Clyde and Faun with a nod. "Come on in, Clyde. Sit where you like. I'll get menus. And everyone gets a coffee and a cup of instant oatmeal." He looks to the girl with rhinestone glasses.

She casts her gaze down, cheeks going even pinker. "Of course they do."

"Thanks, Rashid." Clyde doesn't pat the man on the back the way he did with Barney. There seems to be more distance between them, but the man nods, and Jenny takes note of this.

It's certainly a contrast to Faun, who doesn't appear to have much interest in meeting any human in the eyes unless she's yelling at them. One would almost call her shy if, of course, one hadn't been kicked in the ribs by her.

They find a table at the corner, right where the window meets the wall. The table is affixed to a floor tiled in red, black, yellow, and blue.

"So." Clyde sets the phone down. It appears to have a long crack in the surface that Jenny doesn't remember from before, but the color and shape are certainly the same. "Let me ask you what you asked me. What are you?"

Jenny glances back at the waitress and the man, Rashid. They're at the other end of the restaurant, but her keen ears pick up the young woman informing the man, "Look, they better not stay here all day. Remember the old woman with the bags? She threw food at people!"

"Yes. When they throw things at other guests, you have my permission to kick them out. Not before, all right?"

Jenny turns back to Clyde and pitches her voice low. "Which name do you want?"

"You already gave us Jenny." Clyde's brows meet. "How many do you have?"

"Thousands." She beams at them. In her mind, she reaches for the words of the man who stumbled into her bower, who she needs to find in his own surface-dwelling. They are printed on her heart. "I am the Swamp Woman who entices men to drown, Peg Powler, rusalka, nymph, goddess—"

"I bet others call you 'Pain in the Ass,'" Faun says with a note of what might be fondness. "What do you call yourself?"

Last time she walked among humans, she was in Boston in an uncomfortably starched dress and underwear. They didn't like her names much except for Jenny. She leans back in the seat, which squeaks, and spreads her hands. "Jenny Greenteeth. I like it better than Swamp Woman."

"Right." Clyde taps the phone. "How long have you been below Boston?"

"Since before it was called that. It has so many rats, I knew I wanted to stay! Before then, I was in Lancashire, but when I ate the rats there, I would get sick sometimes." She pauses to think about that. Beneath her feet, she feels a train rumble past, the floor gently quaking, as the restaurant sits on top of another tunnel. "I used to move around more, then. I use the waterways between to do it. You call it 'nexus'?" She tilts her head and smiles.

Clyde gives a curt nod. "Are you master of it?"

Faun's mouth twists. "I doubt this one's master of anything."

"I am the inheritor of it." Jenny summons confidence into her words. "My mother made the waterways when she slithered into the world. She is old and powerful and huge. If there is a queen of the waterways, it is she."

Clyde looks like he's bitten into an unripe apple. "Is she still down there?"

Jenny straightens her back and bursts out, "Of course she is!"

He startles. She can hear the clatter of plates as the pink waitress does, too.

"You can find her yourself if I let you down there," she says quickly. "You need me to travel anywhere at all."

"Do we?" The corner of Clyde's mouth quirks upward. He invites her friendship, as he seems to do with the men.

Jenny laughs, low and soft. "Down there might as well be a river of dog's piss to you. You can't travel in it as I can."

"You have to be the one to open it?"

"And help you through the gate, yes."

Clyde frowns once more, deeper this time. "Fine. I don't suppose we can travel as you do. We spent a good while splashing around before you came up out of the water. And I noticed the train station isn't exactly an Olympic swimming pool. It's shallow. You were traveling in those waterways, weren't you?"

Jenny debates lying and then dismisses it. "Yes. I was in a cenote."

"A what?" Faun is bored. She picks up a small cylinder that contains salt. She examines the holes at the top.

"Water caves?" Clyde tries. "Like in Mexico?"

"Yes. That's where I was," says Jenny.

"All the way there?"

"Of course."

Clyde lets out a low, soft whistle and then gives a shake of his head. "That's exactly what my associate and I are looking for: a gate to a network of water."

Faun rolls her eyes at "associate."

Jenny considers him. "Do you wish to use it to get somewhere or to use it to hide something?"

"Neither. I want to find a thing that's lost. It's down there, waiting for me. Or calling to me, really," he says. "Finding it by normal means has been a challenge."

"He's not much of a detective," says Faun. When Clyde turns and smirks at her, she returns his look with a long sigh. "All right. Fine. I'm not much of one, either."

"Then give me the phone and you can find it." Jenny steeples her fingers. She imagines they want something boring and shiny: a crown, perhaps, or gold coins in a sack. Faun and Clyde aren't human, however, as they have more than shown themselves not to be. Beyond enough clothes to ape mortals and some food to eat, what need have they for human treasure?

Rashid comes over with menus and three mugs of coffee. Jenny ignores hers while Faun greedily takes her cup and drinks. Clyde continues to appraise Jenny.

Then, with a nod, he slides the phone across the table to her.

Jenny picks it up happily. She presses the circular button on it so she can watch the screen light up again. Perhaps his name would be there? The tongue of Boston has come back to her quickly enough, so she hopes the written words are there in her head, too, ready to spring forth. When the phone's square face ignites, it still has a large blot over it like spilled ink. She wipes at it with her thumb, but the ink doesn't go away. She presses the screen, and the hairline fracture she noticed before stretches like a terrible smile across a mean face.

She immediately looks up at them both, expecting to see them with ludicrous grins, leering at her. "What did you do to it? It's broken."

Clyde looks perplexed and tilts his head.

"That's how it was already, sweets." Faun arches an eyebrow. "They break easily. You knew that, didn't you?"

"Of course not." Jenny looks down at it. She taps the screen once, twice, and then furiously stabs at it. Taking her cue from otters and rocks, she slams it on the table.

She finds the hands of Clyde and Faun clamped down on the phone, pressing her hands flat. Clyde looks to where Rashid and the girl stand staring. He manages a furtive smile in their direction. Faun also grins nervously their way, revealing teeth that look like mismatched keys in a pianoforte.

"Stop that," Faun hisses. "What are you doing?"

Jenny feels a prickliness behind her eyes. She steels herself and exhales, steadying her body. "I just thought it would lead me to the man."

"Who?" Clyde is utterly perplexed.

"He dropped this in the tunnel." She feels her pink face heat along the cheekbones, which is deeply humiliating, and here they are to witness it. "I thought it was a star at first. Then I saw a man."

Faun looks thoughtful. "How old was he?"

"I don't know. Not old and not a boy."

Faun leans forward. "Would you say he was handsome?"

Jenny remembers the plush pillow of his mouth and the magnified brown of his eyes, fearful and flickering. Her lips become a snarl, and her answer is dragged from her throat: "Yes."

Clyde looks away as he sips his coffee, like he's intruding on a private discussion.

Faun chuckles. "I have to say, I'm surprised, especially with the way you talk about humans. What kind of man do you find handsome?"

"The kind that would make a handsome meal."

Clyde chokes on the coffee, which means it splashes back over his broad nose. He places his mug down and wipes his mouth with the back of his hand. "You don't just eat rats?"

"Mostly. I like to eat humans if they disturb me. And that's what he did." She waits for Clyde to challenge her. If he does, she'll tell him she also eats people when she wants to or if they're already dead.

He just raises his hands as if in surrender, or as if to wash them from any of this. "I like humans. A lot. But if he stumbled across you, and that's the rule you live by, well, all right. I won't stand in your way."

Jenny glares down at the phone sourly. "There is no standing in my way because, right now, I have no way forward."

"But you have his phone now," says Clyde. "You'll find him."

The phone, to her, seems as useless as rat bones.

"And you still have to hold up your end of the deal."

She stares up at him. The sun shining in through the window catches the different shades of his skin and the moles scattered across his face. He looks hopeful.

Jenny slides the phone back to him. She cheerfully squashes his hope. "What deal?"

Clyde's jaw works and she can hear him grind his teeth. "You said you would open the nexus in exchange for it. That's not fair."

"Neither is the fact I can't find the man who, rightfully, should be my food!"

Faun glances at Jenny and puts her finger to her lips, indicating she should bring her voice down. It is an unwelcome suggestion, though a sensible one. "So, you want us to help you find him? Then you'll open up the nexus?"

Something in Jenny's chest grows lighter. They would be excellent to use for this purpose. "You know more about the ways of humans today than I do." She gives a definitive nod. "If we get him, and you're looking for something in the waterways, I'll find it."

Clyde's eyes momentarily widen. Then he shakes his head. "It's just for me to find." Then he seems to realize he's slipped and his eyes go to Faun. "Except with you, of course," he rushes to add.

"Sweets, you let me team up with you years ago, and I had to beg. I know this is your grand, stupid quest. You don't want us to go on forever playing Faunie and Clyde."

Clyde looks pained. "Never call us that again, please. And I would prefer the fewest people to know about me as possible."

"She ain't people. More feral than anything."

Jenny raises her chin. "You're not human, either, goat girl."

"Satyr," says Faun. "On my father's side. They don't live much longer than humans, but my mother? Oh, she was a minor goddess, a follower of Dionysus, another one of his maenads."

Unbidden, a memory rises in Jenny's mind's eye, a box opening up that she had put in a corner of her brain: a sign swinging over a tavern. A woman is painted on it, tilting her head back as she drinks from a cup held in one hand and holds an abstraction of grapes in the other. Her breasts are bared over a tunic. "The drunken wild women."

Faun lights up. "The wild women of the hills, driven mad with wine and worship for a god!" She looks past Jenny, smiling at the motes swirling in the morning light. "Childhood was a wonderful, wine-soaked blur. I went naked and slept in the grass. You know what that's like, yeah?"

"I have drunk wine." Jenny remembers darkness in a cup and bitterness spreading over her tongue. Then there were headaches and a terrible dizziness.

"Oh, sure, but there wasn't"—Faun makes a long, dismissive motion toward the window—"all this. City nonsense."

"There have been cities for a long time." Jenny remembers the wash of heat when she first broke the surface near the shore of Eridu in Mesopotamia. It was one of the first times she saw a boat constructed by humans, expansive and floating beside the shore, with people laughing and drinking on it. Farther on, she saw a place where people lived tightly together, loud and smelling strongly of livestock that snorted their heavy displeasure. Women sold fried, greasy meat and men danced. Children threw dirt and screamed with joy. How did that many humans exist in the entire world at once? Jenny was so terrified (yes, she can admit that's what it was now) that she fled back into the water.

Faun has a mouth that has sucked on a lemon. "The cities are different now, though."

"They're always different. Humans change and grow like mold."

"Yes, right. Humans and their cities have changed together. They're harder. Meaner." She looks sharply at Jenny, nostrils flaring. "If you do anything to catch the attention of the police, I'll kill you. It will be like you getting your rocks off by killing that little rat. But I'll be the one pulling you apart. I won't even hesitate."

Clyde elbows her. "Faun!"

Jenny simply frowns. She is not ignorant of human violence, police or not. It has come in the form of knives and muskets held to her head by terrified farmers and confused night watchmen. She has dodged rocks from bored drunks, arrows from hunters, and even the machinations of her beautiful, fierce huntress from long ago who gave her plenty of reason to be wary of anything like love. Once, a woman pulled out a long shotgun, and Jenny stared at it until it fired. The bullet hurt like a bee sting soaked in flame and Jenny had had to dig it out herself.

"Of course," Jenny says. "I won't draw attention to us."

Faun's breathing is quicker. As Jenny watches, Clyde puts his hand on her shoulder. His fingers curl and squeeze. She squeezes his hand with her own. Then her breathing slows and she exhales. "Good."

Jenny thinks Faun has been shot at, too. If she was hurt with something worse, she doesn't want to think about it.

Clyde looks at Jenny plaintively as he releases Faun. "The thing I lost was taken by humans, too. It was, um . . ." He leans forward, his eyes briefly flicking over to the girl and the man at the counter—chatting with each other amicably, it seems—before he finds hers. "My skin."

It clicks into place. "You have a skin you can put back on again, then?"

He gives a nod. "When it's taken away, I can't return home. I need to find it."

Jenny locates the right box in her mind and shakes it: a rocky beach and a damp, gray day in Scotland. Seals sat on the rocks, soft, friendly lumps with great whiskers. Then the clouds rolled back and the sun shined down. As she watched, the pleasant creatures split like pea pods, and women and men stepped out and stretched, hands spread as they greeted the sun. "You're a selkie. The seal people. I've seen your kind before."

With growing hilarity, she sees Clyde flush, his brown skin growing a little darker.

Faun's moodiness shifts from despair to frivolity. Her smile inches back onto her face. "That's exactly what he is."

"Guilty," Clyde manages as he picks his coffee up once again. He drinks it studiously.

"I have heard people tell stories of those who can remove their skins," Jenny begins.

"A woman, usually," he interrupts, now irritated, having explained this all before. "And she's a selkie who's removed her skin, and she's just sitting there on the shore, naked, and a man sees her and wants her and he takes her skin and he makes her live with him and be his wife and have his children. Then, one day, a child opens a chest in the house, finds the skin, says, 'Oh,

Ma! Ma, what's this?' and she puts it on and runs away." He takes a long sip, a deep line between his eyebrows. "Something like that?"

"You have even more reason to despise men than I do." Faun overturns the cylinder and angrily shakes white grains into her coffee. "They stole your life. Or, you know, one of them did." She shoots him a glare.

"We're not talking about that right now."

Jenny tries to press this all into her memory, opens another box and puts it all inside before hiding it away until she needs it.

Faun has an aversion to violent humans.

Clyde has an aversion to stories about his kind.

She picks up her own mug. When she sips, it spills chocolate-dark heat over her tongue. Too hot. She puts down the cup and spits the coffee back into it.

Faun snickers. "Lovely."

Clyde wrinkles his brow. "Some people who aren't humans dislike human food. Or is it that you can't eat it?"

"I can eat it," she says immediately. "Sometimes. Mostly when it's made of meat." Her eyes trail up to the window. Above, on the street, she sees human legs, pink, dark, tan, and, due to their garments, sometimes green or blue. They wear sandals and shoes with white laces. The day must be growing hot again because now they bare themselves to the sun like those seals, limbs touched with sweat, skin shining. Tender. Soft.

Her mouth waters. She can feel drool threatening to drip over her lips and down her chin.

Clyde clears his throat. “And what if it isn’t meat?”

Jenny keeps her eyes on the window. Why turn away from such a delectable sight? “When I ate brambleberries, I grew purple and bumpy, like I was covered in boils. I’ve eaten cheese and gone sallow and milk faced.”

Faun snickers. “You are what you eat?”

“Yes.” Above her, she watches legs clad in tan slacks, likely a man. On his feet she sees the sort of man’s shoes that have hit the grate above her head often with their thick leather soles.

Clyde chuckles. “That’s funny.”

Jenny is confused and doesn’t look at them. “What’s funny about it?”

“Well, it’s because, um. It’s like a slogan? Do you know what that is?”

Jenny watches the man in the walkway above the restaurant drop a pair of spectacles and bend down to pick them up. She sees his broken nose, his full mouth, dimples, and by the time she registers his brown eyes, she is standing up.

He’s moving away from her. That’s wrong.

She reaches across the table and grabs the broken phone.

Clyde yelps. “Hey! What are you doing?”

“Jenny?” Faun asks.

She’s out the door and thudding up the stairs.

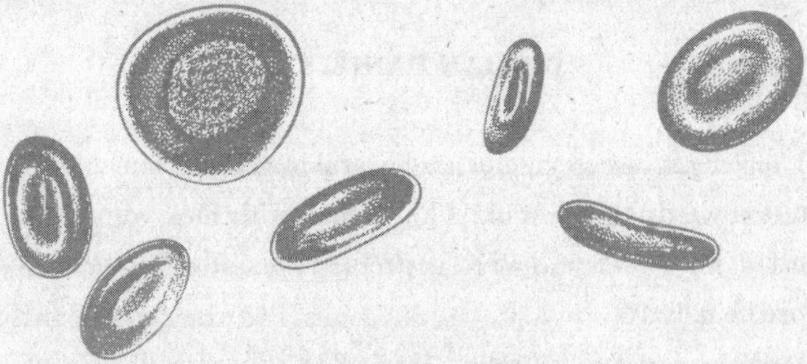

Chapter Six

BLOOD

When she reaches the sidewalk, there are far more people out now, smelling of sour sweat and sickly sweet chemicals. Her green-tinted hair hangs around her face in tangles, and her pink skin looks a little too shiny and new compared to everyone else around her. Jenny sees the man—her man, she's sure of it, scrubbed clean, upright—continue to step down the street. His glasses catch the morning light and reflect gold back into her own eyes.

The air is thick as she runs toward him. Going fast is impossible with the crush of people. There's a group of starch-smelling children in uniform moving listlessly, led by a man with a sign that says FUTURE IVY LEAGUER TOUR; a pale man bouncing along on his morning constitutional with a large baby carriage in front of him; tall golden-brown- and pale-lily-fleshed girls standing on the corner, crowing and laughing with one another as they throw their hands up like birds winging over their heads; someone with cropped purple hair staring moodily down at a phone. She passes another man wearing one of those long-billed hats, and he yells at her as she pushes his arm to get past him and he teeters toward the sidewalk. The woman with him, who has a cloud of black curls and wide, distressed eyes, steadies the man before he falls.

Jenny passes a place called Hong Kong that smells of beef, chicken, and all the most unsatisfying meats she's ever tasted. She runs past the Harvard Book Store Est. 1932. Across the street, the walls of a university rise up with bricks, black gates, tunnels, and doors opening onto thick trees, climbing ivy, and prattling scholars.

All the while, he walks in the center of her vision. A big, solid man, with his long-sleeved shirt that has buttons on the wrists. His hair—curls touched with threads of gold in the sun—is licked and played with by the breeze. She can see his shoulder blades crouching on his back, his buttocks in his trousers with a pocket on each side, and she wants to leap forward and bite him. Everywhere.

"Zeke!" a woman shouts.

Jenny goes absolutely still.

He turns around toward the direction of her voice. Smiles. All teeth and goodwill beaming from his crinkled eyes. "Selene! Morning!"

The sleek, lovely woman has smooth brown skin and a head of springy black ringlets. At her throat is a jade necklace. "Morning, stranger! We grabbing coffee?"

"Now we are!" He is a bird, chirping at her with recognition and pleasure.

Jenny is transfixed by them both. Their clean clothes, their bright eyes. They look natural together.

"Good. I want the bitterest stuff they have." Selene sighs theatrically. "I've spent a morning staring at essays and hating them all. Why are these children wasting our time?"

"Dunno, but I always wrote bad essays. Still do."

"Bullshit. They were great."

"No, no. Most of them were nothing." He laughs. "My motivation for every essay was the due date."

"You published the one about the impacts of early education on democratic thinking!"

He relents. "Okay, that one was good. Like, very good."

"It was! Before I forget, you're helping me move the Saturday after next, right?" She puts her arm around his shoulders. Squeezes.

Jenny is incensed.

"Of course!" He looks pleased and doesn't remove the arm. "I love moving stuff."

She laughs. "I adore you, but you're a freak. No one loves moving things!"

Look at me, Jenny thinks. Turn around. Look at me with your eyes and I'll look at you with my eyes. Then I can kill you. But look at me first.

"If you're ordering pizza, moving's great," he says.

"Suck-up."

"Who doesn't like simple tasks followed by pizza?"

"Hmm."

"I also accept payment in actual money."

Selene smiles and drops her arm. "Pizza it is."

"Good. But first? Coffee."

"Oh, always, Zeke." She knocks her shoulder against his.

"Zeke" is his name! Jenny wants to snarl it but feels wan. She only manages to move her tongue along the syllable, exposing her teeth to the air. Her green, sharp teeth, she remembers too late.

A freckled stranger with bright pink hair and large headphones looks her way and, stricken, crosses the street.

Her stomach roils. She ran blocks to watch him talk to a beautiful woman who isn't her, while she's regarded as a plague victim.

Zeke and Selene walk into a shop. It smells of warm coffee and sickly sweet sugar. The woman's laughter is too loud. In his hands, the light catches a new, different phone.

The drops of the hot, dark coffee Jenny herself swallowed come charging back up her throat, and she has to look away to swallow the acid down. Standing in the wash of humans, Jenny feels fire rise through her veins. She grips the phone so hard, a tremor begins in her wrist and moves up her arm. The plastic case cracks further under her fingers.

She hears Faun behind her before she makes herself known. Even in a crowd of people, Jenny can make out that uneven, clip-cloppy, goaty gait.

Enraged, Jenny twists around to look at her.

Faun's gaze is steady. Jenny doesn't know what is in her own face, but it prompts Faun to say, "Let's sit down, sweets. Come on." She takes hold of Jenny's sleeve with her weathered brown hands.

They find a metal table with chairs. Beside it, groups of men and boys are playing chess.

Jenny feels like she's breathing out steam.

"It's okay." Faun is careful. "We're all right, aren't we?"

She won't answer that. Right now, she is sick of the briny blood stink of humans. Her chest feels torn open, her ribs cleaned of flesh and muscle.

Clyde arrives shortly afterward with a paper cup that holds, based on its smell, his leftover coffee. He studies Jenny. "You saw the man, didn't you?"

She just hands the broken, useless phone to him. "I no longer need this. It's yours."

He doesn't take it. "Keep it. We have plans to make, Miss Greenteeth." He leans over her with a startling warmth. "You know, you remind me of me."

"Yes." Faun grins at Clyde. "You just love eating people. I forgot."

Clyde clucks his tongue and swats her hand. Jenny thinks it's a challenge to fight, retaliation for an insult, but Faun's expression remains the same.

"I'm not much for human flesh, no." He twists his cup in his hands uncomfortably. "But I've very much wanted someone from the mortal world before, too."

Jenny thinks he might be talking about the thief of his sealskin, but she's lost interest in questions and answers. She feels low, drawn thin. The rat was not enough for her to walk among the humans, she realizes. She needs a better source of protein that isn't as diminutive or, she thinks as she picks between her mottled green teeth, whiskered.

From Harvard, they walk together to Central Square. She feels less ill on her feet, the bodies around her thinning. The character of the city shifts. Fewer young people with their friends, and more people with children. Men and women line up outside of restaurants. They laugh and elbow one another in the same companionable fashion as Faun and Clyde. Or Selene and Zeke.

Not lovers, Jenny insists to herself as she lags behind them. More than associates, though. If she could smell pheromones, it would be pouring off them, the assurance they have mingled their fluids and panted into one another's mouths. Do Zeke and Selene want each other?

What a name! Zeke. It burns in her and she hates it and wants to rip the word out of anyone who says it.

Clyde pauses, waits for Jenny to catch up. He offers his elbow.

Eventually, she links it with hers.

"So, I've been thinking." He attempts a smile. "Now that we know the phone doesn't work, Faun and I will help you get to the man directly."

Jenny narrows her eyes and bristles with suspicion. "You just want your gateway."

"I do." Clyde looks pleased. "I also want you to be happy as a clam, as they say."

"Who says that?"

He ignores her question. "No sense in any bad feelings between us."

She's unsure what he means about shellfish being happy. They've never seemed particularly cheerful to her. They're just food or, if one lacks a knife and her drawn claws aren't sharp enough to cut, a potential weapon.

Regardless of the comparison, Jenny sees, yes, Clyde likes people to be happy with him, whether they're immortal as he or hapless mortals who will be dead, hmm, when? Within a couple centuries? Something like that. Clyde thinks people living peacefully together makes things smooth. This is a tactic Jenny once tried in sputtering spurts and starts but has never seen through to the end. When she has consorted with humans in the past, she has often been hungry. She tried to live among them a century ago in the boardinghouse and eight hundred years before that along the Irish Sea, really tried, but the humans never want to be particularly close to her. Something makes her wrong, even if they don't understand what it is, even if they don't see her tear open someone's throat. Even when her teeth aren't green.

"That man will not let me get near him." Jenny focuses on the pavement beneath her boots with a burn of shame. She hates hunting when her pride is wounded. She feels ludicrous and raw with humiliation.

Faun falls into step with them. "Lucky for you, we have an expert in the art of seduction with us." Jenny looks up to see her wink at Clyde.

He looks away at the suggestion. Of all things, he's bashful! "I got experience I can put to good use."

"With Elspeth?"

Clyde's Adam's apple climbs his neck and bobs back down. "Let's talk about something else."

"Aw. Why not? Don't you still think about her?"

Jenny can smell the sweat before she sees it break out on his forehead. "We're not talking about me. We're talking about Jenny." He fastens his eyes on her. "You said you saw him the first time—when?" Clyde asks. "Evening? Morning?"

"It was night," she says.

"Moon out?"

"There were streetlamps." She remembers his glasses catching the light from above the grates.

Clyde claps his hands and rubs them together. "Good. It was dim. He probably won't recognize you when he sees you again."

"I just need to find him without anyone else about." She had him all to herself that first time but had hesitated. She fears it will happen again, that her teeth will be bared and she won't bite. This time, she needs to find him alone, a place where she can keep him very still. Hold him. And, once she has grown bored and satisfied, eat him. The details are blurry but leave her full of desire.

"No. You just need to look different." Faun reaches up and takes a lock of Jenny's green hair. Gently, she tugs it. "This needs to be a different color."

"And we need a better set of clothes." Clyde inspects her.

Jenny growls. "You found these for me."

"And now we'll find others," he says. "And clues to where the man actually lives. You didn't happen to hear his name, did you?"

"Zeke." It's burned in her mind now along with his gaze. "Someone was with him."

"That's a start." Clyde strokes his chin. "Who was his friend?"

Jenny remembers how close the woman was with him. "He called her Selene. They talked about children wasting their time."

"His children? Maybe it's his wife?"

"No!" Jenny is too quick and too loud. She catches herself, sees the look on Clyde's face, and tries again. "No, I don't think she is his wife. They talked about essays with . . . with . . ." She remembers the men who used to knock on the doors of great houses to offer tutelage to the gentlemen therein. Zeke didn't look like that, exactly, but she suspects there are some students still left who desire a tutor of some sort. Or at least tutors who desire students. "Essays. Published things."

"Oh, a professor in Harvard Square." Faun looks bored. "How unique."

"Professors have web pages nowadays." Clyde's smile is wide. "If this Zeke is a teacher, he might have one of those."

Jenny has a picture in her mind of spiderwebs and pages in a book, but she can't fit them together.

"We have a lot to go on." He counts three words out on his fingers. "Zeke. Professor. Selene. Good. Let's go to the library."

The Central Square Branch of the Cambridge Public Library (according to the red sign above the doors) is in a squat cement building. It looks like one of those garages where vehicles are stored. Clyde walks through like he's there every day.

Faun looks circumspect. She dithers at the entrance. An olive-skinned woman with straight black hair and her freckled child come out. Each has piles of books in their arms and doesn't seem to see her. Faun is forced to step out of the way and, so, steps right into Jenny.

"Ouch." Faun sucks her teeth and glowers as if Jenny is the one who stepped into her. "I hate them."

"Just them?" Jenny studies the woman and child as they walk down the street. The girl jumps over a gray puddle. Her mother laughs.

"All of them." Faun motions toward the humans who Clyde walks past with such ease. Her lip curls as she steps through the door. "Like fungus. They're mold. They trapped me for years, you know. I was so happy at the beginning of the last century! Do you remember carnivals?"

Jenny, baffled, nods.

Faun smiles as she looks into the distance. "I thought I could make some money as a circus freak with my goat legs. I met with talent agents, all of it. Instead of the sideshow, though, uniformed men brought me to a holding facility. They poked and prodded and watched my body not age or die." She rubs her forehead. "But I felt pain. They didn't care much about that. I think some were just overjoyed they found a woman they could hurt endlessly."

Jenny can smell her fear. It's the same fear that threaded itself through Faun's words when she spoke of human authorities.

"When I escaped long afterward, I only hated uniformed men for a long time." Faun looks at the ground. "Now they all make me sick. Clyde doesn't understand why."

Though she finds this terribly interesting, Jenny realizes Faun doesn't want to say more about it. Did they cut her open? Were her guts removed? Did they grow back? Instead of asking these questions, Jenny looks for the shelves of books. She will see if Faun will tell her more another time.

Clyde doesn't say anything. Instead, he immediately slips over to the front desk. He smiles in a friendly way at the stout woman sitting there. She's slope-shouldered, with a sharp ferret nose. They speak of the weather, how it's gotten so warm today, and are the computers available? The woman smiles back and nods several times. He nods, too, and goes and sits down in front of, and becomes engrossed in, one of the machines in a row along the wooden table. Each has a bunch of buttons with letters on them, and when he presses them, they make a satisfying clicking sound. This appears to manipulate the images on the flat glass window in front of him. The images move too fast for Jenny to understand what they are. Clyde manipulates them impressively. Effortlessly.

Jenny has been in libraries many hundreds of times. She learned to read Latin in the oldest one she was inside, where she had to cut off her hair so the clerks there thought she was another scholar. She has picked up Chinese and Arabic by similar means. In the last handful she visited, under the gray skies of the British Isles and the busy, cramped streets of horse-smelling Brooklyn, she taught herself how to read English. Not well, but capably. Her favorite part of those times was the card catalog, which seemed to have all the world's knowledge under her fingers.

She does not see any wooden chest that would serve the same function now, which is troubling. Without it, the shelves look anemic. She walks toward them and can't help but notice the humans there, eyeing her mismatched clothes in a way they did not seem to when she was just walking with Faun and Clyde.

Jenny picks a book at random. The cover crinkles when she touches it, so she draws back. On further inspection, its outside is preserved in a sheet of plastic. The pages are not confined in such a way. She turns them at random and finds she is reading about a woman on a beach with a man. Water crashes on a surf, a woman admires the taste of a man's tongue (nothing to be particularly excited about, in her experience), and wonders whether or not their love can be "true."

Curious, Jenny reads on, but an explanation on how love can exist as something "true" is not forthcoming. Does that mean there's such a thing as false love? Can she use it to lure in the man? She flips pages forward to find more detail, but instead just reads about the woman eating "a muffin that was absolutely heavenly." An explanation of the muffin's relation to ecclesiastical matters is not explored.

Also, the description of humans eating food reminds her that the rat was awfully small. Looking at her fingers, she sees they now have a greenish hue again. Her instinct suggests it's time to eat once more.

Jenny puts the book back on the shelf where she found it. She looks up to see if Clyde is done with his machine, but he is not. He has a small smile on his face as he pokes the buttons.

Faun stands near the doors, her arms crossed. Her face is like a brick wall.

A young, golden-skinned woman with big, wet blue eyes and even bluer hair stumbles into Faun with a heavy cart of books. Her glasses magnify those wet eyes and remind Jenny of the man.

She mouths his name: "Zeke." If she can't taste him, she can taste that.

While the young woman apologizes profusely, Faun's face turns a fascinating shade of red.

"You fucks are all the same!" Her voice fills the space, and some of the library's inhabitants look up. Jenny suspects Faun is not really talking to this woman but the humans who, long ago, were all too happy to imprison and prod her body. It must have driven her mad. "And don't you dare cry! You're not allowed."

In a fascinating show of disobedience, this command prompts the blue-haired young woman to flush as well. Enormous tears pour down her face.

Jenny watches with intense curiosity. She wonders if Zeke cries like that. If not, can she make him? How? Would he whimper? Would she need to remove one finger at a time or would that cause him to pass out too quickly?

The woman Clyde talked to at the front desk comes up to them both, gingerly walking with quick, little steps. She asks Faun in a low voice what the trouble is and would she like to sit down?

Faun yells at her, too. "You get away from me! Am I making trouble? No!" Jenny can hear her blood thundering through her veins, the raw panic. Faun is here, in the library, and she also isn't. She's in a windowless room and cruel humans loom over her with starched uniforms and sharp cutting implements. Her eyes are like those of a panicked salmon, seized from the river and fluttering on the shore. Or like a child falling under the water, struggling to swim.

Jenny, curious, joins her side.

"Our library," says the sharp-nosed woman, revealing herself and the blue-haired girl to be librarians, "is not an appropriate place for yelling. I think you should leave."

The girl with blue hair wipes her face hurriedly and interrupts her associate. "Ma'am," she says, addressing Jenny, "is there something you need?"

Jenny considers this. "I think I need to leave, too," she says, eyeing Faun. "I am also not appropriate for this library."

"You're not? Why?" The blue-haired girl must feel a misguided kinship with Jenny because Jenny's hair is also not a standard human color. The fact this woman thinks she's also mortal disgusts her. Far from being aware of such an insult, the young woman just looks baffled.

"Oh, you're polite to her, huh?" Faun looks as if she's about to spit.

The blue-haired girl holds up her hand. "Now, listen—"

Faun recoils. She's certain the woman is about to strike her.

Jenny doesn't think this is the case, but her hackles are up all the same. She takes the blue-haired girl's hand in hers and brings it to her mouth. The woman stares, seems to think it's about to be kissed, but Jenny bites instead.

It's not hard, she doesn't break the skin, and it's just for a moment. She just needs to show dominance! But the girl's eyes go wide in horror. Then anger.

Silence descends on the four of them. Even the ferret-nosed woman is shocked.

"Get out." There are no longer tears on the blue-haired woman's face, just anger. "Right now. Get out!"

Jenny smiles, lips closed. With more than a little satisfaction, she walks toward the door. Faun clip-clops after her. Clyde, as far as Jenny can see, is still happily tapping away at his machine, blissfully unaware that anything has happened at all.

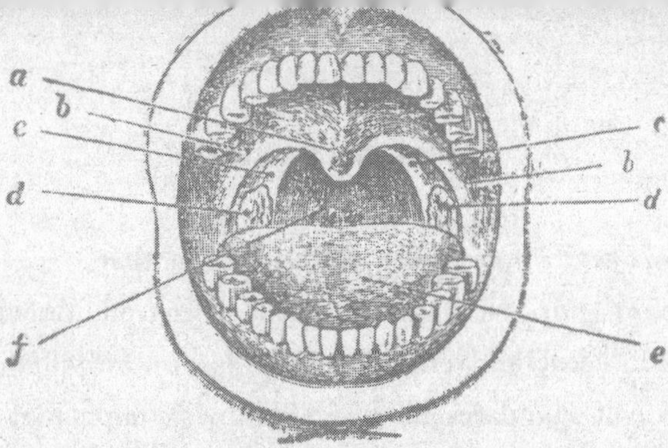

Chapter Seven

PALATE

Jenny walks away from the library and down the block. She laughs as she goes because the air tastes sweeter out here, and the world looks brighter. She put a human in her place! How utterly satisfying.

Faun catches her elbow. "Why'd you do that?"

"Oh, I did not like her," Jenny says.

"Why? 'Cuz she bumped into me?" There's a deep line between Faun's white eyebrows.

Jenny's breath catches. "I do what I want to who I want when I want."

Faun presses her lips together. "Is it because you're lonely?"

She stops, twists, and glares at Faun. "What?"

"I didn't like her because I'm an angry old bitch who's met the worst sort of humans imaginable." Faun's heart is loud, still a panicking gallop. "You got angry because you like having me as company."

Jenny inhales sharply. "How dare you."

"No, I get it. One grumpy old bitch to another."

"You do not." Now she shows Faun her teeth, drawing back her lips in a cruel and terrible sneer. This creature with the wrong bottom half who dares call herself Jenny's companion! Jenny is too great to be understood.

It's midday, and Jenny has been among humans far longer than she's used to being around anyone in years. Decades. She's exhausted, and with the sun straight over her head, she's hot. Mostly, however, she's hungry. Soon, the green blush on her skin will regain its fishy beauty. She has maybe until the sun is at its apex in the sky.

Faun stands straighter, chin up, dress belled out to show her hidden hooves are far apart. It's an intimidation stance. Jenny thinks she could be a warrior. Perhaps, in another life when she was pleasantly drunk on wine, long before she yelled at librarians who startled her, that's what she was. "I do understand you," she says. "What, you think you're so special?"

Jenny knows she's right. She likes Faun and it's awful. Will Clyde accuse her of the same thing when he catches up to them? Of liking them both? It's so much more comforting to cocoon herself within chilly water and her own self-regard. It's better to not be with other people.

She grows enraged. If Faun is squaring up to fight her, wouldn't it make sense for her to return the favor? Her bruises from earlier no longer hurt, at least not too badly. Her cracked rib has already knitted back together.

A man across the street howls something at them, startling them from their standoff. They both look toward him. His head is pink, with white hair crawling along his scalp. He's wiry, but something about the red hue of his cheeks and the sunburn of his arms strikes Jenny as, well, juicy.

He's swinging a box with glass bottles of brown beer in it. That beer is clearly inside him, too. She can smell it on his sweat. His red face is joyful and his eyes are screwed up in laughter as he repeats himself: "Hey, sluts!" He proceeds to hold up two fingers and lash his tongue between them. Then he breaks into a wide, happy smile, proud of himself.

Jenny's anger is blown out like a candle snuffed in a puddle. She suspects she should be revolted, but mostly, she's simply confused. Last she knew, "sluts" were lazy women and sleepy milkmaids. The gesture is, however, certainly one of sexual innuendo. Perhaps his hand is supposed to be a woman's nethers and his tongue a penis? She's unsure.

Faun, meanwhile, seems to vibrate. Her pupils are pinpricks as she quivers with rage. "Asshole."

The man must see her lips move because he cups a hand around his mouth and says, "Two whores looking to pull some tricks!" He then points at the hem of his trousers, holds a loose fist in front of his zipper, and pretends to masturbate himself.

Jenny wonders if he's bragging about engaging in self-stimulation. What a pathetic thing to boast about! She's seen humans, often ones who think they're alone and unobserved, do just that since the beginning of their ridiculous civilization. By the distance he keeps from them, the whole street between them like a river, she suspects it's an insult. He's just like the drunks she's seen leave bars and taunt passersby, carelessly weaving along the street. He doesn't wish to tempt a slap or, in Faun's case, a kick.

And indeed, Faun jumps forward, clopping onto the black street. She seems ready for a battle.

Jenny touches Faun's shoulder. "Wait."

"He deserves a beating." Faun's accent shifts, her tongue wrapping around the edges of consonants and touching vowels in ways she must have left behind long ago. Her grip on the present moment is slipping again and she is back in a laboratory with cruel men.

"I'm hungry." Jenny gives the barest smile, showing the edge of her green teeth. "Like with the rat."

Faun's eyebrows lift. Her gaze flicks to the man and then back to Jenny. Then she smiles, too, understanding filling her face with warmth.

They swan across the street to meet him. Jenny remains aloof while Faun has become all smiles. For a moment, his face is perplexed as Jenny begins to walk with him, matching her step with his. He walks carefully at first, and then with more confidence. A pleased grin appears on his face, sunrise-bright, innocent as a child's.

"Greetings!" She returns his brightness.

"What's your name?" Faun's voice is breathy.

"Ralph! Last name McGish." He throws the arm holding the beer around Jenny's waist, which is a deeply strange sensation, especially when his pink fingers rest on her hip. He eases her forward like a prized cow. And, oh, he is elated! "What's yours, ladies?"

Faun doesn't answer. She just giggles. The sound is so false, Jenny expects him to be suspicious, but he looks too happy, too overjoyed.

Ralph McGish agrees, just like that, to take them to his house. He regales them with times in his past when he brought other women home, one after another. "It's all confidence," he says. "I know I'm a catch, right? So then, you know what? They do, too."

"Yes." Jenny smiles with great sincerity and doesn't throw off his arm even though she wants to desperately. "You are a catch."

"I'm a fighter, you know." His teeth, to her surprise, are all very straight, and he smiles like a man on a magazine cover. For a moment, he is handsome. There's a hole in that smile, too, a missing piece. He sticks his tongue through the gap when he notes her staring. "Lost that in a fight at the Cantab. I wasn't boxing anymore. After the head injuries, the cauliflower ear?" He points to his ear, which is, indeed, misshapen and bumpy. "When I'm doing bad, like now? When I'm drinking again? I like to fight. I'm not even that good anymore. My ex-wife, she was a waitress when I met her at one of those joints, and she told me, you know, she couldn't respect any man who didn't want to fight for something they love. I was a good Catholic kid. She was Catholic, too, but she seemed to like having something to confess, you know? You both Catholic?"

He reaches and squeezes Faun's buttocks with a large, square hand. She flutters her white eyelashes like moth wings and giggles again. "No, but I've been to Rome."

"Aw." He nods slowly. "I'd love to go some time. See the pope."

Faun shakes her head. "It isn't like it once was."

"World travelers, huh? You don't happen to be students, do you?" Ralph McGish doesn't wait for them to respond. "As long as you're legal, it's all fine with me."

They turn a corner and the restaurants they pass become tall, narrow houses. Trees are dotted along the sidewalk, their green leaves beginning to yellow at the edges. They stop in front of a gray door with a rusted knob.

"Ground-floor suite!" He moves his beers under his arm and begins to claw inside his pocket. Eventually, as they watch him fumble, he pulls out a set of keys. He attempts to push one into the lock, misses, and has to try again. He laughs at himself. "If you both left my drunk ass right now, I'd get it. Just a silly old man."

Jenny knows drunk. She's seen many humans and animals screaming, fainting dead away, and, memorably, somersaulting. This man opted to do none of these but, instead, decided to stand in the street and be vulgar toward the both of them, she reminds herself firmly.

She prefers the drowned victims, the ones who can no longer talk.

He finally opens the door and brings Jenny and Faun inside, where it smells damp and vaguely fungal. The hallow way—which humans, in the last century or so, had begun to call "hallways" and use as rooms meant only to connect other rooms to each other, very wasteful in her opinion—is dark, with a pile of shoes near the door. The windows are speckled with what is most likely beer that has dried to the glass. He throws his keys onto a small table, but they slide off and onto the floor. Leaning forward to pick them up, he laughs uproariously as his trousers begin to slide down to reveal his ass.

Ralph stands up again, swaying. "I got beers, but if you want to get things started right away, I won't mind."

"All right!" Faun stands in the hollow way and rolls down the waistband of her skirt until the entire thing falls to the floor in a puff of fabric, revealing her goat legs with their backward-bending knees. She grins, wicked and hairy.

Ralph McGish drops his box of beer. One of the bottles cracks, fills with foam, and the bubbles geyser upward.

Jenny, however, in seeing Faun's hairy legs in their full glory for the first time, finds her eyes tracking up to her waist. There, along her brown belly, is scar tissue. The skin is thick with it, knotted, bubbled flesh. Jenny herself is able to heal from burns after a hearty meal, but she remembers fire and the horror of smelling your own cooked flesh. Faun, it seems, cannot heal herself so completely.

"What the fuck?" Ralph McGish whispers. "Are those real?"

Faun answers by kicking his legs out from under him.

Jenny hears the snap of a bone.

Ralph McGish begins to scream. He falls to the floor, arms wrapped around his ankle, like he's protecting a small animal. "What are you?"

"You said it yourself." Jenny stands beside Faun and manages to smile, too. "You're a catch. You're our catch."

"God," he begins.

Jenny squats down and, with as much might as she can muster, punches his nose.

It bursts like a boil, but instead of viscous, yellow pus, blood runs down into his mouth. His face twists in pain. He looks more like a squalling infant than a man, and, surprised at the sight, it gives Jenny pause. It's been many years since she's watched a man cry, really cry. The tears on his face are like bubbles under water after you jump in, clinging to one's fingers. He looks awful.

Faun thumps her hoof down on his splayed hand. Ralph howls. It immediately swells, his fingers turning thick and pink as if the blood in his veins is screaming against the skin. She keeps kicking, breaking the man, his shins snapping. Ralph McGish's mouth wails. Faun doesn't seem to remember that anyone else is even there.

Jenny reminds herself that this is the sound of pigs rutting in farmyards. It's among a range of thoroughly mortal sounds. She thinks of the many babies in carriages who have been rolled over her head, screaming like cats in an alley battle. Crying out like this is a thing humans are born knowing how to do. This man is only reiterating it, like he's singing a chorus in a long, primal song.

It just happens to be a repulsive song that right now knots Jenny up inside. It lingers and nauseates her.

Panting, Faun falls back. She mops the sweat off her face with her arm.

Jenny takes the opportunity to jump forward. Her nails become claws and she lands on top of the man. She does what she wished she had done in many unsleeping hours since she met and allowed Zeke to escape. Crouching on Ralph McGish's chest, she snarls into his face. He quails. Then she dips her head and snares her green teeth in his throat.

Jenny bites down into sour, damp flesh salted with blood and fear. His skin burns with alcohol. The pulse under her lips sputters. When her teeth sink in farther, they meet the cords of his neck and the spongy give of his windpipe. The muscles battle her teeth. He really is a fighter.

Jenny clamps her jaw down harder and pulls. Electricity crawls across her skin, like during the last turn of the century when she ran her fingers over an electrical socket at a circus that smelled of salted caramel and horses. Euphoria sings between her ears, and the world is good.

The destroyed, rough meat she jerks out leaves a dark trail of arterial juices. It runs over her chin, hot and steaming in the cool doorway.

Ralph McGish doesn't scream anymore. His body looks up sightlessly, goes slack. The air around him is filled with mundane, human smells.

Now he looks like a proper kill. It makes her hungrier. She begins to eat his throat. The meat is tough, but the taste—like pork, marinated—is delicious.

"Hey! Damn it." Faun pants. "I wasn't done with him!"

For a moment, Jenny feels shame. She sits up while straddling the man. Taking the gore from her mouth, she considers it as one would consider a particularly grisly apple. "I said I was hungry."

Faun remains annoyed. Her arms are crossed and her face is dark with anger. "You're not very good at being on a team."

"I told you we weren't the same."

"We are! We're gods among scum!"

Jenny agrees. She thinks that, in her years of living, she has managed well so far without intimate associates of her own age. Of course she has seen them, deer with the faces of women and men underwater with pig snouts and tails, but she usually gives them a wide berth. "Does Clyde help murder people with you?"

Faun sits on the stairs and watches Jenny continue to sit on the body. "Doesn't go in for this kind of thing." Sighing, she digs in her coat pocket. She takes out a cigar and then a book of matches. "He's Clyde. Humans are precious creatures who share custodianship of this realm or something, even when they mess it up and torture everyone on it. Even when they cook the world in flames and smoke and foul excrement. Even when they do what his girl did to him." She seems indifferent, even bored by the cooling body. It's lost her interest.

Jenny, meanwhile, gets to work removing the man's clothes. She pulls his shirt over his head. "What does he say when you do this?"

Faun bites off the end of the cigar and spits it out. "Nothing. I think he suspects, sometimes, but I don't do it a lot. Only in the company of people who also want blood." She levels a gaze at Jenny and then an arched eyebrow.

"So, when you return to see him, you won't tell him about Ralph McGish."

"Who?" She runs a match over the bare wood of the stair. It ignites in a hiss of flame that she touches, deftly, to the cigar.

Jenny pulls off his loose trousers and messed underwear. "That's what this man said his name was."

The smoke is thick and good. Faun exhales a gray cloud of warm, woody tobacco through her nose. "Well, then, no. Their names don't matter to me, sweets."

Jenny sees Zeke in her mind, staring straight at her, knowing who she was after a sea of years when she was a nothing, a grain of sand whirling under the waves.

"Know what I'll say when I see Clyde?" Faun takes another puff. "I'll tell him I needed a moment to calm down. If we get separated from each other, we meet in front of the Dunks in Central Square. No idea if he saw us get kicked out, but I'm sure he'll meet me there whenever he's done. Probably when the library closes, knowing him." Her eyes narrow as she looks down at the body. "I haven't beaten a man in a very long time. It's been even longer since I've killed anyone. The first time I enjoyed it was to a woman, you know?" She takes a deep, unsteady breath, smoke curling out of her nose. "To get out of where they kept me."

Jenny doesn't want to know more than what the belt of scars on Faun's abdomen already reveal.

Faun sees Jenny looking at the scars again. Immediately, she throws her arm over her belly as if hiding it removes it from Jenny's memory. Her eyes cast downward as her cigar snows ash onto the stairs. "They wanted to see how I worked. Like what some humans did when they found the first platypus. They thought it was a prank and they took it apart, like someone would spend their time sewing ducks and beavers together." She puffs again. "I need a drink."

Jenny studies the meat beneath her. When she pulls people down into water, their bodies eventually become bloated, soft, and easy to tear into bits. "It's going to take me a long time to eat him."

"I'm sure he's got a fridge you can shove him in."

"A what?"

"Like an icebox?"

Jenny shakes her head, trying to think. She knows what "ice" and a "box" are, individually.

"Lords. How long were you down there?" Faun pauses. "Do you know what refrigeration is?"

"Storing meat in the cold?"

"Exactly. It's a storage place that keeps meat cool. You eat what you can and put the rest in there. When Clyde and I sneak into motels and hotels, they have tiny versions. I don't like them because they buzz when I'm trying to sleep."

"And you're sure he has one?" Jenny didn't see them when she was last parading about the surface world, masquerading pathetically as a mortal.

"It's probably in the kitchen." Faun pushes the cigar into the corner of her mouth and stands. Her legs tremble momentarily, and then, after a few deep breaths, she finds her footing. Perhaps the death of the man has not left her as cold as Jenny thought. "Come on."

Jenny stands and follows, lapping the blood running down her palms. She nibbles at her fingernails to dislodge the gristle under there. As she swallows, she feels her energy grow in her belly. Her face flushes hotly, and she watches her hands blush pink once more.

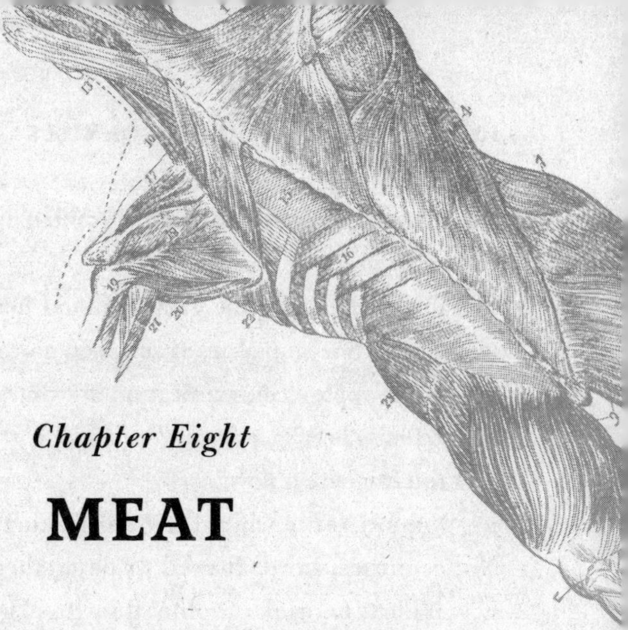

Chapter Eight

MEAT

Faun shows her a large set of white double doors on the front of a cabinet taller than Jenny is. When they open it, cool air ghosts out and kisses her skin. The fridge, as Faun calls it, has a little bit of food and libations inside: red apples that are far too shiny, a wilted head of lettuce, boxes of margarine, and cans of beer stacked on top of one another.

Jenny is shocked. "All this food is his?"

"Ours now. It can be where you keep him, too."

"He shares all this with family, certainly."

"I doubt it." Faun nods toward the mail stacked on the wooden table, a sink piled high with pans and plates caked with food, and a tiled floor that's a dull brown but, as Jenny studies it, appears to be dreary yellow tiles covered in grime. "This is a bachelor. He probably wouldn't have brought home a couple of women if a wife was here to yell at him."

Jenny isn't sure of the mysteries of marriage, but certainly more than one wife has overheard her husband and another woman and thought better than to interrupt. Yet, indeed, the place appears to be empty.

Faun reaches into the giant box and her fingers brush one of the cans. She stops herself and then moves to one of the too-bright red apples. She picks it up and bites, crunching loudly. "God, I miss beer."

"You can have it now."

"Nope. I really can't. It's been making me sick for years. No, centuries. Lord. It used to be mother's milk to me and now it hurts to drink. Another thing to blame on those men in uniform, I'm sure." But Faun doesn't sound sure at all. Jenny picks out one of the cans and examines it. Plenty of cans have made their way down into the flooded train station over the years, but they tended to be empty. She's unsure how they open. She plucks at a circle of metal at the top, but it doesn't do anything.

"You drink?" Faun asked.

"No." Jenny puts it back and examines the colder of the two doors. There is meat there, though sheathed in plastic and plucked of skin and entrails.

Jenny leaves the fridge open so she can examine the kitchen counters.

She finds a wooden block stuck with knives. Some, she is loath to admit, look sharper than her teeth. "I can skin and dress him, but that will take time. I need to cut the meat from the bone."

"You could cut him up and boil him."

"I don't see a fireplace."

"What? Oh, sweets. No. You don't need one." Faun clops over to a metal box, where she explains the burners on top, and how the dials can be used to produce fire. She demonstrates.

Jenny jumps back.

Faun, for the first time since they arrived, appears genuinely amused. "God, no wonder Clyde wants to help you. You're like a lamb. Well, a bloody lamb, but a lamb. You've seen a stove before, haven't you?"

"They didn't used to look like that, all smooth and pale." Glancing back to the front hallway, Jenny chews her lip. "He won't know about the man I killed?"

"Not if we don't tell him. He'll get scared and start worrying about the police." Faun's mouth twists. "And I know you don't want to be arrested, right?"

Jenny remembers a night once, long before automobiles and streetlights, when she was stopped by a constable who was angry she wasn't wearing clothes. He threw a scratchy horsehair blanket over her body. She repaid him by dropping on all fours and biting his ankle. Then she ran away. "No," Jenny says.

"Good. We just have to leave here after a couple weeks, before the neighbors decide to check where he is—if they check on him, anyway. Humans are strange like that. Also, you should probably clean up." She jerks her chin to Jenny's clothes.

Jenny looks down. The front of her hoodie is splattered with blood. She wipes at it with her hands, but that only produces a long, gory streak.

Faun wanders out of the kitchen. From the other room, she whistles. "Damn! This place looks big enough to house you, me, and Clyde. We could tell him it's yours, some odd house you found years ago and managed to keep empty. Or something."

Jenny runs her hand along the mail on the table doubtfully. All of it has some form of "Mr. McGish" or "Mr. Ralph McGish" printed on the envelope. She leaves behind sticky red fingerprints.

"You should throw those in the garbage." Faun wanders back into the room. She languidly points to a bucket next to the kitchen counter. "He probably wouldn't believe you have a friend who's loaning you an apartment, either, huh?"

"I don't have friends."

"I'm aware." Faun brushes her fingers back through her hair. "I'll think of something. Let's clean up the mess in the front hall."

The mess she refers to, of course, is the body. Faun regards it as an obstacle and seems unconcerned how long ago it stopped drawing breath. She suggests covering the kitchen floor in sliced and flattened garbage bags. Jenny has only seen the black, flimsy plastic when full of trash, or so full the sack is split like a fish's belly. Faun finds what she calls "a roll of tape," which unspools into flat, fragile ribbon with adhesive on one side. She asks Jenny to stretch the plastic on the floor so she can stick it down.

They then move what was once Ralph McGish out of the front hall. Jenny holds the legs and Faun grabs the arms. The head lolls to the side. Faun laughs as it droops and bounces against the floor.

Jenny is annoyed. She wants her food as unbruised as possible. When she sees the manic joy in the satyr woman's eyes, however, she's reminded of when she and her sisters used to delight with one another in the hunt. She doubts Faun would celebrate as they used to, all wet, slippery lips and tight, slimy embraces, but Jenny's face cracks into a smile in return.

"I know I'm going to regret this later." Faun laughs. "But gods, I don't care. Watching that bastard die felt amazing."

"I don't regret getting food."

"You still might. Does that disgusting man really taste good?"

Jenny's lip curls haughtily. "You don't need to have any of him."

"Of course not." Faun sighs through her nose. "Whatever you do with him, we have to wash the front hall if we want Clyde to spend more than a minute inside. He'll smell the blood immediately."

Wash? The water had always taken care of cleaning anything for her: fish, combs, shells, interesting rocks. On dry land, of course, water only occasionally falls from the sky. Much less convenient, but when it washes the land, really washes it, it's clean or, at the very least, flooded. No trace of any bodies left.

Beneath the sink, they find a treasure trove of soaps and concoctions in brightly colored bottles. Faun and then Jenny scrub the front hall with clothes from the man's bedroom. The fluids smell of perfumes or the runoff from fortified citadels and factories. Also, incongruously, lemons.

Jenny grows impatient with this ritual cleansing. She wants to eat more. They're on their hands and knees, toiling and grunting.

Just when she thinks they're done washing, Faun points at another drop of red-now-brown liquid on the floor.

When Jenny rises, her knees ache. The rags are pink and her shirt is spotted and befouled as if she simply laid down to scrub the floor with her whole body.

"He has a washer in the room behind the kitchen. Come on."

The "washer," it turns out, is yet another metal box. It produces cold water from an unseen spout. First, Faun puts her own clothes inside the box, along with more chemicals. When she stands before it naked and hits a button, it begins to whirl around.

Jenny examines this process clinically. Through the small window, the clothes spin in bubbling water, cycling like one of those funfair rides she's always stared at with what she won't admit is envy. What a miracle machines are, doing things just because humans command them to do so. Humans are inferior animals, true, but they have excellent ingenuity.

Uncomfortable with her momentary appreciation for the kin of apes, Jenny goes back to the kitchen to eat her fill. She flips Ralph onto his stomach, revealing wide swaths of rosy pink skin burned red by the sun. She pauses to wash him, splashing him with water from the faucet.

On the wall of his kitchen, she sees a photograph of him when he was young. It's the same face shape and the same hungry eyes and smile. She knows he really must be younger because he looks buoyant and hopeful. His ear is not yet deformed. Beside him is a woman with a white veil and a sprig of small flowers in her hair. She smiles, too, but is more focused on cutting into the large, layered cake in front of them. The glass of the photograph is, to Jenny's surprise, polished clean and well-kept. He loved this picture. Now that he's dead, that love and care he put into maintaining it has evaporated into nothing. The thought, to her surprise, makes her sad.

Faun yells when she returns to the kitchen. She doesn't like that Jenny has left his body naked in the middle of the floor. "Eat what you can and store the rest in the bags I showed you! Shove him in the freezer. No parts showing, okay?"

"Freezer. Yes," Jenny says much more confidently than she feels.

A man is much like a rat. A rat that makes clever machines, but a rat nonetheless. And yes, rodents sometimes have dark, lovely eyes and sweet little whiskers, but they are still beneath her. She focuses her mind on this as she unsheathes her claws. She refuses to think of his eyelashes, like those of the people who fell beneath her waters, either by her hand or theirs, and drowned in front of her. Jenny turns away from the photograph on the wall.

She eats.

All the thoughts in her head leave her for a few glorious minutes.

When the remaining meat sticks too firmly to the bone, she takes out his knives and cuts. Arm from shoulder, leg from body, head from neck. He is already rotting and the smell is sweet. She splits him open to remove the colon and throws it in a stinking clump into the refuse bucket. With relish, she pulls out shining ropes of his intestines and the prize that is his stomach and kidneys. She drools as she bites into them, grinning as juice runs down her chin.

When her belly swells and distends, Jenny sits back happily. She's full and, as she always is after eating, satisfied. Clumsily, she rolls each leftover piece of the man's body in the plastic on the floor. His head is partially sheared of its skin and muscle, but still recognizably a head. The bones she doesn't need to pick her teeth or comb her hair? Well, she will have to bury those, she supposes.

Jenny leaves the kitchen to find Faun.

Faun now dries her clothes in the machine next to the first. This one washes her garments in hot air, not water. Then Faun dresses once more, covering the scars on her belly; her round, drooping breasts; and her goat legs.

Faun directs her to wash her clothes, too. "Wow. You're a mess. Throw his clothes in with your stuff, too, okay?"

Jenny strips without a thought. For the second time that day, she stands naked before one who is essentially a stranger. "Why didn't you wash his clothes with yours?"

"Because you're washing them with yours. I didn't kill him, you know?" Faun looks disgusted. "Also, I don't want to."

Jenny appreciates the honesty, but it's mean and petty. She sits in front of the washing machine, contemplating her clothes mingling with those of the man she's killed, her buttocks bare on the tiles as she pulls her knees up to her chin.

Faun stretches, arms raised high. "I'm going to make up a cock-and-bull story and tell Clyde one of his connections has a place," she says. It's as if no one has died at all. "When I come back, please just agree with anything I say, all right? I know how to lie to him." For a moment, her brow knits. Guilt? Perhaps, but the guilt isn't strong enough for her to pause for more than a moment. She cuts her eyes to Jenny and motions at her own mouth. "You should take a bath, too."

Jenny touches her chin. When she looks down at her hand, she finds gristle, still slick with fat.

"Back soon, sweets." Faun stops awkwardly in front of her and squeezes her shoulder.

Are they sisters now, wedded to each other in blood, though they have only known each other's names for a few hours?

But Faun says nothing more, drops her gaze, and leaves.

Jenny eventually sees the darkness beyond the windows. Night is here, and the streetlamps blaze like orange fires. Naked, she returns to the kitchen. Instead of washing his filthy pants, she decides to put them in the trash. She pauses when she holds up his trousers. Something heavy sits in one of his pockets. She pulls out a phone, just like Zeke's.

On the screen are several words. She sounds them out slowly: "New. Voice. Mail. Sister. Charles."

For a moment, her insides are cold, like the gray slush of winter has been packed down between her ribs. He had a sister? Jenny traces the word with her bloody thumb, and to her shock, the screen changes.

A woman's crisp, gentle voice erupts from the phone: "Hey there, Ralph. We haven't heard from you in the group for a week now, but I wanted to let you know we're thinking about you. You're stronger than you think. I promise." The sister breathes out a laugh. Then the phone is silent.

Jenny is seized with an urge to run out the door and down the street, whether constables find her indecently exposed or not.

She stills herself. The phone reproducing a human voice is alien to her, but it's just another too-clever device. A mechanical parrot. She has seen toys like that stretching back centuries, metal birds with real wings, and full-grown dolls shaped like gentrified women in enormous wigs who play the pianoforte for enamored audiences. They are less useful than ovens and washing machines.

And if she leaves now, Faun and Clyde will be angry. They won't help her. She would have to find a human she trusts to be smart enough to help her and resist eating them.

Jenny keeps the phone close as she looks for a washtub. She finds one through the master bedroom, where there's a window with a spiderweb crack in the glass. This was where Ralph McGish had planned his unlikely seduction of her and Faun. Seeing his dingy home and old nuptial portrait, she suspects he didn't have much opportunity otherwise. She wonders if he woke that morning and had a premonition it would be his last. Or perhaps he only thought of women and what he would shout at them when he left his house.

Beyond the bedroom is a more promising find, a washroom with a white tub inside it.

She leaves Ralph's phone on the tiled floor as she climbs in. Stop thinking, she tells herself firmly as she fills it. Experimenting with the faucets, she realizes that one gives only hot water and the other cold. It takes her a while to find the right temperature. Unable to locate a stopper, she instead covers the drain with her foot.

When she reunites with Zeke, she will not torture him the way Faun tortured Ralph. She's sure of that. She also doesn't want to kill him right away. What is the middle between those states? She wants to keep him with her, chained up, kneeling down in front of her, forehead pressed to the floor as he begs her for his life. And when he looks up, it will be to say her name and look only at her.

She wants to keep him like a toy.

Jenny submerges herself for what feels like an hour. The blood comes off in brown, disintegrating shreds. When she sloshes above the surface, she sees the phone once again, its condemning screen with "Sister Charles" on it. Someone who thought of him, is still thinking of him, and may come looking to see where he went.

Human meat is delicious, yes, but rats are less complicated.

Downstairs, the front door swings open.

"You have to ask me before you do things!" Clyde is snappish.

"I'm impulsive, sweets." Faun's laugh is tight and even sounds uncomfortable. "Isn't that what you love about me?"

"Not at all."

"Little too late to tell me that," says Faun.

The bathroom catches all the sound, a sinkhole where Jenny can swim in words without being required to reply back with her own. She finds she likes that. It's soothing to hear people so clearly after years of straining underground for fragments of conversation.

Not that humans ever talk about anything overly interesting, of course. The weather seems to be an enormous topic of conversation. So does alternating between shouting at and soothing children. Also, sporting events and annoyance over rats in garbage. Humans want to talk about everything. Like Ralph McGish, they are an idiosyncratic mix of simple and complex.

She sinks down farther in the tub, the water far too clean for her liking. It sloshes over the side. It feels good to be as deep as she can be.

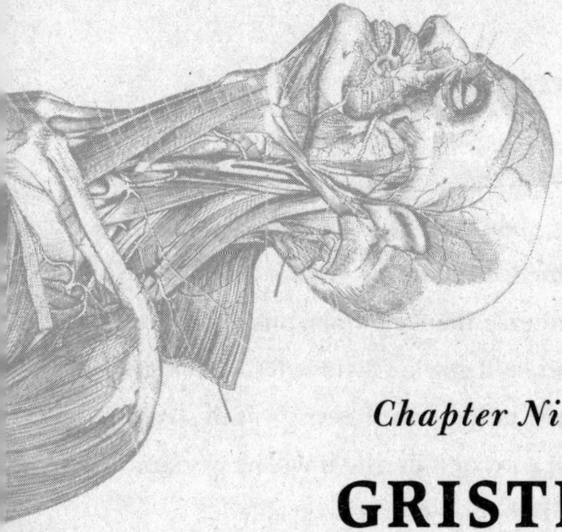

Chapter Nine

GRISTLE

When she breaks the surface, she can hear them. Their words spear her with something like fear.

"You can't just walk into someone's house and decide you live here." Clyde stomps down the stairs.

"Just a few days! A week, tops. If he comes back, we claim we're squatters."

"How do you know a man lives here?"

Faun pauses for too long. "I mean, look at this place. There's a layer of dust on the carpet. And not a stick of furniture matches. Men can't match anything with anything."

"No, no, no. We've holed up in plenty of places where you're the one who's brought home chairs and cushions and nothing ever looks good together."

Faun laughs. "That's because I don't have a social secure-what's-it and can't get a job."

"Social security card. And you can find a job without one, but you have to get to know humans and ask them about things, and you don't like that."

A silence stretches between them.

He knows Faun is lying, Jenny thinks. He knows something so much worse has happened here, yet he isn't saying anything about that. He'll open the freezer, then tear open one of the pieces of meat in black plastic, and he'll gawk. Clyde will turn on Jenny with the same human horror in his eyes that she's seen so many times right before she either runs or kills. But it will be worse now, because she's already tried to fight them and she failed.

"Anyway," Faun continues on, "what about squatters' rights?"

Clyde exhales and it's a casual, gentle sound, like a horse wuffling. "You have to live in the same place for twenty years."

"Twenty years isn't much longer than twenty minutes, sometimes. Don't you think?"

"For me, you, and the other one, sure." Jenny can hear each individual step squeak as Clyde nears the bathroom. "Where is she?"

"I'm sure she's here."

"Please say she's not out biting more people."

Jenny doesn't want to call to them. She's had a habit of not calling out to people for centuries. It's not her way, with the recent exception in mind. Instead, she splashes in the tub, swatting the water around like she's trying to hit an incessant fly.

"Ah," Clyde says. "Of course."

It's a hard thing to admit, but Jenny would not be alive for as long as she has if she didn't know fear. What if he throws open the door, sees some speck of blood on her face, and immediately knows what she's done? She scrubs her face with the water and then, in the blur of her eyes, sees the phone on the floor. She reaches out and slides it across the tiles to sit under the sink.

Instead of opening the door, he pauses in front of it and strikes it gently. "Jenny? You in there?"

Even though she's wet, her mouth is dry. "Yes," she manages.

"May I come in?"

"Yes?"

He swings open the door, sees Jenny is again without clothes, and blocks her from view with his hand. He seems to have truly absorbed the human propensity for shame. "Do you need to be in water every day?"

"No. I like water. That's all."

He wears a half smile that she can see peeking out between his fingers. "Thought you'd get bored of it after so many centuries."

"No." She sinks down, protective. "I would never." He doesn't know, she thinks, and with it comes a wave of nausea, as if the eyeball she pulled out of the man's face is staring up from her belly through the tunnel of her throat.

"Ah. Right. Listen." He meets her eyes now that her body is mostly hidden from view. "His name's Ezekiel Fuego-Eckstein."

The one she resurfaced to find in the first place.

"Or Zeke."

And he has reduced that name to a single punch of a word, a surprise: Zeke! It makes her laugh. With a rush of tub water, she sits up. "How do you know?"

"First of all, you had a lot more information than you thought. Secondly, I remember him from years ago." He looks away from her breasts, as though they are the glare of the sun.

"What?" Jenny gawks at him. How dare this man exist before he came looking for her?

"He used to write these 'investigative reports' online about monsters and urban legends. He was probably, I don't know, thirteen at the time. He wrote some pretty canny stuff about fair folk, mermaids, and, of course, selkies." Clyde motions to himself and gives a little bow.

Of course he had known her name, Jenny thinks. He had researched people like her for years.

Clyde still keeps his eyes away from Jenny's body. "Humans, when they write about us? It comes out strange. Some people are clearly writing about themselves, their obsessions, their, uh, physical interests."

"Sex." Jenny remembers tracts about witches dancing naked and riding brooms in ways that did not suggest flight, things she was unaware magic women had much interest in doing.

"Yes. That." He frowns, distressed by the word. Clearly, he's spent too long dwelling in the company of Faun's embarrassing honesty. "His work was at least clinical, thoughtful. Collated data from books. Treated us all like we were more real than fairy tales. Some of the most reliable stuff I've seen online."

"What line?" Jenny thinks about train lines. She's lived long enough in a station to know what those are. "Is that where he lives? Can we go there?" She stands, water sliding off her skin.

He fully turns away from her. "No, Jenny, please. I don't have any of that. I couldn't find his address. It's not listed."

"I don't need to know how to address him. You said his name. That's enough."

He frowns. "'Address' is another word for where he lives."

"Oh. Yes." Jenny slowly sits back down in the tub, miserable. What good is a name if it's not attached to a person who they can find? And what good is all her years of knowledge if the world of now is still a confusing morass?

"But that's just why we can't go off and find him right now, you see. You need to learn some things first. We need sort of a script for you to follow, right? Like a play. Do you know what a play is?"

Jenny is mortally offended. She draws herself up to her full height and swings her arms out grandly. "Yes, I know what theater is!"

"Ah. Clearly." He *ahems*. "So, we need to figure out some things for you to say to him. Pick-up lines, right? Then we figure out what to do about your teeth. And we need to make you more, um . . ." Clyde, still looking away, holds up a box with a photograph of a woman on it displaying long, silky black hair. "Human."

She curls her lip in disgust and doesn't move to take the box. "Tell me what else you know about him."

"He's a fellow—er, well, they call them 'teaching fellows.' He works for a professor, Selene Harrison. They teach something called 'public policy.' I don't know where he lives, but I think I know where he works."

"And he's there every day?"

"I don't think—"

"Do you think he's there right now?" Jenny feels like a pigeon has gotten caught in her chest and keeps fluttering to get out. Her heart sings. "When can we go?"

"Not 'we.' I don't think we can all be there. I think it has to be just you. And we have to fairy-godmother you into someone more like him first."

"Yes. All right. When do we start?"

"Why don't we find you a towel?" Clyde shuffles out of the room. His eyes never stray to the phone once.

Clyde and Faun, to her horror, have trained themselves to sleep the way humans do: every night, from after dusk until dawn. While they do, they ask her to sit in front of a mirror that looks like a phone, but bigger. Faun suggests she watch as many "shows" on it as she can while they're asleep.

Jenny wears her black hoodie again and a pair of underwear while she stretches out on the floor's carpet, staring at the box.

"Look at how people talk and react to each other. Don't do everything they do, of course, but just. You know." Clyde looks past the mirror and examines the books on the shelves. He pulls one out and flips through it, a large volume full of photos of people hitting one another with gloves. Their faces are variously mashed and bloodied. More than a few of the men smile like Ralph did, an attempt at roguish charm soured into belligerent confusion. "Listen." Clyde puts the book back down. "Watch the humans on TV, their habits, the way they speak. Practice saying things aloud to yourself if you can."

Faun yawns abruptly, dramatically. "Though not too loud. I want to sleep."

Jenny represses her disgust for human things and instead stares at the screen. "Fine."

"You change the channels with this." Faun holds up a black bar with large buttons on it.

Channels like waters, she thinks, taking it in hand.

When Clyde leaves, Faun leans down to whisper, "I told him we found an unlocked house where the person in it has been clearly gone for weeks. In fact, we found so much mail in the slot and under the door, we could barely open it. Try not to contradict that, all right?"

Jenny's eyes cut to the door. She wonders how sharp his hearing is. "You're certain he doesn't know?"

"Yes." Faun huffs at the implication she would be doubted. "Of course he doesn't know."

She both likes and is infuriated by Faun. She both likes and is frustrated by Clyde. If their plan to help her find Zeke doesn't work, she decides she will be gracious and, rather than try to kill them again, turn from them and run. She doesn't think it will be shameful, because she will simply wait to never see them again. Unlike humans, she suspects they will take much longer to die.

Jenny grits her teeth. This is all too complicated.

Faun mistakes her expression. "It works like this." She touches several of the buttons and the TV brightens.

Jenny watches a woman with white, even teeth, enormous eyes, high cheekbones, and the glossiest hair she's ever seen. She shows off diamond bracelets and pearls and all sorts of things humans collect. She says they're worth money. Numbers appear at the bottom of the screen.

"Night!" Faun sweeps out of the room. She must know what theater is, too, because she has the presence to match.

Alone and fascinated, Jenny picks up the black bar and pushes down on one of the buttons. When the screen changes, she jumps and drops it.

On the screen, a man and woman eat at a table covered with a stiff white cloth. Again, the woman has straight white teeth. The man has thick, full lips and glasses that seem like the ones her man wears—Zeke, yes, she has to think of him by name now. There are lit candles between them, though Jenny knows humans created electricity to replace candles long ago, so it's curious a couple would use them. They have food in front of them, but rather than eat it, they talk.

Jenny's memories of the theater are old, but the actors there acted. Here? They speak quietly, conspiratorially to each other. The man tells her he'll protect her. She says she knows and kisses him. They move their noses away from each other like experts and open their mouths in a synchronized fashion to accommodate each other's tongues.

The next instant, the screen changes. They're in bed, kissing just the same, but now having sexual congress. Blankets shield the meshing of their sex organs from view. It's such a ridiculous moment, him heaving atop her, pretending to mingle their fluids.

But how awful, how strange, how wonderful that it quickens Jenny's pulse. She feels her mouth go ajar and her heart thudding against her ribs.

This. She wants this from Zeke, before anything else. She feels a shiver start inside her and work down to her tightening sex.

Then the TV changes again. The details of the act are confined to mystery. Now the woman stands in an overlarge shirt—clearly the man's—while in a clean white kitchen. When he enters, wearing just a pair of undergarments that show off the curve of his buttocks to excellent effect, they grin at each other with their smooth teeth. Or, rather, she grins first and then he follows.

Jenny finds herself grinning as well. She stops when the people in the TV begin to kiss once more. She doesn't have the white teeth that they do. She needs to fix that. Once again, Clyde and Faun have proven their use and wisdom in the human realm.

Jenny strokes an incisor. Should she start the change with that? Or one of the molars? The molars hurt worse. It won't make them hurt less to save their removal for last.

It doesn't matter, she thinks. She needs to find the man and figure out what innate quality kept her from killing him. It shouldn't make a difference, and yet.

She pushes hard against the incisor and then plucks it forward like the string of a lute. Then she seesaws it until it begins to hurt. She takes the pain and buries it in the saltwater caverns and snaking crevices of her mind, where her memory of French, Old English, Arabic, Latin, Aramaic, and Chinese sit nuzzled up together, where she remembers seeing her first fortress and her first light bulb, the time she first saw a wheeled cart, and the time she first saw a merry-go-round with smiling, still horses.

Somewhere in there is a box that contains the numbness of her waking hours in the flooded train station.

With a pang and a final twist, she yanks the tooth out.

Jenny holds the sharp green nub in front of her. The tooth is darker at the root, like a piece of grass pulled from the soil. She laughs at its smallness.

Her tongue pushes into the gap where the tooth was, exploring the gums eagerly. It tastes a little like human blood, but distinctly briny and her own. The teeth will grow back new and white, of course, at least as white as the teeth of the man cooling in the freezer. Ralph has left her a gift even if he didn't mean to do so.

The humans in the TV stop kissing so that the woman can talk into her phone. The screen changes to indicate she is speaking to another man. It's all suddenly very boring. She wants to see them kissing again.

Gingerly, Jenny picks up the remote and touches another button. The TV turns black. Panicked that she has broken it, she presses that same button. She's relieved to watch it turn on once more.

Touching more buttons shows her more images of men and women kissing one another—never men and men or women and women, it seems. There are rules here, she thinks, though they seem arcane and silly. Every civilization has them, she supposes, but those all fall apart eventually.

She watches a man yell at a woman and then the woman yell back. They kiss. This doesn't seem quite right, but the actors performing it seem happy enough.

Jenny watches a story about a teenage girl with thick eyebrows and rough, greasy hair who continually prays to her god for help. She watches another program about men who steal money from a train and seem far more interested in spending time together than they are in the woman who stays with them on a farm with horses.

In the bedroom, she hears Clyde and Faun rustle together. Whether they're fighting or fucking, it's hard to say. The films seem to suggest one can do both.

As the hours pass, she pulls out her green teeth one by one until her mouth is blood and meat. She spits onto the carpet a couple times because there's too much to swallow.

In the kitchen, she finds a small knife, the kind used to remove the delicate bones from fish. It can help replace her teeth in their new state should she need to bite anyone. Her experience suggests this may indeed be needed.

When light comes in through the windows and Clyde stirs in the other room, she's excited to show him all she's learned about humans and their romantic inclinations and seduction behaviors. She decides to mirror his expression the way she saw all the actors mirror one another's.

He comes into the room, sees her, and gives a slow, almost sad smile. He looks sleepy.

She smiles back, blood sluicing down her bottom lip.

He yells.

"I had to remove my teeth. They grow back," she says carefully as their absence changes the shape of her words. It sounds like "Ah hahd to womove muh teef. Dey gwow bach." She doesn't even have to do it again if she eats human meat often enough!

"Oh. Yes. All right, that makes sense." He stares at the pile of pointed green teeth on the floor like they're mouse droppings.

Jenny gives a great, withering sigh and acquiesces to his comfort by pushing them beneath the couch behind her.

He remains ill at ease. "At least you have a start on what we need to do today."

"Wha?" She wipes the film of blood that's gathered on her pink chin. "I oo?"

"Yes." He holds up a catalog of some sort that contains photos of thin, wide-eyed women, as if they're all for sale. "If you want to get near a man, we're going to make you look as human as possible."

She is going to see him! She is going to see Zeke and flawlessly, or at least as flawlessly as possible, trick him.

Jenny jumps up and spreads her hands in celebration. She spins, which reminds her she has not stood in a very long time, but she doesn't sit back down. She dances, stumbles, and laughs. Clyde, to her shock, laughs, too. She dances about like a toothless witch in the woods, bounding around a fire with a cat.

Faun descends the stairs in what she assumes to be the former master of the house's seaweed-green robe. It smells like smoke, and she strolls in it like a queen. "I was asleep," she murmurs, low and sounding more murderous than she did when she committed murder. "Be quiet next time."

Jenny smiles gummily up at her sister in arms, her fellow hunter. What a relief to once more find people to whom she belongs! She simply has to get the man, then open the tunnel up for them, and all will be well. She, Faun, and Clyde could even go on being good friends afterward! She doesn't need them, of course, she assures herself, but what a relief to be near others again.

The next day, the first of her lateral incisors punches through her gums while Faun dyes Jenny's hair. Clyde tried his best, but the black gunk he was supposed to comb through those lank green wisps crept over his gloves and got on his shirt. He looks horrified as he attempts to scrub it out. Faun steps in with a great indignant huff.

Jenny smiles at her with her one tooth hanging over her lip.

Faun's mouth twists but does not return the jolliness.

In order to practice her human interaction, Jenny mirrors Faun's face.

Faun seems to misunderstand what that expression means. "It won't take long. I promise."

When her third molar makes its way through, it's evening, and she and Faun are examining her drying hair. Faun winces and glowers. "It's not black."

Jenny agrees, but she doesn't care. She just runs her tongue over the blocky white bones coming into her mouth. "Brown hair is fine." Momentarily, she piles it on top of her head. She twists her chin back and forth, admiring her reflection with its long neck and jutting chin.

When Zeke sees her, he will be agog at her beauty. He will gasp and say, "Who are you?" and she will take him to a separate place to tell him. There will be no people around and they can have each other's company for hours. Perhaps a whole day.

And when, Jenny wonders, did she start wanting to impress him? She's just going to eat him anyway.

Clyde calls from the other room. He asks about getting food to put in the fridge.

Jenny goes very still.

"Oh, it's disgusting in there!" Faun laughs a little too loudly. "The smell alone would make your nose hairs curl. Don't open it!"

He doesn't.

Later that week, while the three of them watch TV, her second canine knifes through her gums in a jet of warm blood.

Faun informs her of a new fact: "They're not white. Or, well, not as white as they could be, sweets."

Jenny examines the yellow cast to the teeth. A sheen like the reflection of mint on water crosses the enamel. "They eventually change back to green and get sharper." Still in her euphoric mood, she puts her index fingers on either side of her mouth. She pretends she has mandibles of a great beetle, which she thinks is very amusing.

Faun's mouth just twists. "Is there a way to stop it?"

"I just need to, um. Eat."

Putting a softly wrinkled hand on Jenny's shoulder, Faun cuts her eyes to Clyde. He's busy considering the television.

"No." Faun is firm. "We'll have to bleach them. I'll go out and get bleaching strips for when they're all in."

Jenny hates the sound of that. Then she sees that Clyde has taken the computer machine of the apartment's previous owner. Another contribution by Ralph! She walks over to him to admire it.

Clyde has it open on his lap. On the screen is a photo of Zeke.

"Yes," says Jenny. "Please."

When she accidentally bites her tongue with one of her new bicuspids, Clyde is counseling her on how to talk with humans. "Eye contact." He points at his own eyes. "If they start to say something confusing, something you don't understand, keep that eye contact, nod, and smile."

"You always know what they're talking about!" Faun calls from the kitchen. "You actually bother to care about them."

"I always *look* like I know what they're talking about," he corrects her. "That's not the same thing."

Jenny stares at him hard and refuses to blink.

Clyde grins warmly. "Your teeth make you look like you just lost a fight."

Jenny sours. "They're growing back! And I would never lose a fight."

Faun cackles from the other room. "Sure about that, sweets?"

Jenny snarls. This whole process has begun to take too long.

Clyde shakes his head. "I'm not being literal." He sighs. "Just pretend that when people talk, they're all telling jokes. Then wait to see if someone laughs."

"That's terrible advice," Faun announces as she clops through the door. She holds one of the CVS bags from the last time she left the house to run errands. "Voilà. Teeth whitening strips!" Through the plastic, Jenny sees a box with a disembodied grin that leers at her suspiciously.

Jenny doesn't think this is worth anything like the word "voilà," as it's neither particularly special nor much of a surprise, but she does as Clyde instructs. She just nods, smiles, and waits to see if someone laughs.

"I also got you a new dress." Faun pulls out a dark, slinky cloth without sleeves and lets it drop like a dead bird out of the sky in front of Jenny. "And you're going to figure out how to do makeup, because I don't have a clue in all the seven hells."

The next week, as the last of her incisors creeps into her mouth, Jenny accidentally smears the end of the eyeliner brush onto her eyeball as she leans in to the bathroom mirror. She hisses at the sting until Clyde gives her a look, cautioning her not to hiss any longer. "Now," he says from the door, "Professor Harrison's room number is listed as 4-E here and then as TBA here. So I'm not sure where she is in the building."

Another molar grinds up through her sore gums as he explains to her what deodorant is.

Her last tooth slides downward as Jenny uses the plastic-handled razor Clyde got her to slice the hair from her armpits, her legs, and along her belly.

Faun is at least ready with the whitening strips. They taste bitter.

She wishes she felt that bitter about pretending to be human. She still looks down on them, she tells herself. But when Faun removes the whitening strips, when Jenny stares at her reflection, she sees her own blunt little teeth like glistening pearls, a necklace held between her lips.

And it's fun to see her face smile back at her.

Unfortunately, she's running out of food now. The last of Ralph is meat and gristle stuck to gory ribs and thigh bones, some muscle clinging to his skull. Despite the miracle of electric refrigeration, Ralph has begun to taste old. She has to hunt once more.

When Clyde and Faun bed down for the night, she decides to leave the house for the first time in almost two weeks. She needs air. Also, Clyde seems to know they're keeping something from him, casting quiet glances at them both sometimes. At least he's kept away from the fridge, fearing it's full of mold and rot. Faun, for her part, is being more affectionate, pulling him into bed with her at the end of each day.

Jenny goes out wearing the hoodie over the long dress Faun gave her. There's a chill in the evening air, but it's mild. It may not be a very lovely costume, but she feels beautiful as she walks along a sidewalk choked with humans. Some glance her way and, when she smiles, she's delighted when they smile back.

She walks to the Charles River. Farther down the shore, there's a boat ablaze with lights and bubbling with laughter. Here, near the bridge, it is quiet and dark.

Except for a man and woman standing in the water up to their thighs. The man is large and dark skinned, with lush rolls of fat cascading down his lovely back. The woman is similarly fat and soft. They giggle and splash each other. Happy.

Isolated from everyone else, Jenny thinks.

When he gives a particularly loud cackle, she recognizes him. It's the man Clyde talked to in order to get her clothes. Barney was his name, right?

Jenny pushes the name away. He is food, and that is all there is. She shucks off her shirt and dress, leaving them next to a bed of mulch-smelling flowers. She kneels down to pick up the knife she hid in the hoodie's front pouch. This startles a large Canada goose squatting nearby, who reels up and beats his wings at her in anger.

Barney looks up. His smiling face goes slack. "Baby?"

The woman startles. "You good?"

"We got to go."

"Did you see something?"

"Heard something. If something's there, I'm not risking shit."

"All right, Barney." The woman takes his hand and they slosh to the shore together.

Jenny hesitates, staring at their intertwined fingers as they escape. Her chest feels hollow, empty.

Slowly, Jenny puts her clothes back on. She feels weak and stupid for letting them get away, but it's different, isn't it? When she's in the water, she uses that to her advantage, pulls people down to drown them. It's different when they're the ones in the water and she's on land.

A cloud of whiskey slides through the air into Jenny's nose. She turns and sees the old woman from the church, Mags. Her cheeks still have that empty look, free of the teeth that Jenny herself has cultivated with powers Mags doesn't have.

"Going for a bath?" She gives Jenny a blurry smile. She sways and so do the items in her plastic shopping cart. It rattles as she pushes it over the grass. "Barney's here, I think. Good thing your eyebrows have grown back."

"Yeah." She rubs her arm, surprised the woman remembers. "They do that."

Mags giggles and hiccups, the noise slurring into her words. "Where are your little friends? Clyde and the short one?"

Jenny shrugs, aware that besides Mags, no one else is around now.

Mags throws out her arms expansively, a scarecrow's limbs with barely any flesh at all. "Everyone at the shelter likes him, and everyone hates her. Of course, they're together! Isn't that funny?"

Clearing her throat, Jenny leans toward her. "I don't know if they like or hate each other most of the time."

"Oh, both, I'm sure." Mags waves her hands. "They're not like us. You and me, kid, we're women who are good at being alone."

Jenny's face heats and she breathes deeply. She's angry now, humiliated that someone has seen through her so quickly. She shows her by pulling out the small knife and pushing it into Mags's throat.

Mags doesn't move. Her eyes just go a little wider as arterial blood sprays down her threadbare jacket and onto Jenny's dress. She opens her mouth to let loose a scream, but even that is silent. She stares at Jenny past the point of seeing her and her beauty, past the point of seeing anything.

Jenny releases the knife. It remains in Mags's throat as she falls forward. She doesn't bother to remove it until Mags is still. Then she flips her over, removes the knife, and feasts on the soft, still-warm neck.

The whiskey in Mags's blood causes Jenny's world to tilt and fill with heat. There's a lot of it. Her rage is snuffed out as she devours, like a matchstick thrown into a pond.

When she's done, she pushes all that remains of Mags into the river and then throws her cart after. Her body is embarrassingly light, even lighter than her things.

Jenny is sated and, for the most part, pleased with herself, but all she can think about on the way back to Clyde and Faun is how Barney held hands with his woman. It was so gentle. In her mind is also Mags's hazy stare, her assessment of Jenny's loneliness searing and true. But that, like many of her memories, recedes into the depths inside her.

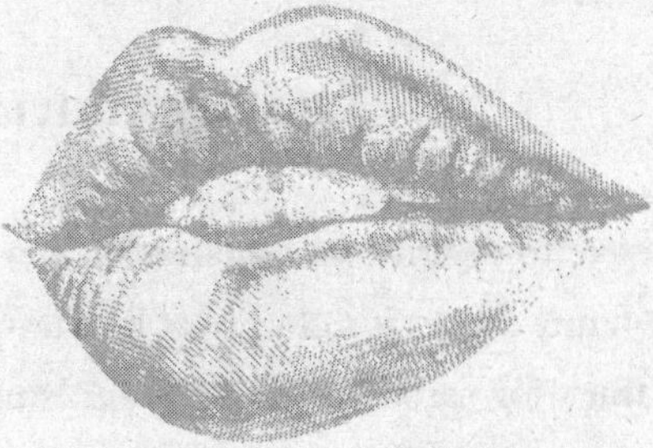

Chapter Ten

LIPS

Jenny's jaw aches as she stands, alone, outside of the John F. Kennedy School of Government. She wears a light camel trench coat over a loose shirt and jeans that Clyde brought home for her. Across the street, she sees him and Faun sit at a donut shop with "DD" over the door. They regard her and continue to eat pastries. Clyde nods indulgently and shoos her with his hand.

It's a cool, sunless day, the skies gray and solid as slate. She knows which window belongs to Professor Selene Harrison's office because Clyde pointed it out to her. She focuses on it, sharpens her ears, and hears the name "Zeke." Her heart flutters and she becomes achingly aware of the old woman's meat, still sitting in a great lump in her stomach.

"Zeke, please," says the woman's voice. "Just go ahead and kill me now." She makes a strangled sound, pretending to choke on her own spit.

"Let me think about that. Hmm. Kill my boss? Go to jail without paying any more of my student loans?" Zeke chuckles. "How about next week? I'll kill you after the next paper is in."

"I have to rewrite my syllabus." There is a sigh of fabric on fabric. Jenny thinks it's clothes at first until she realizes the fabric is too thick for early autumn. It sounds more like furniture. The woman, Selene Harrison, has shifted in her seat. "I hate this. I don't want to do it."

"I can rewrite it for you. You need to add the Hefferen paper, right?"

"And the one on urban center development. The one on crime, too. The one that Sturges added an addendum to recently?"

"Foster."

"What?" Another shift of fabric.

"You're thinking of the Foster paper." He sounds so pleased with himself. "She added a section on the failure of prisons to reform inmates due to unclear expectations put on the populace."

"No, that's definitely Sturges," she says crisply. "They're similar, so it's easy to confuse them, but Foster did that deep dive on solitary confinement."

"Yes, Foster did." His insistence is gentle, helpful. "Then she incorporated it into her earlier research to correct initial assumptions about the intelligence of the prison populace."

"Oh, fuck," she says. "You're right. I can't keep any of this shit straight anymore. See that pillow over there?"

His answer is tentative. "The one with 'If you want to find a prince, you have to kiss a lot of frogs'?"

"I made it." She seems proud. "Could you suffocate me with it?"

"I would, but I think my scholarships might be compromised."

"Yeah, yeah." She gives a theatrical sigh.

"I know." He consoles her. "Do you have the two thirty appointment booked out with the problem student yet? Huang?"

"I would if that asshole would respond to my emails."

"He didn't?" For the first time during this exchange, Zeke sounds genuinely surprised. "He responded to mine."

"You're a man, and the kid's kind of a closet sexist. He could also just be stupid."

He sighs. "Or just being a teenager. We need to stop accepting undergrads to this course."

It's not the conversation that Jenny would expect between Zeke and a potential wife. They're also very familiar with each other. Not overly familiar, but she seems to know him.

Jenny is sad that she so obviously does not. She's still fairly sure she wants him dead, but not before they have the chance to talk.

When this is all over, and she's done what she likes to Zeke's remains, she'll sink back down into the flooded station. No more need for sadness. The stink of humans will leave her and so will any lingering regard for them. She won't emerge for two hundred years this time, she assures herself, leaving only to occasionally hunt and eat. Maybe, by then, most of the humans in Boston will have killed one another in some sort of war or have been driven from their houses by floods. She thinks of them running and screaming, scrambling like ants, and smiles to herself. Boston was her home before most of their forefathers were infants. She outlives not just their shortened lives but also their fragile townships and cities, her superiority spelled out in every year she thrives beneath their feet.

She enters the door beneath Zeke and Selene Harrison's window. It opens immediately under her touch and she's met with another glass door, which does not.

Between the doors is a man at a desk. "ID?" He nods toward a black box on the wall.

Jenny glances at the box. It doesn't look remotely like anything associated with a scholar at an institution. She turns to the guard and practices her smile, the one that punctures dimples into her peculiar pinkish face. "I'm not a student here."

"Are you delivering something?" He glances at her coat, as if expecting her to produce a bouquet of flowers or a brown package where there's none.

"I'm here to see Zeke Fuego-Eckstein. I need to return his phone." She says it clearly, loudly, like she and Clyde practiced.

"You can leave it here with me."

Her nostrils flare and she feels her heart speed up. "No. I need to give it to him."

He raises his white eyebrows at her. Then he shrugs. "Sign in, then." He points to an open book with lined paper. "Name here. Then the date and time. Remember to sign out when you leave."

Jenny grasps the pen with discomfort. It's far too light in her hand. The last time she wrote her name was at the request of a night nurse in a white hat, someone who seemed concerned when she walked by with blood splashed across her dress. The nurse had been correct to be concerned, but only because Jenny planned to use the hospital to procure a helpless meal for herself in the form of a sick human.

In script, she writes, with a shaky hand, JENNYFER GREENE. When she asks the man at the desk for the time, she feels a rush of confidence. She writes, TWO O'CLOCK, looks up at the man, this guard, and beams.

His eyebrows are bunched together over his nose and he shrugs. He presses a button on his desk, and the door produces a *click*. "Do you do that thing? Uh, calligraphy?" He tilts his head toward her. "You write nice."

"No," she says firmly. "I have no patience with tanning cow hides and little talent at painting them in ink." She rewards his bafflement with a smile before she heads up the stairs.

As she climbs, Jenny's ears find Zeke's voice. Attached to him is that smell. Vanilla. Cinnamon. Utterly artificial, something he anointed his body with to mask his primal sweat. She follows his scent now, too.

The hallway has flyers for what are termed "speaking engagements" and "study groups" on the walls. She passes a sapling-thin dark man in a suit chatting animatedly with a young, prim woman who takes careful notes.

"I ordered the lunch for the workshop Thursday," says Zeke as she nears their door.

Jenny pauses. Something that she refuses to recognize as fear builds in her chest.

"Are they going to have the chicken and pasta?" Selene sighs.

"Oh." He sighs, too, put out by some mysterious obstacle. "No. I think it's too late to change it. I just got the vegetarian pizza."

"Pizza? Oh no. Not pizza." She laughs. "The ones they make are awful!"

"Soggy." He's mournful. "How can anyone ruin a pizza?"

"It takes talent."

"And spite."

Jenny knocks and, without hesitation, pushes open the door.

Selene Harrison looks up from her seat on the couch. She has a computer like Clyde's. It's opened in front of her like a clamshell on her lap. Up close, Jenny sees the woman has threads of white running through her black curls. The woman regards her with a small frown over wire-frame glasses. Where she was warm and open to Zeke in the privacy of the room, she's imperious as Jenny stands on the threshold. "Can I help you?"

Jenny looks away from her to Zeke. He's as arresting as when she first saw him, his hair somehow messier than it was in the station. Now he leans against the wall, arms crossed. His shirt is different than it was the other day, now a sky blue with buttons. She can see he wears another shirt underneath, neither of which hide the fascinating jut of his collarbones. He looks at her, head cocked. He pushes off from the wall, falters, and stands, hesitating to dust off his trousers.

His lips look softer than she remembers.

He squints at her through his own glasses, his brow wrinkling. Does he recognize her? Jenny's heart swells.

"Ezekiel Fuego-Eckstein? Zeke?" Jenny enunciates this clearly. She practiced that with Clyde, too. From her coat pocket, she pulls the cracked phone and displays it with the hauteur of an officer flaunting a badge. "Is this yours?" She makes sure to smile.

Zeke's eyes narrow to a squint. There's a sheen of sweat prickling along his throat now, and it makes him shine like a leg of mutton shimmering with fat. He takes a cautious step forward. Infuriatingly, he is not looking at her but the phone. "That's mine?"

"Yes!" She grabs his hand and his pulse jumps beneath her fingers, the blue veins of his wrist running with beautiful, thrumming life. A seashore teeming with fish and salt. She lays it in his palm. "See?"

He retracts his wrist and, because she must not be greedy—not yet—she lets him go.

Jenny dislikes letting go. She hates the wave of desire that rises up and speeds her own pulse. And she's close enough to smell the sweat on his skin, the vanilla, the mint huff of his breath. She just wants to be closer. It's awfully humiliating, but she reminds herself he can't see the hunger beneath her skin, not in the way she can hear the *wub-dub* of his heart.

But the beat of that muscle in his chest slows. He touches the button that changes the images on the front of the phone with ease and presses it several times. "Oh." He smiles a little and looks up at her. His eyes are a studied squint, but the gratitude shines out behind his glasses, out of him. "Yeah. It is. Thank you. How did you know?"

Jenny smiles wider than she has in many years. She and Clyde worked on the story together and she recites what he told her to say: "I used to work at an apple store. I had a coworker look up the cereal number of your phone. Then I found your profile on Lincoln." Clyde was very firm about all of this: apples, cereal number, Lincoln.

Zeke's eyebrows meet in the middle and he nods. He understands. His beautiful mouth is in the shape of a small frown as if he's trying to piece this all together despite the fact she's just explained it. She doesn't like how he hesitates.

The silence must be stretching too long because the woman takes pains to fill it. "Zeke helps teach one of my courses. He has a desk down the hall, I'll add." The woman remains seated, but her soft edges have gone firm. Her smile is smaller and tighter than Jenny's. "I'm Professor Harrison. I was supposed to meet with a student at about this time. I don't know if he's still coming, but . . ." She lets the words hang in the air.

Zeke looks at Jenny with a furrowed brow and, to her delight, chews on his bottom lip. She supposes she's delighted because that's exactly what she would like to do to his mouth. The difficulty, of course, comes in keeping him still while she does so. How far away are they from the river?

"Do you want to get coffee later?" He's shy, his grin tentative. "I'd say let's get some now, but I have work."

"Oh no, you don't." Now the woman has turned her attention back to her laptop. "I have it."

Zeke looks distressed, which is fascinating. His forehead wrinkles sweetly. He looks younger somehow. "Don't we have to talk about . . . ?"

"No." The professor smiles and doesn't look up. "It can wait. I promise."

Jenny is awed by the kindness of this woman, giving her assistant up to a stranger! She watches him sink into himself like a hermit crab. Oh, the sublime euphoria that will sweep across her when she gets him alone, cracks him open, and devours the softness inside! The chill creeps up her spine deliciously.

Zeke jerks in surprise. When he looks at Jenny, his eyes narrow behind his glasses. He regards her closely, a man of science trudging through tide pools in oversized, shiny boots, eyeing every sea star and urchin like it's the first time he's ever seen one. He wants to take note of her.

All Jenny can do is mirror him, tilt her head and nod. She feels off-kilter, flushed. Hot. But this is exactly what she wants. She waits for him to speak.

"How about we just grab some coffee in the Smith Center?" Zeke tries. "My desk isn't that private. It would be good to talk for a sec." He looks away with his long, lovely lashes, bashful. "If you want, anyway."

Jenny nods greedily. She agrees with him that, yes, they should go somewhere private. Whether it's to unleash her claws and plunge them in between his ribs or to kiss his lips into a purpled bruise, she hasn't yet decided. Ideally, both, and if he screams, no one will be there to take note of it.

"Great." The professor yawns with an exaggerated broadness. "I'll see you tomorrow."

"Oh, no." Zeke shakes his head quickly. "I'll come back after to finish grading the essays."

Selene is amused. "We didn't promise them the grades would be up until next Thursday."

"Yeah, but you know they'll ask."

"Some of them are already asking." She gives a great, withering sigh. "These type A's. I swear. They need to figure out sooner or later their emergency isn't ours. Also, unless they're about to flunk everything, it's a grade. Not a death sentence."

"Okay. Yeah, but you remember being that age." His smile is weak. Jenny wonders if he was that anxious, small scholar.

"Oh, yes, and I was just as tightly wound. The best corrective is to tell them to chill the fuck out as gently as possible. Anyway, Zeke, I'll see you. Enjoy your time with . . . ?" She looks at Jenny expectantly.

Her name, she realizes. Faun warned her about how to dispense it, because, of course, when she finally guts and devours Zeke, someone will come looking for him. She prefers murder to be anonymous, the deaths of Ralph and Mags intimate and unmarred by her name.

But Selene Harrison is looking at her and waiting. She has an air of authority. In the interest of being human, Jenny can't be silent.

"Jenny." She gives her a dimpled smile. "How-nice-to-meet-you." Stiffly, she extends her hand.

"Mm-hm." From her seat, the professor doesn't notice. Or she dislikes being interrupted when speaking with an apprentice. Perhaps she can tell something is wrong with Jenny, that her skin doesn't fit, that however much deodorant she's anointed herself with, she still smells of rainwater and oil slick and rat guts. Or maybe she doesn't want to get up. "Nice to meet you, too."

If Zeke can smell the grime on her, he doesn't give a sign. Instead, he leaves the office, allowing her space in the hall so she can follow. "Jenny? Jenny what?" He leans toward her. Conspiratorially, she thinks.

"Jenny Green." Warmth rises inside her as he absorbs this name without ire.

"Jenny." He reveals his teeth to her. The bottom set are pushed together like reeds sunk in a bog. They're as beautiful as those flashes of ivory when he says her name. "Have you been to the Smith Center?"

She shakes her head.

"It's a couple blocks away. I'll buy you a coffee there."

"Yes. You will." Jenny is enthusiastic even though she hates its acidity, the way coffee burns her throat. "Just us two, yes?"

"If you don't mind!" Zeke glances back at the professor's door and sighs. "Sorry about how awkward that was. Selene's great, I promise. She kind of gets into my business sometimes, though. She thinks I should date more. I think dating feels a lot like endless job interviews, you know?"

Jenny has no idea what this means. "Does it?"

"Not when you like the person." He glances at her, smiles, and then quickly looks away.

Jenny is confused, but she just laughs and tucks her hair behind her ear. She makes sure to lean close so that the rest of the office, with its rows of doors, with the laughter of students and professors in other rooms, is blocked from Zeke's view. She doesn't have the power to seep into minds and command them, but if she could, she would creep into Zeke's and fill him up so full that there would be no room inside him for anything else.

Zeke gnaws his lip once more, which makes her jealous that he has access to chew his own mouth when she hasn't yet done so. He looks around. "This is weird to ask, but did you see something when you picked it up?"

Bitter fate! He is oblivious to her expert seduction. "What do you mean?"

He exhales. "I'm not sure. Let me get my wallet and my phone. Well, my new phone."

She watches him go to his desk, which is out in the open, surrounded by nothing but a flimsy gray wall that, when unused, appears to fold in on itself like a screen from the Orient. So, not very much privacy to devour him there. A map of the Boston transit system is pinned to that wall, with each line color-coded and covered in small notes with dense handwriting. Beside it is a photograph of him and a freckled young woman, perhaps a family member or past lover. Jenny hopes she's past, anyway.

He pulls out a leather shoulder bag hanging on a chair. It has buckles on the front. When he loops it over his shoulder, she's reminded of messengers on the backs of bicycles. If only he were riding one when they first met! Then she could have hit him over the head with it until he stopped moving and dragged him off to do what she liked to him.

They walk back down the stairs. At the door, Jenny remembers to pause to write the time on the paper again. In the column that reads "Time Out," she writes, FIFTEEN PAST. This seems to be sufficient because the guard says nothing, though he looks like he wants to.

Outside, to her surprise, she sees Clyde and Faun still across the street at the donut shop. They devour sweets, their heads hunched together. She tries to catch their eyes, but they only see that which is in front of them, which is food, an urge that Jenny understands.

She understands less when she sees Faun touch Clyde's hand, the fingers poking out of worn gloves. Clyde doesn't look up at her as he pulls away. Their romance, such as it is, seems to be something Faun wants more than Clyde.

Jenny looks to Zeke, who is squinting at the lines painted on the road that denote where a pedestrian may make his way across amid the sea of cars, usually without being hit by one. He glances at her cautiously. "When you got the phone, what did you see?"

She thinks about this for a moment. He must suspect she was wandering the condemned station as well, her eyes also casting about for inhuman under-dwellers. "Something strange." It's the right thing to say, because she can hear Zeke's heart speed up.

"You saw her." His eyes go round with delight and he grins. He can't believe his luck!

"I did." It isn't a lie. She's perfectly capable of seeing herself by lifting her arm and glaring at it, for example.

He nods quickly, adamantly, and, still looking at her, begins to walk across the street. One of the cars screeches to a halt and honks at him, but he merrily ignores it, which leaves her impressed. She may see him as tender as a newborn rat, but he has no fear of being smeared across the pavement. "I've spent my adulthood studying public policy and writing about government. I thought that was the big-picture stuff in life, you know?"

"It isn't," she says with confidence, because empires have collapsed around her like kindling in a fire. A few generations, a famine, some storms, a plague, and time are usually enough to wipe out anything raised by men. Some places still stand in Rome and Damascus, but the centuries have gnawed on them like dogs on bones, stripping away the color and grandness. Humans, in their brevity, are very good at building and making much of dust. His studies are nothing to her and, as far as she can tell, nothing of value.

"There's so much more! But I convinced myself there wasn't." On the other side of the street, the arm that isn't burdened by the bag is empty. Perhaps she can sneak her own arm into the bend of his, and then they can stroll together.

Jenny raises her hand. He doesn't notice, too enraptured in his own words. She imagines him finally recognizing her inhumanness and then pulling away in disgust, so instead of grabbing him, she slides her hand right back into her coat pocket. Sadness sweeps over her until she forces it away.

"You really did see her?" His whisper is too loud, his joy radiating out of him.

This startles her. "Of course I did."

Zeke is delirious with pleasure, his face open and his cheeks dimpled. "I thought it was a regular woman, just covered in mud.

But did you see the teeth? Were you close enough?" He sees her affirming nod and swells with joy. "They were reptilian. Feline. Full-on predator! I've never seen anything like that, not in a human face. I kept waiting to see the stillness you get with a rubber mask or some kind of ripple you get with silicon. But that's not what happened. And the eyes!" Zeke spreads the fingers on his hands, gesticulating broadly.

Jenny enjoys his admiration.

They turn past a pharmaceutical store where she believes Clyde and Faun got most of the makeup that's on her face now. Briefly, she studies a woman through the window who wears more makeup than she does, her eyelids a vibrant green, and the kohl beneath her lids shaping them in a way reminiscent of a tiger's. She's seized with the urge to go home and put on more. Her face isn't wrong—she knows this because she worked hard on cultivating its humanness—but she wants to underscore what makes it attractive so that Zeke's attention will be that much more transfixed. She wants him to be driven to her face like a moth to a guttering candle.

Because, she realizes sourly, that's how she's drawn to him. Even with him talking about his encounter with her in her natural form, Jenny realizes she wants even more of his attention. She wants him to see her again, really look and know her. It angers her how quickly she has grown dependent on his regard.

Disgusting, she chastises herself. Leaving your comfortable life to seize prey rather than let it come to you! She is confused as to why she has upended her solitude for such an inconsequential creature. He's handsome, yes, but why does that matter so much to her? She has devoured a bevy of handsome men before him.

"It's this way." Zeke leans close enough that she can feel his minty breath ghost across her cheek. He points down the road. "Mass Ave, not Brattle."

Street names are difficult to keep in mind. Impermanent. Some don't even outlast the paving on the roads.

Her distaste must show, because Zeke's brow knits together. He misunderstands her. "There's a lot of coffee places around here. I don't have to choose if you have one in mind. I'm not, like, a huge Starbucks fan, but if that's your thing, that's fine." Zeke's friendliness seems more strained now.

She suspects he's trying to make her comfortable. It's a surprising thought and floods her with relief because, well, isn't that proof she has the upper hand? He's ceding control to her, which is funny, because she's been so pleased to be in his presence, she's forgotten that the object of their journey couldn't mean less to her. "It doesn't matter. I don't like coffee, anyway."

And it's the wrong thing to say, because new color infuses Zeke's face. Now he seems shot through with some flavor of shame. "Oh. If you want to go elsewhere, that's fine. It's too early for a beer, but . . ."

"No. You want coffee. We can get coffee."

"I mean, I always want coffee." He laughs nervously.

"And I want to talk with you, just the two of us."

When he smiles this time, his eyes crinkle, which makes his lashes seem longer. He's happy to have her regard.

She demurs, bowing her head and pushing another lock of hair behind her ear. It feels as soft and dry as a feather as she sweeps it back over her cheek. "If you want."

Then he laughs. What a lovely sound, like a fissure that widens into a canyon, revealing precious stones embedded in the rock. "I like that we're both so busy focusing on what the other person might want, we're not even asking each other what we actually want to do."

She flushes. He's far too perceptive. "That's right."

"Perfect." He chuckles. "Come on."

When she said "just the two of us," she imagined a room with soft chairs and carpets muffling their feet, a waiter to bring a pot of coffee and then disappear behind a curtain to treat others. Perhaps, conveniently, the fabric on the chairs and on the carpets would be red. If she left blood behind, it would be days before anyone realized the discoloration on the material. She would just have to take away the bones and viscera she didn't wish to digest.

Instead, the Smith Center is mostly open floors and glass: glass windows, glass doors, all sitting in metal frames. She can even see up through to the floor above, where scholars slouch over computers and sleep in chairs. Everyone can see everyone in the space in front of the coffee shop, where the floor is unrelenting stone and the chairs don't have a pillow in sight. They are metal and plastic things, nothing that looks like it would be particularly comfortable for one's buttocks for any period of time. There isn't a curtain in sight.

Jenny should make her excuses to him. She should tell him that she would prefer to chat another time, that she forgot she had a particularly specific yet ill-defined task that would take her far away from here. She considers claiming she needs to go looking for a family heirloom, like a locket with a lover's curls inside or a golden comb or a scroll sealed in a tube of ivory. Something precious and recognizably human. Maybe she could say she's looking to retrieve her own phone from another train station?

But she looks at Zeke. The lights that string along the ceiling put a glimmer in his eyes. They are a beautiful gold now. She wants to set those eyes in amber and put them inside a locket around her neck so she can carry them with her, always. When she's lonely, she can look down at them and see him look back at her.

Jenny realizes she is staring. Rather than averting his eyes, Zeke stares right back. To her wonder, his tongue darts out and he licks his bottom lip. Then he seems to realize what he's doing and looks away quickly for an empty table. The blush that burns across his face is exquisite.

He spots one and takes her arm to lead her to it. Her sleeve slides up and he finds her skin, the one she stole by feasting on the man whose pieces are in the freezer wrapped in black plastic, and the woman who's at the bottom of the Charles River.

His fingertips seem to buzz where he makes contact with her. Even when he releases her arm so they can sit down, the place he touched is pleasantly warm. She runs her own hand over it.

She has been touched.

"You're smiling." He laughs. "Something funny?"

She feels warm. "No."

He looks skeptical. "All right. Well, if I can't get you coffee, what can I buy you?"

"Pie," she says at once, thinking of a particularly salty meat pie she had on the shore of the Nile. It was, she remembered, made of dormouse. Perhaps another rodent. It's unlikely that they'll have exactly this. "If they have it," she adds, hastily.

"Pie! I can check!" Zeke gives her a smile that not even predators in the wild would mistake for a challenge. There is something honeyed about him. She sees a natural gentleness to him now.

She watches him go and gazes at his haunches. How do you eat with someone who you want to eat more than anything else?

The noise of the place fills her when he's gone. Jenny grits her teeth through the caterwauling of an infant and the laughter of a tableful of adolescents who, in between shrieks, pop gum and pull smoke from a device they covertly pass between them. She feels annoyance hiss up her back and throat like steam. She is a teakettle, a pot over a hearth, a can over a campfire, heating and ready to husk out ragged breaths of vapor. They all smell of vile human fluids, the baby adding the scent of old milk to the air.

She sees a pigeon that's gotten into the building. It jerks its head as it steps across the floor with pink, scaly feet and red, horrified eyes. Watching it trapped inside with her, she sees herself in its panicked gaze.

Steady, she thinks. You are human, like them, so you must not be made red-faced and angry over what humans have produced all their lives: useless noise and chatter. She doesn't need the fury growing in her gut like a pond bursting with scum.

She thinks of Clyde and Faun, who have been so kind in helping her. For them, she will meet her goal of cornering and devouring this man, this boy in the face of her titan strength and years, and she'll open the waterways for them to sluice through to their hearts' content.

Zeke returns with a cup of earth-bitter-smelling coffee, a plastic cup of water, and a paper plate with a round pastry on top of it. He walks in quick, excited strides, and his eyes—oh. They are bright with satisfaction, a hunter who has returned with food for his clan. His smile is small and smug, she sees with a shock of pleasure.

Jenny warms up again. She parts her lips and says, "Thank you," even before he sits down. The words taste strange to her, too soft, like a gutted fish washed up on the shore.

He puts the plate and the water in front of her. "They just had a raspberry pecan muffin. Hope that's okay."

"Yes."

"Great!" He curls both of his hands around the paper cup. "Then it's official: Thank you for finding and returning my phone. You're amazing."

"Well, I didn't want to keep it."

He laughs like she's told a joke. His eyes crinkle again as he does so, which she finds she likes. A lot. "So. Tell me about you."

"Tell you what?"

Zeke's grin is irrepressible. "Where did you grow up?"

She imagines the hot swamp she was birthed into, the way the waters crawled with scaled, toothy creatures that have long since died away. It was hotter then, or at least it felt like it was in her memory. "I don't think about it often."

"That bad?"

"No, I just try not to think about the past. I think about now."

He cracks up. "What's that like?"

"Freeing." She hopes to leave it at that.

"Like our friend." His smile has not moved, but he speaks in a lower, more serious register. "Tell me what you thought when you saw her."

Jenny does her best to give him a magnanimous look. "She is perfect. A spectacular predator."

He looks surprised but nods in agreement. "I guess so!"

Does Zeke not believe her? How rude of him! "You didn't think she was deadly?"

"Of course I did. She tried to kill me."

Jenny feigns innocence. "Really?"

Zeke looks off in the distance, smiling. He doesn't seem particularly frightened at the memory. If anything, he's excited, transported back to the cool dampness of her lair. In order to trek through those tunnels voluntarily, he must have a passion for the dark. "It was the best moment of my life."

She gawks. "It was?"

"I've been hoping for something like that to happen for years."

"Getting killed?"

"Seeing something that was beyond human knowledge." Zeke is caught up in his own thoughts. She realizes, with mounting horror, he has forgotten she's there at all.

Jenny seeks to rouse him back to their conversation. "When I saw her, in the train station, she wasn't wearing clothes."

"Train station?" Zeke frowns, a line appearing between his brows. "I thought that tunnel wasn't in use anymore."

"Of course not. It's sealed. That's why she makes her home there."

"Oh. Yeah. Makes sense," he says carefully. Jenny hears his pulse galloping in his veins. Is it because of the memory? Has that muscle been thudding this hard since they sat down? He keeps his voice low. "Do you think there are others like her?"

Jenny's innards go cold. He's looking at her, but she has a terrible sense he doesn't see her. It hurts being mistaken for a human when she is so much more.

Yet, though he doesn't really see her, Zeke sips his coffee without breaking her gaze. He has the look of an obsessive, pupils blasted wide and black, nearly devouring his eyes. If only that obsession was turned on her. "When I was a kid, I read everything I could find on cryptids. We seem to have that in common, right?"

Zeke says the word like it should mean something important to her. "Yes, of course. Cryptids."

"Yeah!" His grin is broad, silly. "You're a practical person. You worked at Apple, you know? So I get it if it's not your thing."

Jenny suspects the little Clyde told her about the fruit store was not enough. She also wasn't paying a lot of attention to him. "I like stories."

"Stories?"

"Myths."

He brightens even more. "And urban legends! Like the Jersey Devil, the Mothman, the Loveland frog—I loved reading about them. My dad sent me books from Mexico even when I wasn't talking to him." He pauses to blush and clears his throat. "I researched Snopes and all the websites I could find that existed back then. I wanted to be a slayer or something. Like Van Helsing or, I don't know, Buffy."

At *slayer*, Jenny winces. "You wanted to kill them?"

He bursts out laughing. "It's just a hobby. I wasn't even sure about them existing until I saw her up close!" He guzzles his coffee. "You really think I could overpower something like that?"

She furrows her brow, remembering spears and fire. "You might."

Zeke senses he's said something wrong and shrinks in on himself. "It's not like that. I wanted to see that they existed, first. I'd heard rumors about the student who disappeared a while back. One of their friends posted about seeing a green woman in the flooded train tunnels, but they didn't add a photo. She's proof." He jabs his index finger into the table. In his face is the shadow of an enamored lover, but also a carnival barker, a man mad with his own pride in what he loves made real to the world. "The truth is out there, right?"

Jenny primly crosses her legs under the table. Her stomach is tight with fear. "How is this woman who attacked you proof of Mothmen?"

He falters. "It isn't."

"So perhaps it's only one person? One woman?"

Zeke's smile becomes small, just the barest curve of his mouth. "The native people here have called her Pskegdemus. The English say Peg Powler and Nelly Longarms. Or Jenny Greenteeth."

Jenny is overjoyed to hear him say it again. She preens.

"But it doesn't matter what her name is."

The spell over her breaks. She feels stung. Everything inside her rings bright, new, and confused.

"What's important is that she lives in fresh water, she swims too fast to be caught, and she'll never die." Zeke scratches his chin, which has the ghost of stubble along it. It's so slight, it could be dirt. She wants to run her fingers over the sandpaper texture and watch his eyes widen at her boldness. He, however, is ignorant of her intentions. "So, if the phone was in the water, how did you get it back?"

Now it is she who falters. "It was there."

"Not just in the train tunnel, but in the water. How did you get down there?" The way his smile doesn't waver. The way she can see a slip of his teeth. He holds his cup in his large hands and looks so pleased with himself. For a moment, she's sure he trapped her, and she didn't even realize he had set up a snare.

"I was taking a walk there." Beneath the table, she folds her hands into fists.

"Underground?" Zeke tilts his head, pressing further.

Jenny's knuckles are white. "I saw it in the water and got it."

He's questioning the story now. She can see it in how he squints, his mouth wavering in and out of a hesitant smile. "You just jumped in?"

She schools her face to be as relaxed as his. He has practice in looking terribly clever, probably due to teaching at a university and all, she realizes. It's infuriating. "Yes."

He steeples his fingers. "So you saw her but were able to get the phone yourself?"

"She must have had somewhere else to be. She left."

"Where would she go? She was naked."

If he goes on much longer, she'll have to run, or she'll have to kill him and cause everyone else here to scream, smoking teenagers and baby included. But Jenny is struck with a thought. "You just remember her being naked? Is that all you saw?"

Zeke's smugness collapses—he's mortified! He's been caught being what he is, a lustful, dirty human, and it's so very gorgeous. He drops his eyes. "It was a little distracting," he says softly. "I guess she could have found another tunnel."

"Or clothes."

He looks at her. Really looks at her, up and down. At last, he's in the same room with her, seeing her, even if he doesn't know her name this time. "Yes. Maybe she found clothes and left her tunnel."

Jenny is pleased with her cleverness. She's also pleased that Zeke looks shamefaced. In celebration, she picks up the dessert he was foolish enough to give her and takes a bite. Just a small one. The taste of tart berries breaks over her tongue along with cinnamon, sugar, and all manner of other spices. Candied fruit and nuts seem pretty far from a meat pie, but it's buttery and good and ignites her taste buds.

After she chews and swallows, she exhales. "Oh," she says, touching a crumb on her bottom lip.

Zeke raises one of his eyebrows. "Like it?"

"A little." When she looks down, she sees that, in her euphoria, she finished the pastry.

"Have you eaten today?" he asks. The look of soft triumph on his face is annoying, she decides, but she got to eat the first good human food she's had in ages because of it, so she finds she isn't angry at all. In fact, she finds his investment in her dietary habits endearing.

"Not properly. I haven't had anything that good in years." She thinks about that. "It feels like years, I mean."

"Sure." She can sense his heart pulse, strange and erratic. "Don't you think you should eat more regularly?"

"I'm trying, yes."

"Oh, good." He sips his coffee again in a nervous way, and she tries to see under his placidity. He's about as easy to see through as a lake full of peat, dark as a lens of onyx. This is exactly the kind of place she loves to hide in and the very worst place to hunt.

Jenny runs her fingers over the plate in order to pick up each crumb.

Zeke sees this and chuckles. "Are you in school? I used to do that."

She abruptly stops and forces herself not to eat another crumb. "What do you mean?"

"I barely had any money when I was getting my master's degree. Hungry grad student, you know?"

Jenny doesn't.

Zeke tries again. "Where did you go to school?"

She and Clyde didn't rehearse this. "Is that important?"

"No, no, of course not!" He sees her confusion and looks uncomfortable. "I didn't really have a lot of money before I got the gig with Selene. I had to live with a lot more roommates and make some really embarrassing phone calls to my mom to ask for cash." Zeke laughs at himself, but there's a tightness to it. "I boiled a lot of ramen. I can't eat it anymore, even when it's from a nice restaurant or something. Do you like ramen?"

"I don't think so." She is curt.

"Oh." He looks crestfallen.

This is not someone who suspects her of being a bloodthirsty monster. She's sure of it. He's confiding something to her, something vulnerable. She thinks of the warmth of being held by her sisters. "I do like to eat a lot," Jenny says.

"Me too, like more than normal. For a while, I didn't even pay attention to the flavor or anything, but that's because I spent a few years real depressed when I realized I wasn't happy with what I was studying anymore."

Jenny wrinkles her brow. "Depressed?"

"Oh, yeah. Government policy's real depressing once you realize how little you can change on your own, you know? It all takes so much time and enthusiasm, and I don't think I have any of those anymore." He laughs casually, but his eyes have an unfocused quality to them. "I don't think I was that hungry no matter how much or little I ate, just filling the void."

"Filling a what?"

He frowns. "Like an empty space inside of you? Inside of everyone."

She licks the last crumb off the tip of her index finger and looks at him while doing so. "What am I trying to fill? Tell me."

His surprise is so appetizing, so funny, she wishes his blushing cheeks were tart cherries that she could pluck from his face and take between her teeth, roll over her tongue. "That's not what I meant." He looks at the stinking, murmuring, laughing humans around them.

Human relationships, she's gleaned from TV, are made up of rituals. Seductive overtures are an important one.

She lowers her eyes and looks up at Zeke through her lashes. "Why not?"

His breath catches. His dark pupils expand with what is clearly desire.

Kiss me, she thinks, as loudly and forcefully as she can without pushing the words out of her mouth. *I don't care if you shouldn't be worth anything more to me than a meal and a fingerbone with which to pick my teeth!*

"I—thank you. Wow! But, well, I'm sorry, we just met. You don't really know me." He scratches his neck nervously. "And I don't really know you."

It's as if someone cut her open, dropped stones into her stomach, and sewed her back up. Dimly, she realizes she's afraid that he'll get up and leave her, disgusted at her forwardness.

Zeke looks apologetic. "I didn't mean to give you the wrong idea."

She jolts upright in her seat and pushes the plate away from her, toward him. "What idea? I don't have any ideas at all!"

"No ideas?" He looks at her as if suppressing a smile he's too polite to send her way in case it's taken in scorn. Then, miraculously, he gives her the expression anyway.

"No."

"None at all? No ideas in your head?"

The wash of bitterness over her mouth dilutes the shame. "You're making a joke."

"A little." He's entertained! Entertained at her expense!

If he suspects she and the woman he saw are one and the same, sharing a name and an identity, he plays at innocence so sweetly, it makes her thighs clamp together. If he doesn't know what she is, nor her designs on devouring his flesh, she wants him all the more.

Behind them, a scream rises up and then trills away into laughter. One of the groups of adolescents shouts as the pigeon flies low overhead. The bird flaps its wings in a terror as it swoops over a neighboring table, and then another. A woman shields her infant, now stone silent, from the bird's complete incomprehension. It knows only fear.

A young scholar stands up with his knapsack. He whirls it over his head like a spiked morning star. His companion yells at him. "Dude, no! C'mon, sit down!"

"That thing's going to get killed." The softness of Zeke's face that she enjoys so much? It sharpens. He looks sad, resigned.

She wants to ask "Why?" because they wouldn't be killing it for food when there are tarts and cakes available so near that would fill them much better. But as she watches the wide eyes and open, jeering mouths of the humans around her, she remembers her sisters killed for the sheer frivolity of it. She frowns. If his only hesitance toward becoming more intimate is not knowing enough about her, she will show him her boldness. "No, he won't."

The bird flies toward the front of the building. Evidently, it aims toward the windows that gleam like cut crystal. To that creature, they must look like pieces of sky. It flies straight into them with a thump.

Instead of falling down dead like a stone, it stutters backward. It feints and appears determined to try again. Before it does so, it swoops lower.

Jenny jumps up on the table with muscles in her legs that humans don't have. Zeke makes a choking sound, which is a strange thing to hear from someone when she, indeed, wants to be the one choking him. She glances down to see him looking up at her, gaping. His coffee has spilled on his shirt. Instead of being impressed with her courage, she realizes he's likely to be more alienated from her by her strangeness. Also, she has perhaps ruined his clothes.

No, she tells herself firmly. In this moment, she doesn't care. Her object is now the pigeon.

The bird, in flight, tilts its question mark head toward her. They lock eyes. Then she is all creature and instinct. She jumps upward, vertically, to grasp its fluttering body.

Jenny lands not on the table, but on the floor beside it. She crouches as she does, the silence spreading across the room. Everyone—every scholar, mother, and child—stares at her.

In her hands, the bird stills like prey knowing it's about to die. Its little heart pushes out between its ribs in immediate, quick stabs. But she's full, she tells herself firmly. She doesn't need to eat.

She looks at all the humans and, to her shock, watches them raise their hands. They applaud. Some laugh, as if grabbing the bird is a great folly.

Jenny stands, relieved she didn't decide to eat the bird in front of them.

She turns to Zeke, holding the bird tightly, as if he were a coyote or snake that wants to take it away from her.

Zeke stares at her, then the bird, and then her again. He is awestruck. Rightly, he has realized, yes, she is a very impressive creature. He laughs, but not in scorn. It sounds the way sunlight ought to sound when it hits water.

With his head, he motions toward the door. "Come on. Let's get him out of here." He stands, grabs his bag, takes his paper plate and coffee cup, and charges forward to push the door open for her.

She follows him with the bird in her hands. At the press of wind and air on its feathers, it struggles in her grasp.

Once she's under the now gray and moody sky, Jenny opens her hands in an imitation of the poses in which statues of saints are fashioned. The bird jumps to the ground, hops forward, and looks around vacantly. Then it flies up. It becomes a curved bow and then a speck of gray among rolling clouds.

Zeke can't stop smiling. He claps twice as he nods in approval, and the sound is more wonderful than the cacophony inside. "Impressive!"

Jenny glows at the praise.

He pauses. "Oh, Jesus. What's on your hands?"

She sees specks of red appear there. No—pink. Pink specks blossom across her knuckles into a rash.

He leans closer, eyes wide and horrified. "Is that from the bird?"

Have birds changed so much since she was last walking among humans? But no, she sees the way the skin puckers. The texture of nuts and berries or, more specifically, raspberries and pecans. The contents of the muffin. She thought she had more time between digesting it and its effects on her skin.

Jenny's face grows hot. "This happens sometimes."

"Oh, damn." He moves to touch her and then hesitates. "You aren't allergic to pigeons, are you?"

She needs to leave. Now. "Yes." She takes one hand in the other, as if to shield it from his gaze. Already, she can feel the skin of her face percolating, ready to erupt in the same pattern.

He speaks low, eyebrows meeting in concern. "Do you want me to take you to the hospital?"

Jenny flinches, imagining witch finders, clerics, and doctors who laugh as they cut people to pieces. "No!"

Zeke startles. "Oh, I'm sorry, I didn't mean to, um . . ."

She interrupts him. "We can see each other tomorrow."

His mouth becomes an *O*. Then he asks, apparently very shocked, "Here?"

"Yes," she says brightly.

He adjusts the strap of his bag over his chest, then plucks it nervously. "I guess I have to get back anyway. We could meet at the same time . . . ?"

She nods quickly. "Yes! I would like that!"

"Is your job okay with you taking off in the middle of the day?"

"Yes, yes, absolutely!" Jenny does not ask him to clarify. She is full of panic that he will see beneath her human mask.

Zeke reaches out and squeezes her arm beneath the shoulder. It's gentle, but it sends a jolt like an arc of lightning through her entire body. "Thank you for finding me." He smiles. "See you tomorrow, okay?" He turns and leaves, glancing back after several paces. Then he continues into the entrance of the Harvard train station and disappears.

Where he touched her buzzes pleasantly. As she stares, spots run up her arms.

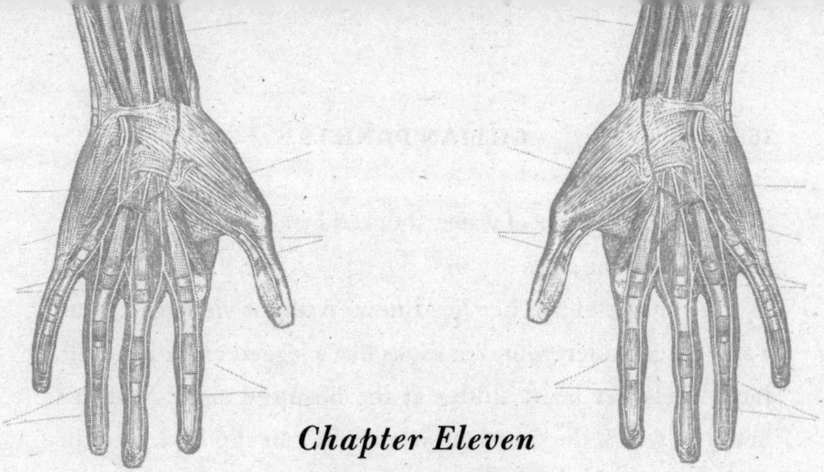

Chapter Eleven

HANDS

The first thing Jenny wants to do is tell Faun and Clyde of her great success. She will get Zeke alone yet! To her surprise, they didn't wait for her in the donut shop. She pushes open the front door with its bright pink and searing orange symbols that threaten to burn her retinas. A woman on the street in the same uniform as the guard sees her and pulls away, which tells Jenny that the marks have spread to her face.

She frowns and leaves.

Above Jenny, the gray clouds converge. The air grows thick with the promise of rain. Water begins to *plip-plip-plip* on her forehead and her fingers. Then it begins to fall at once in a hush.

She's entertained, as she always is, to watch humans run for cover. They scowl and shield their hair with opened books, flat computers, paper, and plastic bags for dog leavings, all while running around like ants. Some scrub the insides of their bags for things that extend and unfold into umbrellas. Humans have been living on this wet, hot rock for so long, and still they're terrified by an occasional sputter of water, shocked by a fork of bright lightning splitting the sky.

One surges above her head now. Without viewing it from a safe place underground, it looks like a jagged crack in a wall. Jenny feels her heart stutter at the beautiful sight. Still, it's better to watch the rain from where she can slip back into the dark, scummed-over water, where a storm in the outside world is just a volley of drops on the surface of a makeshift pond.

Her hair hangs heavy now, and her jacket no longer makes her exposed skin feel safe and warm. In fact, she's cold. She prefers the amniotic warmth of being underwater. Rain falls too fast to drain into the sewers, and the street runs with new streams. Her joy begins to evaporate. She deflates.

Jenny wraps her arms around herself and trudges back to the house. She keeps her head down as water leaks into her eyes like tears, just colder, and very much not her own. She lifts her gaze only to study familiar landmarks: a brick sidewalk that turns into smooth pavement; a shop with vibrant, false flowers hanging over a patio; and a sour-smelling dumpster spotted with rust.

When she gets to the front door, she knocks, but nobody opens it. So she stands there, waiting for Faun and Clyde, unsure if she's being ignored or they have yet to come back home. She is now as pathetic and low as a half-drowned cat.

"Ralph's not in there," a throaty voice says. "I checked."

Jenny spins around, her hair flying out like the tentacles of an octopus. She sprays drops that land on the woman's umbrella.

Like Ralph McGish, this woman has a soft face. Her skin has a tracery of delicate lines around purpled eyes that are as green as the surface of the sea when the wind is still and fish are hiding far below, and a parted mouth with thick lips. Her hair is white and short. When she sees Jenny studying her, she smiles, showing a part in her two front teeth. It reminds Jenny of a shy young girl learning to greet strangers. "I've knocked a few times. He hasn't opened up yet. I think he's gone on one of his trips. I really do hope he'll be back soon. I hope he's not lost. Are you his neighbor?"

The rain clings to Jenny's lashes, but she remains so still, she won't move to wipe them away. This woman has caught her in a moment where she is as vulnerable as prey.

She remembers the phone screen. Sister Charles.

Jenny keeps herself cool, detached. "I'm not a neighbor."

The woman's face warms. "But you know Ralph?"

She sticks her chin out. "He called my friend and me whores."

The woman is quiet for a moment and then looks at the ground. "I wish that surprised me."

Jenny doesn't need more proof this woman knew him. "Did he call you that, too?"

"Not to my face. I was a waitress when we met. None of the regulars at the bar where I worked liked him." To her surprise, the woman gives a gentle laugh. "Not a lot of people do. I knew him when I was Mary-Cat Charles and he was Ralph 'Fuck You, Very Much' McGish. Now I'm Sister Mary Catherine Charles and he's still Ralph. He's sort of Peter Pan, you know? 'All children, except one, grow up.' That's Ralph."

"Peter Pan?"

"Never mind." Sister Charles rubs her chin. "Ralph has good days and bad. For a while, we were married. And I started going to the program, got clean, and I left our life behind." She meets Jenny's eyes. "He got sober for a while, too. He was better. Kinder. But I think it made him afraid."

Sober. The way the woman says the word, it sounds like a new religion. Maybe she's a nun for it. Jenny can't meet her gaze and itches the red spots on the side of her face. "I see."

"I check on him, once in a while. To make sure he's doing all right." She reaches into her bag and pulls out a stick with cloth wrapped over the end. Without hesitating, she hands it to Jenny. "There you are, dear."

Jenny stares at it, confused, until she recognizes the sleek texture of the fabric. She hurries to unwrap it. An umbrella.

Sister Charles steps close, her body radiating warmth, and helps Jenny locate a button on the side of the stick. When they both press it, the umbrella unfolds between them. Awkwardly, Jenny raises it high over her head the way she sees humans do. There's no reason for the nun to give her a gift like this.

"There." Sister Charles dimples. "Have a good day, won't you? Stay dry, if you can." She raises her own umbrella again.

And Jenny should go after her, snap her neck, gnaw her throat until the esophagus is bloody and exposed, because this woman may come back and have others with her. It would be the smart thing to do.

But she gave Jenny an umbrella and told her to have a good day. So she watches the woman walk into the rain until she's swallowed up by the downpour.

Then Jenny's alone with her new umbrella, freely given, unsteady in her grasp. It rocks above her head, spilling droplets around her but, more importantly, not on her.

Jenny feels a warmth spread over her from the inside out. Like being with Zeke. Humans are so strange.

She touches the doorknob, turns it. It doesn't give.

Now that the house is locked, she can either wait or she can go back to her train station and shelter beneath it. For a moment, she pictures the torturing government people Faun told her about. Jenny feels like there's slimy duckweed tangled in her mouth. Waiting here would be a terrible idea if officials are lurking about.

She leaves quickly, walking through a puddle by accident—and then a second, on purpose, just to show she meant to walk through the first one if anyone saw her. If any police are about, maybe watching her from behind the bushes or beyond the sheets of rain, she hopes they see and know she's a woman unafraid of puddles.

Jenny likes swimming in water so much more than walking in it.

By the time she reaches the familiar grate on the ground with her train tunnel underneath, she's only a little less soaked, by the grace of the stranger's gift. Her thighs ache from walking so long without stopping.

Then she hears them.

"No, it's here. It has to be here!" Clyde sounds upset.

"Maybe she lied." Faun is simply bored.

"But then where did she come from?"

"She said she's old, older than Boston."

"The waterways are here," Clyde says firmly.

"They have to be, right? Otherwise, we're at square one."

Jenny decides it would be best to interrupt them directly rather than wait for them to come back out. She pulls up the grate, squats and looks at them, standing in her tunnel. Behind her, she balances the umbrella, but water still manages to slide under her collar and run down her back.

Faun looks up at her. Her jaw goes slack. Then she looks away.

Clyde just stares.

"I told you. You can't use it without me," Jenny informs them airily.

They don't say anything to her for a moment. They seem small, standing beneath her. The quiet oozes like a drop of sap along tree bark.

Jenny sighs and breaks the silence. "Do either of you have the key to go back to the house?"

Faun finally looks up at her again, raising her pale eyebrows. "Yes?"

"Good. Let's go back, then. We'll come here again once I get Zeke."

"You didn't . . . get him?" Clyde wrinkles his brow. "When we left you to find him earlier?"

"No." Jenny tries to push wet strands of hair out of her face. "There were too many people around. I'm very powerful, of course, but it would be annoying to fight every human I come across. Also, as you can see," Jenny continues, dramatically pointing to her cheeks, "I ate something I shouldn't have."

Jenny feels the rain slow to a lovely, light mist.

First Faun uses a rusted ladder to climb out of the tunnel, her hooves hitting the metal oddly. When she gets to the top, Jenny puts out her hand.

Faun cracks a sheepish smile and takes it. "Didn't think I'd see you again."

Jenny wrinkles her brow, confused. They really did think they could get somewhere without her! "Well, you are."

"I am! What's wrong with your face?" Faun is trying, and not succeeding, to conceal her amusement.

"It happens sometimes." Jenny waves this question away. "I still need your help."

"You really do. You look a mess, sweets."

"Yes. I would like to use the dryer again for my clothes. They're uncomfortable and I don't like them right now." She plucks at her soaking jacket in distaste.

Clyde follows Faun up the ladder. He looks baffled. To Jenny's amusement, he seems to be clenching his jaw. She can hear his teeth grinding against each other. "I know we had a deal, but you must understand that we—I—have been waiting a long time."

"Of course it makes sense you would try to go there on your own. It's what I would try." Jenny is benevolent.

"You're . . . not angry at us?" Clyde looks at her, trying to see into her watery soul. The raindrops in the tight black coils of his hair look like pearls in the glow of the streetlights.

"Why should I be angry over something I would do, too?" Jenny begins to walk back toward the house, and they walk with her. She attempts to share her umbrella, but Faun holds up her hand to dissuade her and Clyde shies away. He's waiting for her to leap forward and break his neck. "I told you I'm the only one who can open the waterways," she tells him. "Of course you would want the same power I have. But sadly, you aren't me."

Faun smirks, giving Clyde a side glance. "A terrible tragedy."

"Well, it is!" Jenny sniffs. "I'm very gifted and good at what I do."

"Aren't you supposed to be good at eating people?"

"I'm good at hunting them. Hunters know there's a right time to strike."

"Do they? And when are you looking to strike at the boy?"

"When I want to," she says hurriedly. "Anyway, do you know anything about getting humans to kiss you?"

"Oh, gods." Faun laughs. "I always preferred drinking my way through a wine cellar to cavorting with people on green slopes. When I was young, I didn't much like intermingling any of my body fluids with anyone, not even other satyrs. Too many limbs and hairy bits." Faun's face sours at the thought. "Clyde knows more about all that than I do. Don't you, sweets?"

Clyde hunches into himself. "I don't want to talk about that now. Please."

"Not even Elspeth?" She sneers.

"No."

Jenny rounds on Clyde. "Then did you ever court a man? What did you do to make him want you?" She stops herself because her words are clearly coming out wrong. Making Zeke want her is not as important as getting to be alone with him. She hastily adds, "How did you make him trust you?"

"Only girls for me." He says this without joy as he puts his hands in his large pockets. When his coat opens, she can see his pockets have enough holes that his fists are visible. "And you don't make people want to earn your trust. You give them reasons to *want* to trust you."

"Yes! That." She notices the misting rain has stilled to nothing and puts her umbrella down. She tries to close it. "All I've had to do in the past when I saw someone whose presence I enjoyed was rise up out of the water, smile, and wait for them to come to me. Or they ran and I could chase them."

"Sounds delightfully simple." Faun watches, amused, as Jenny struggles with the umbrella. Eventually, she relents, takes the umbrella out of her hands, and closes it for her. "It's an economic approach."

"Yes! I prefer being straightforward." Jenny beams. "Going up to someone when you're naked and smiling is difficult to do these days when you might be arrested." She feels a great distaste. "I just have to figure out the equivalent enticement for the man. He wants to meet me again tomorrow."

"There's a start, sweets." Faun claps her on the back. "You must have done something to impress him."

"I did!" Jenny is proud. "I caught and released a pigeon!"

Faun stares at her, waiting for more to the story.

"Humans were terrorizing it. I saved its life," she clarifies.

"I see." Faun seems doubtful.

"Yes, you're right. You just need to get him alone." Clyde focuses on his feet as he walks. "You can certainly do a version of your usual 'chase and seduce.'"

"But how?" Jenny can hear the whine in her own voice and despises it. "It's much harder than I thought it would be."

"Just tell him you want to be alone with him," Clyde says.

Jenny scowls. "It can't be that simple."

They talk for a long time about the pitfalls of modern seduction. Jenny comes to the realization that they know significantly less than she does. They all avoid the fact that Faun and Clyde were about to abandon her despite their promises. She believes they must be chastened by their own failures to open the waterways. Graciously, she doesn't shame them further.

They arrive at the house. Faun feels each of her pockets before fishing the keys out of one of them. She leans over the doorknob to unlock it. "Home again, home again, jiggety-jig," she announces.

Inside, Jenny starts toward the washing machine and dryer but pauses to stare at the kitchen, where Clyde is now looking through the cabinets. He frowns, not finding anything of interest among the soup cans. Eventually, he closes the cupboard door and lingers momentarily at the fridge. She feels a twist of dread in her gut as she watches him, as if her stomach is attempting to strangle her kidneys. He decides against opening it, it seems, and squeezes past Jenny to return to his computer.

She looks at the fridge, where the rest of Ralph McGish sits. Zeke is made of those same pieces, she tells herself. It will be easy.

Jenny makes sure Clyde is busy, opens the door, pulls out a piece of Ralph McGish—a hand sheathed in a glove of plastic—and breaks off a finger. She's shocked how fresh the fridge has kept it! Savory, marbled with fat. She gnaws until she hits bone and then cracks that open to drink the slight marrow inside. Now, this she would prefer was still warm with life, but oh, it's so much better than rotting flesh!

When she's done, the red spots on her hands have vanished.

Jenny studies her face in the gleam of the faucet and sees there are dots of brown blood dried on her lips. She runs the water and splashes herself with it until she's clean. She dislikes the rosy-pink skin, missing her beautiful green body, but she wants to be a human among humans for a while longer. She supposes she should eat more but she's full now, and she doesn't plan on spending too much time with Zeke tomorrow. Not while he's still alive, anyway.

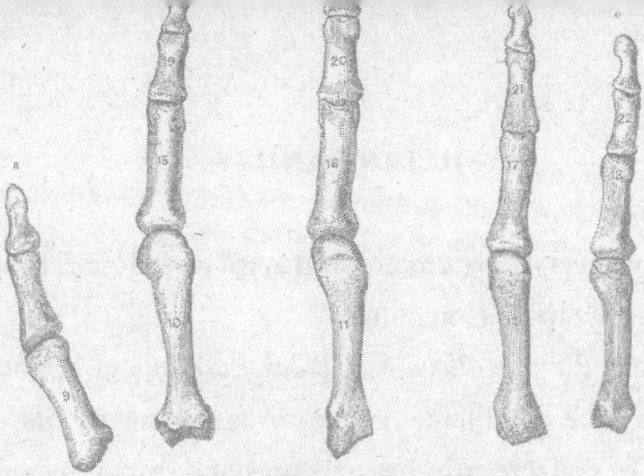

Chapter Twelve

FINGERS

Faun settles down to watch a film on the TV. "Oh, look, the idiot box," she calls it. The couch wheezes under her rolled-up skirt and furry haunches. It emits a cloud of dust.

Clyde lingers on his computer, and then stares out the window. His breath fogs the rain-flecked glass. For a moment, with the windows touched with rain, she can pretend they're bubbles. They're all under the water together.

Jenny wipes her mouth. She made sure to wrap up the finger bone tightly before putting it in the garbage. Then she slides down to sit on the couch beside Faun.

"I remember this in the theaters." Faun points to the screen, where a glamorous woman is glamorously murdered. "I hid in plain sight then. I knew how, even when they came out with the skirts that cut above your knees! And then higher than that!

"I went to a new city every few years. I had friends, told people my legs were just a bit funny, and then the old gang and I would do just about everything a metropolitan gal would like." Her smile dulls then. "It's been a long time."

Faun calls the film *Blood and Black Lace*. It's in bright, saturated colors like none Jenny is used to seeing in real life. Music pours out of the screen in heavy drums and horns. A murderer with black gloves follows and kills various women in increasingly unlikely ways while he inflicts specific, peculiar tortures. Jenny doesn't have much interest in keeping track of the plot. Instead, she gets distracted by the pinch and pull of faces on the screen as they change expression—the shapes of mouths, and the wrinkles that pucker and soften around eyes. The words don't quite match the lips speaking them, the sound clearly recorded separately.

Human faces are, when you begin to live among them, terribly unique. She has forgotten and remembered that before. Some of the ways the actors grin or pout remind her of Zeke. It's the slanting of an actor's mouth, a squint of an actress's eyes so that they sparkle in a charming fashion.

Jenny imagines chaining Zeke up in the laundry room, just a circle of metal around what she imagines to be a shapely ankle and a short chain soldered to the wall. Not too short of a chain, of course. She wants him to move about the space, at least until she decides it's time for him to die. What if she decided to eat a little of him at a time? Bite off his fingers one by one, like Ralph? His arm to the elbow, and then to the shoulder?

It would be painful, though. And, oh, each wound she inflicts would very likely become full of infection and pus, and his face would be a constant twist of terror, probably even fury. Not just a pinch between his eyebrows but a face full of constant, panicked fear. No more charming smiles for her, not unless she tortures them out of him, and then they would be strained.

"All of this just to eat me," says the Zeke in her mind, smiling with bloody, split lips in an awful, cruel grin. "Aren't I lucky?"

Jenny wakes and realizes only then she had fallen asleep. It's a peculiar sensation to sleep outside of water, not least because it feels as if something disgusting has fallen into her mouth and died.

Faun is also slumped over, face slack, another victim of sleeping in the open air.

She looks over and sees Clyde is gone. Instead, she hears him upstairs, shouting.

Jenny climbs the stairs quickly. Has he opened the fridge? Does he know now that he's been living in a slaughterhouse? She pauses when she hears Faun give a yawn that turns into a long, harassed groan.

"Not again," she murmurs. She clambers to her hooves and pushes past Jenny to get to the second floor.

Jenny hesitates and then follows.

Clyde breathes laboriously and twists in his sheets, but his eyes are still squeezed tight. He's in bed, acting more human than either of them. Sweat covers his dark brow. "Give it," he says. "Give it back."

Faun leans over and shakes him.

His eyes open and cut across the room, whites flashing to iris and pupil. When he looks at Jenny and Faun, he recognizes them. His face becomes more measured, distant.

"Again? Lord." He throws an arm over his face. "You ought to hit me, Faun. I haven't been hurt within an inch of my life like you have, but here I am, fussing like a child over some dreams." Clyde laughs, but there's a heaviness to it.

Jenny realizes he's crying. There are long wet streaks on his face, spidering out from his covered eyes. He's smiling at the same time, which makes Jenny uncomfortable and a little confused. She didn't think of Clyde as someone who had two minds about anything.

"It's all right," Faun says, and it's raspier than how she usually speaks.

"When I get my skin back, you won't have to put up with this anymore. I promise."

"Aw, gods. It's fine." She takes Clyde's long hands in hers. Squeezes.

Clyde swabs his face with the corner of a quilt covered in brown and yellow squares. He doesn't move his hand for a moment. Then he squeezes back.

Jenny's face burns. "Yes. Don't cry and upset people anymore."

Clyde raises an eyebrow. "Oh, I'm upsetting you, then, am I?"

"No! Of course not. I'm never upset! But you shouldn't cry or feel bad. When I feel bad, I just stop thinking about it. I pretend my brain is the waterways and I find a tunnel and shove whatever I'm thinking down there."

"Right." His lip curls. "I used to do that. It builds up over time, like water in a dam."

Jenny breathes out slowly. "It's good that I'm myself and not a dam, then."

Clyde wipes his nose. "I wish I was as self-assured as you are."

She doesn't bother to correct him and say she isn't self-assured at all, that she pretends she is until she forgets she isn't. "Of course you do."

"Want me to stay up here?" Faun's soft brown skin has a golden glow in the light of Clyde's bedside lamp. Strands of her white hair gleam.

"No, no." Clyde tries to shoo her away. "Don't trouble yourself. Go on."

Jenny turns and leaves. When she's at the stairs, she realizes Faun has stayed behind. She speaks low to Clyde in words that Jenny can make out just fine. "I promise. We'll get your skin back soon."

"You can't promise that," says Clyde.

"It takes as long as it takes. She'll help when she's ready. I know she won't run."

"You sure?" Clyde sounds strained.

Faun chuckles to herself. "We tried to get it today without her, and she didn't even think of leaving us behind. You can tell she's lonely."

Jenny's jaw unhinges. It's as if flames erupt under her skin and her blood begins to boil. The nerve! She trudges down the stairs and considers leaving through the front door. And she imagines peeling off her clothes and going back down into the train station as if none of this ever happened.

But she wants to leave them about as much as she wants to stop pursuing Zeke, which is to say, not at all. Jenny has made a promise to herself that she must eat the man. She is a creature of honor, she assures herself, and takes seriously the covenants she makes with herself.

But lonely? No. It's never occurred to her to be lonely before. Why start now?

Jenny sits down in front of the television. It's now playing a film where a man turns into a wolf creature with white shaggy fur. He's under a curse, apparently, which seems to be activated within the proximity of women he finds attractive. Jenny realizes that she's under a curse, too, and it makes her drawn to Zeke. It's awful.

She's so angry, she refuses to fall asleep again. Jenny has betrayed herself, because, despite what she told Clyde, she can't think herself out of it. Inside she is a tumult of rage, hot and unquenched, and embarrassment because she is not the self she once was.

Jenny doesn't turn when Faun comes back into the room.

"Let's find some clothes for tomorrow," she announces.

"For who?"

"You, sweets. I look perfect." Faun says it in such a solemn way, Jenny realizes she's teasing. "We're going to help you seduce your man. We promised." She goes to one of her plastic bags and pulls out a balled-up length of black leather. As she unfolds it, Jenny sees it's trousers. "I found these and fantasized about cutting them up to sew into a coat, but I think we can put them to better purpose, don't you? I haven't seen you wear that dress since I got it for you, so I figured you're not a fan."

Jenny thinks about the blood that soaked it through after she murdered Mags near the river. The stains were so stubborn, she hid it, sure that Faun and Clyde would be angry with her messiness. She instead focuses her attention on the pants and frowns. "They look narrow. Are they a child's?"

Faun clucks her tongue. "No. See how long they are?"

"A tall child?"

"They're supposed to be tight. You see it on television." She nods toward the screen as a wolf man runs against the night sky. "A woman wears some nice, tight pants and every man stares at her. It makes them imagine her ass and legs."

Jenny opens her mouth to suggest she not wear anything at all if that's the case, saving time for everyone, but closes it again when she remembers, no, she should definitely wear clothes.

"Come on." Faun shakes them out. "Let's see how these fit."

The answer is that they fit very tightly indeed, but they make the muscles in Jenny's thighs look good. Faun has convinced her to wear a loose green shirt with a black camisole beneath, the shirt draped so that one of the straps is visible. Both are from a bag she keeps with her of clothes and fabric scraps she has fished out of various garbage receptacles.

Faun assures Jenny, as she leaves the house the next day, that her buttocks are shown to great advantage in this outfit.

"I doubt that will matter," Jenny says, even as she remembers the way she's leered at Zeke's haunches.

Faun snorts. "Well, you haven't bedded him yet, have you?"

Jenny's mouth twists. "Before I eat him, you mean."

"Yes, yes, before you eat him. I know. Good luck!" Faun bolts the door shut, leaving her locked outside on another overcast morning.

Jenny feels peculiar as she walks down the street. Once long ago, out of boredom, she swallowed leeches and swore she could feel them grasping at her insides. Then she had, for some hours, the mucus-slathered, dripping skin of a slug. At first, the experience had been novel, fascinating, but as slime slid down her body, as her skin became far too pliant and soft, she felt like she had been turned inside out. It was deeply unpleasant.

This is how she feels on her way to see Zeke. The trousers are wrong, like a second skin when she's barely comfortable in her human one.

She's nervous, which is madness. She's stronger than him, faster, and has plans to devour him like a minnow. What does she have to be afraid of?

Today, she promises herself, I'll eat him.

She stands at Harvard Station and looks toward a press of human beings, smelling sour and damp. She spots him not within the crowd, but outside of it.

Zeke arrives on, of all things, a bicycle. It shouldn't surprise her that he would use a mode of transportation that is fast and strange. It suits him well. He jerkily weaves between groups of humans, some of whom give vocal dismay. Once again, he ignores the cars as he crosses the street.

When there is enough road in front of him, he flies. Unlike the other bicyclists nearby, he wears a thing on his head like half of a large eggshell, with holes in it. He finds her eyes and beams.

"Jenny!" With his sleek new velocipede, he capably leaps from the road onto the sidewalk. He stops in front of her and dismounts. His trousers have a slice of oil across the thigh.

She stares at him in horror. "What are you wearing on your head?"

Zeke turns his hand into a fist and knocks the helmet like a front door. "Have to keep my brains safe!" He looks triumphant. "Don't you wear one?"

She panics. "I don't ride bicycles."

"Do you know how?" He tilts his head, like he's studying her.

"Of course not." Jenny shakes her head. She can feel her face grow hot, remembering children on velocipedes. They always seem so free and informal about riding them.

"That's too bad." Zeke pushes his glasses up his nose like he needs to see her more clearly. "Let me know if you ever want a lesson!"

Is such an offer normal? She's not sure. Before she can ask, he continues onward.

"As for me, I wear a helmet because I'm not much use as an academic if my brains are splashed across the street!" He laughs at himself.

"I would prefer you not die." Jenny finds that she's smiling. "Like that," she adds quickly.

"I'd be giving back to the environment! Something can make a snack of what's left of me if I got in a terrible accident." His grin doesn't waver. He's having fun with her, she thinks.

Jenny can feel him looking beneath her outsides right through to the center of what makes her a creature. Her trousers couldn't make her feel more naked.

His eyebrows raise at her silence. "Ah. Sorry. I always do this." His chuckle is sad as he looks down at the street and away from her. "I make things gross."

"No." She clears her throat. Tries her best to play along. "I'm sure a passing rat would think you're very tasty."

To her relief, he's amused. "Not a passing cannibal? I know there are cookbooks about turning roadkill into fine cuisine."

Jenny can feel it. She's being pulled in two different directions. Part of her is horrified at his death, vivid and brutal, but she is also salivating. She swallows down the spit coating her tongue. "You are much too good to ever just be roadkill."

"Aw. I bet you say that to every guy." Zeke unbuckles a strap beneath his chin and pries the helmet off. Under it is his glorious thick hair, catching and refracting sunlight. He tries to smooth it out and succeeds only in making it messier. "So, leaving aside the idea of being a victim of a terrible accident—"

"Which would be awful and not a very good way to die." Jenny tries to be helpful with her interruption.

He laughs hesitantly and continues. "Have you ever been to the aquarium?"

Jenny gapes at the glow in his face, the delight waiting to pounce behind his eyes. "I haven't."

It's the right answer. Zeke pulls two pieces of paper that he calls "passes," bravely holding them out like freshly killed game. He has that same desire in his face, but it's not to snuff out the life of a doe or a hare, but to take her somewhere new.

She imagines glass tanks of fish, dark corners where it might be possible to sequester them both from any kind of crowd. It was much like that when she saw an aquarium at a sideshow once, the least attended, saddest, and grimiest part of the exhibition. The unblinking fish gazed out between children's fingerprints left on the glass. Jenny smiles at Zeke and nods.

They end up taking the train. Zeke runs a card over a small TV and the gate to the platform springs open for him. Rather than waiting for her to do the same, he stands close enough to the plastic wings of the barrier that they won't shut. She follows him and an alarm goes off, but no one looks up, not even the station attendants in their bright red shirts.

Zeke knew she wouldn't have a card, Jenny thinks. He knows she's out of place, probably senses how different she is even if he can't articulate it.

And he wants to spend the afternoon with her anyway. It's a thought that is both embarrassing and endearing to her. What a weak little creature he is!

Zeke uses his bicycle to leverage more space for them both in the train car, looking pleased with himself as he finds two seats beside each other. Outside the train windows, she sees the solid walls of a tunnel. There are probably other stations like hers nearby, waterlogged, abandoned, and walled-off from view. Jenny feels more comfortable in this metal tube than she does above the surface. Admittedly, she would prefer there were less humans here, particularly when a group of young people scream and playfully hit one another as they pass.

They sit and Zeke's calf presses against hers, his legs in corduroy and hers in leather. The fabric sighs as they touch. His thigh radiates warmth.

Kiss me, she thinks with every fiber of herself that is willing to think something so saccharine. It's a loud thought, one that vies for her attention against the wet smell of humans, a stench that knifes into her nose as the squealing train stabs her ears.

Zeke sees her, and everything goes into focus. He just glances at her and grins. His glasses have a smudge along one of the lenses.

Jenny reaches out the way she does—doing something without really thinking about it—and takes his glasses off his face. A small gasp escapes his mouth but he doesn't stop her. She studies the lenses critically and frowns at them. Pulling the cuff of her green sleeve over her fingers, she polishes the smudge away as best as she can manage.

Once she's satisfied, she gives the glasses back to him, folded so that the wings are flush against the frames. "There," she says. "I fixed them."

When he takes them, his hand is hot and damp. His rough fingertips are blazing points of contact. Zeke leans close to her ear, and that breath—smelling of coffee and chocolate and mint and his blood; his warm living blood, right there, running under his skin in boiling rivers—slides along her cheek. He's so close, the timbre of his words vibrates through her. "Just try to take them again."

She shudders. When she looks at him, she sees the gleam of a challenge in his eyes.

So Jenny puts her hand in his and takes his glasses back. She smiles as she pulls them to her chest and holds them to her heart.

"No!" He bursts out laughing. "I didn't mean now!" One of his hands sneaks under her armpit to get at them.

She gently elbows him away.

"Come on!"

Jenny is breathless. "You said 'try.' I tried. I did it."

Zeke giggles. An actual giggle! It feels good to make him laugh. "Everything's blurry!"

"Aren't we going to the aquarium?" Jenny is all false innocence. "You should get used to being underwater!"

"I like my glasses."

"I like them, too. I might keep them forever."

"You're a bully." Zeke doesn't sound upset at all. If anything, he sounds pleased. Still, his eyes are unfocused. No, that's not right. One eye is looking at her, and the other is slanted in the other direction. His smile collapses when he sees her staring.

Slowly, gingerly, she cedes their playful little war and presses the frames back into his hand.

Immediately, in a fluid, practiced motion, Zeke plants them on his nose, but the rest of him has none of the same confidence. His eyes now face the same direction again. "It's. Um." He speaks so softly, the train's noises nearly swallow it. "Have you ever heard of lazy eye? My parents didn't know it was a real thing, either! It's a sort of misalignment? It's normal. Common.

Really common. Tell that to the kids I went to school with, of course! But, you know, kids are going to be kids. They're still learning empathy, right? That's what I think. That's what my eye taught me." He speaks quickly, nervous and sweating as words fall out of him, and she watches his shoulders press inward toward his ears.

She doesn't like that at all. "Spectacles are amazing!"

He startles. "Sorry?"

"Your glasses are just so, you know!" She motions, letting her hand shape the air as she searches for the word.

"Useful?"

"Useful!" Jenny blunders along far too loudly. "Aren't they a great invention?"

"They're pretty good." Zeke touches them, looking shy.

"People used to just have to live with lazy eyes and cross-eyes and warts that sat right on your lid!" She should know, for she had taken advantage of their limitations if she deemed it necessary to entrap and feed. When very hungry, impaired prey is best. "But then people made glasses and now, well, I guess they still have all those things, but it's not the same. It's easier. It's better. All because humans are so inventive and smart." Giving that compliment is hard, but it's deserved.

Zeke smiles again. "Maybe," he tries, and clears his throat. "Maybe ask before taking them next time?"

Her face burns. "I will."

"And yes. We are very smart." His hand brushes hers, just like that, and then he moves away.

The shock runs up and down her spine, making her sit straight. His skin! His skin is so supple! Her knuckles hum with sensation, which is utterly humiliating because it reveals her own awful, tender sentimentality.

Jenny is hot all over the rest of the way to the aquarium. When they switch trains, she considers taking his hand, but then a pale, angular woman with bright red hair grouses at Zeke for having a bicycle with him, and he apologizes with a nervous smile while holding it more firmly against himself by wrapping his arms around it. His hand is unavailable to hold! It's a great disappointment, she thinks as they get off the train.

After Zeke locks up his bike, the aquarium entrance proves a challenge.

Zeke's tickets, according to the ruddy man in the glass booth, have expired. "See the date?" The man at the desk points unhelpfully.

All of Zeke's good humor seems to evaporate again. "I thought they were good through December."

"That's not a twelve, that's a two. They expired in February." The man rips the tickets in half, his face unmoving. "We can give you a discount with a student ID."

"That's at home." Zeke glances at Jenny and then away again. His shame is pungent, sharp, a smell that she doesn't like very much at all.

"Then full price." The man smiles with an eerie, impersonal edge. He doesn't see Jenny, but he doesn't seem to see Zeke, either. If he did, he wouldn't be so unkind.

Zeke grasps for what's inside his trouser pocket. "Hold on."

Jenny notices the tank next to the aquarium entrance, alive with seals. One barks and swims between its brethren. They're sleek and fast, with freckles and liquid dark eyes just like Clyde's.

If Clyde has his sealskin, Jenny suspects he would be much happier.

She points to the tank and asks, loud and haughty, "Can we go to those?"

The booth man yawns. "The harbor seals? Yeah. They're outside. Absolutely free."

"Good." Jenny sweeps away from the booth and is gratified when Zeke stumbles to keep up with her.

"Sorry." He looks contrite. "I'm an idiot. The date's right there! I messed this up."

Jenny finds she doesn't care about the inside of the aquarium, even though she knows it's likely beautiful, with rare fish like jewels and many private spaces for her to eat. "I've seen fish before."

"They have penguins as well." He looks more deeply disappointed at not seeing the waddling, long-beaked birds than she is.

"I've seen penguins before, too. It's fine. I promise." Steeling herself, she breathes in deep, and then takes his hand in hers.

He doesn't pull away. Their fingers intertwine and their sweat mingles together. Warmth explodes out of him and into her. He squeezes briefly, as if to make sure Jenny's real.

Jenny stops at the front of the tank, where a whiskered round seal regards her, blinks in pleasure, and then speeds away with the grace of a human submarine. Much lovelier, of course, for while a submarine is clever, the ones she's seen have been uniformly ugly.

"I guess I haven't looked at the seals before. Not really." She can hear the laughter returning to him, hiding right beneath his words.

Together, they stare at the seals, and the seals, in their blubber and smiling eyes, stare back.

Groups of screaming children and their parents come to watch, laugh, yell, and eventually pour into the doors of the aquarium. Jenny can hardly hear them. There are the seals, their gliding bodies, the lapping of the water against the glass, and Zeke.

When she turns to him, Jenny sees he's not looking at the seals, but at her. He appears shy but so very happy in that moment. His hand in hers is nothing like being grasped at by confused humans who are about to die, she thinks. It's of his own gentle volition. She resists grabbing back so tightly that his fingers break.

They stay at the seal tank a long time.

When she gets home that evening, she tells Clyde with as much confidence as she can muster that she just needs another two days. "That's all," she says, flushed and pleased with herself. She can still feel the caress from Zeke's fingers on hers.

Clyde looks her up and down and raises an eyebrow. Frowns. Then, saying nothing, he goes upstairs. She can smell the impatience on him, coming off his back in a miasma.

Jenny's flush of pleasure becomes shame.

She has called herself a hunter and has spectacularly failed to hunt. What good is she? Jenny has not continued to exist far longer than her dead, devoured sisters because she misses opportunities to feed! She has played with her prey too long this time, entertaining herself because his hands feel good in hers. Because she wants to taste his mouth. The slide of his tongue against hers would be pleasurable but, ultimately, something she can replicate without his body's willingness. Can't she just kiss a corpse and be content?

Depressed, she decides not to go out tonight, though there are still men and women on the streets waiting to be eaten. The meat in the fridge is slight now, just scraps clinging to the bones. Ralph is a refrigerated memory kept alive only in the pictures on the walls.

Cold, chewy ligaments fight her blunt teeth as she tries to chew them to bits. It's unsatisfying, but so what? She wants to be hungry when she finally devours Zeke.

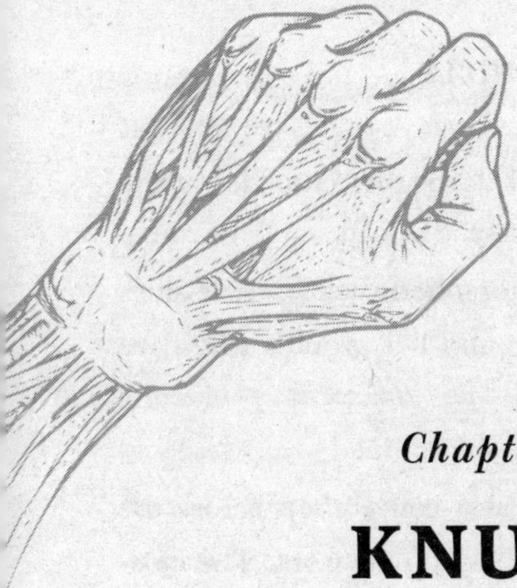

Chapter Thirteen

KNUCKLES

Jenny leans against one of the brick walls that surround the campus grounds. Sunlight filters through the green leaves that climb the bricks, picking out their individual veins, and she watches a cloud of gnats shimmer in the air. On days like this, bright and a little chilly, she can smell the heaviness on the breeze. Swamp and water want to devour the city again, eat it with storms and wind and rain until it looks like it did without humans tending and manipulating the land.

It's in the nature of humans to perish, and it's in Jenny's nature to help them along. She reminds herself of this firmly. Why would someone as old as her need to be reminded of her own nature? She is not as changeable as little men and their little lives, but now she has to insist that to herself. Is something a natural part of you if you have to remind yourself of it?

She waits a long time for him to show up. Harvard Square brims with people, some loud as they laugh and talk, and others hunched over their phones as they wander. They're all distracting themselves from the inevitability of death that crouches at the backs of their minds.

It dawns on her that Zeke has forgotten their date. If she's more important than the people around her, wouldn't he have remembered?

The hour draws forward slowly.

She distracts herself by staring at a coffee shop across the street with a picture of a woman smiling on the front. The illustrated woman has long hair, a crown, and a bisected tail. It takes a while before it dawns on Jenny this is meant to be a mermaid, but one who is more anodyne than any she's encountered. The image has a smooth, doll-like emptiness devoid of anything like venom or sharp teeth.

If he doesn't show up, what will she tell Clyde? That she's lost her prey? She can make him help her find Zeke again, yes, but how much more patience will he and Faun extend to her? She knows they already doubt Zeke is worth the wait.

And then, through sun rays filtering between the buildings, turning the windows into squares of gold, she sees him.

Zeke has no bike with him today. His glasses catch the light and give his flawed, lovely eyes a gooey warmth. He wears a black coat over a white sweater, a concession to the cool day, and trousers that, regrettably, suit him well.

"Jenny." It's more of a breathy acknowledgment than a greeting. She can see dimples in his cheeks from where he smiles and an apologetic line between his eyebrows. "I'm so sorry about being late. Have you been here long?"

"I have nowhere else to be."

"I'm surprised you didn't leave!" His chuckle is uncomfortable. "You weren't worried, were you?"

"I didn't think you had died." She snorts, and even as she says it, she remembers what he said about brains spilled on sidewalks. "I just thought you forgot."

"Jenny!" He takes her shoulders in his hands and leans close, smiling. "How could anyone forget you?"

The way he squeezes her is so careful, like she's glass, that she laughs. "You're right! No one could forget me." The corner of a board pokes her, and she sees he has a white placard tucked under his armpit. Something is written on it, but that side is turned away from her. "Is that from one of your lessons?"

He looks down at it, and a charming shade of red spreads across his cheeks and over his ears. "I don't have classes Thursday," he says, as if she's in the habit of keeping track of the days of the week. She can hear his heart give a strange stutter. "I was, um . . ." He meets her eyes, clearly embarrassed. "At a protest."

Jenny vaguely remembers other times in Boston when people have stood in the streets and yelled. Instead of signs, they have often had muskets. "A protest?"

He nods sadly. "I think it's all sort of naïve these days, honestly. Protests mostly seem to be about getting together to yell and bond while you're yelling. I'm not convinced they change anything on their own, but, you know . . . It certainly feels important. And it's something to do, right?" He swings the sign around and reveals the words on it.

"'Down with White Supremacy,'" she reads aloud slowly. The *H*'s trip her up as they usually do, being a newer addition to the English alphabet, not to mention the peculiar shape of the *W*'s these days.

Zeke waits for her to say something else, to make some comment, but considering she has no idea what his sign refers to, she hesitates to respond. "What were you protesting?"

He beams. "Police brutality! They beat up this Black man the other night here in Cambridge. The officers said they had cause because he yelled at them, but who cares if he did? He wasn't armed, you know?"

She frowns. "Isn't that what officers always do?"

He nods in agreement. "Exactly! That's what I'm talking about. It's awful and it's systemic and none of us notice it anymore. When I was a kid, I watched movies and *Law and Order* reruns without thinking about it. I thought the police were there to stop robberies and solve murders. Instead, they're patrolling neighborhoods and intimidating people with my skin—" He stops himself. "I'm sorry. I'm not teaching a class, and here I am, treating you like a student."

"You're just talking." Jenny is surprised at the flow of words, the passionate burn rolling along his cheeks. "It's fine."

"But I'm talking a lot, right?"

"That's not true," she cuts in, grabbing his soft, lovely hand. "You talk a fine amount. The right amount! I wouldn't say so if I didn't think it."

Zeke looks a little baffled but very pleased. "If I ever talk too much, tell me. Guadalupe—Lupe, that's my sister—she tells me to shut up a lot."

"I don't want you to shut up." When she says it, she feels how true it is. His silence, his death, would annoy her deeply. "Ever."

"Oh." He sets the sign next to the brick wall, words turned out toward the courtyard. The corner of his mouth twitches. "Miss Green, I think you're trying to seduce me."

She is overjoyed that she's doing so well at seduction for him to recognize it as such! "I am, yes! You ought to seduce me back, I think."

Zeke's face develops an impressive blush. "I really should, huh?" He is dazed with all that blood leaving his brain and migrating to his capillaries so quickly.

"Yes! And you should talk to me as long as you like about protests and bicycles and that pigeon I very bravely caught for you. You're interesting." She thinks, too, of how he said her name when he met her, how he knew her immediately, intimately. "And I'm interested in you."

His response is a choking sound followed by a chuckle. "I'm very average. My biggest and most interesting phase was when my parents were divorcing and I started camping behind the house."

"Did you hunt on your own, too?" In her experience, that's mostly what people do when they set up tents, at least when those tents are by rivers and lakes.

His eyebrows fly up. Then he laughs. "Not unless you count stealing food from the convenience store. And by food, I of course mean ice cream and chips. I was awful. Lupe would tell me I was an idiot, even though she was younger." He shrugs one shoulder, embarrassed but also deeply pleased. "But sometimes you want to be wild, I guess."

She laughs at him and his scholarly airs and the way he is clearly a better lover than an adventurer. "Oh, yes. You are ever so wild." Jenny attempts some of the sarcasm that Faun uses so often.

"I have my moments." He rolls his eyes affectionately. "I know you're different."

Jenny stills. Her too-tight pants suddenly feel like sausage casings on her legs. "Different how?"

"What is that supposed to mean?" A pale woman on the brick sidewalk interrupts. She stands in front of them, arms crossed. Her thin legs are far apart as she takes a stance like a fighter. She has curly brown hair and the kind of pale eyes that look like a gray dawn free of sun. She nods at the sign. Then at Zeke. "Are you trying to get rid of white people?" Those gray eyes dart to Jenny, piercing and lovely. "Are you trying to get rid of yourself?"

Jenny gives the woman nothing but a raised eyebrow and a tilted head. She looks to Zeke, waiting for an explanation. Is this a friend? A cohort? But his lips are parted, and his eyes don't seem to comprehend who this woman is, either.

"Well?" Her nostrils flare. "Why are you promoting hate against white people?"

His mouth twists in a new way, an ugly sort of hard, sharp smile. His eyes remain steady on the woman. "I'm not." He pushes his glasses up the bridge of his nose. "You seem a little confused."

The woman smirks. "What do you want? Black supremacy?"

Zeke smiles, too, but without warmth. "No supremacy would be great."

"White people invented civilization," she says, motioning to herself and the buildings behind her.

Now Jenny is amused. "I don't remember Sumerians being as pale as you."

Zeke turns to stare at her.

The woman looks at Jenny like she's mad. "What?"

"I think that was the first civilization," Jenny says. "Or Tanger. Or Luoyang."

The woman curls her lip and looks at Jenny like she's a moron, unfit to hold conversation with her. "I'm talking about real buildings! And classical art! Not modern stuff, either. The stuff that looks like real people."

"People look like a lot of things." Jenny scratches her chin in a mocking manner. "You look like a giant, angry trout but less spotted, I think."

Zeke guffaws and then covers his mouth, as if he's ashamed to be amused.

Jenny cuts her eyes at him and grins.

The strange woman fumes. Entertainingly, she stamps her foot. Jenny expects her to start yelling about the perfection of the empire in which she lives, maybe shouting about the greatness of the Romans, the superiority of the Spaniards, the glory of the Czars. Instead, she looks glum. "I can't deal with you people."

"Jews? Latinos? People with signs?" Zeke motions to himself. Taking on the aspect of a carnival barker, he bows grandly, and a proper sneer appears on his face. "Thank you for your comments. Anyway, my friend and I are trying to talk."

The woman remains in her soldier's stance, with her sour, little mouth. Maybe she's unhinged, or maybe she just woke up and decided to be cruel. It's easy to do the latter, Jenny thinks, when you decide other people aren't as real as you are. It's a thought with which she is deeply intimate. Shame curls through her chest, a weed growing in a soft, dark place, its roots slithering around her insides.

Jenny has had enough of this woman. She reaches out and snatches her pale hand.

The woman gasps. She pulls back, but Jenny won't let go of the long, delicate wrist. She lazily examines the appendage, which has bright red nails and a golden ring on one of her fingers. "He said go away."

"What are you doing?" The woman is afraid, which is deeply gratifying. Her eyes are wild, darting around for someone to help her.

Jenny considers just breaking the woman's hand, snapping fingerbones like matchsticks. Yet being with Zeke inspires her toward a different course of action, though not peace. Never peace if I can help it, she assures herself. The proximity of his body, his warmth, it all makes her quite hungry. She does what she did to the librarian, lifting the woman's hand to bite it.

And Jenny pauses. She recognizes herself in this woman, the fear she has when she thinks about humans physically overwhelming and murdering her, of how she must bite first or be bitten. Or run through with a spear. It's served her well to strike every person she's seen as an intruder, whether adult or child. In her way, is this woman not doing the same thing? Trying to strike first?

Which means, of course, she is also dangerous.

The woman twists but can't free herself from Jenny's grasp. "You're insane!" she snarls. "You're racist and you're insane and you're hurting me! Help! Someone help me!" Tears shine on the surface of her eyes.

"If we let you go, you have to leave." Zeke's eyes continue to seek Jenny's, but his voice is sure. He is angry with the stranger, her willingness to misinterpret him, her cruelty. His anger doesn't manifest as force, but Jenny recognizes his thirst for retaliation lingering beneath his civilized facade.

The woman pouts. "You're so mean."

"*We're* mean? You came up to us!" Zeke groans. "You can go to hell, okay?"

"I'm already there!" The woman howls. At last, someone looks her way. "I'm in Boston, surrounded by overeducated children!"

Zeke sneers. "I guess you're not wrong there."

Jenny smiles, too, and releases her.

The woman's own momentum causes her to stumble backward and land on her ass. Her hair falls in her face.

Zeke bursts out laughing, loud and broad, and it's one of the most uninhibited sounds Jenny has ever heard. It's an animal freed from a snare. It fills her up with joy.

"You!" The woman begins to crawl back to her feet. "You're monsters!"

Jenny is deeply pleased. "Yes."

Zeke looks happy, too. "Bye!" He merrily throws the sign down in front of the woman so that she has to stare at it. Then he hooks his arm into Jenny's and they leave through one of the brick exits away from the campus.

"You don't want your sign back?" Jenny enjoys his happiness.

"Nope. I can make another." He tugs her along. "Come on. I want to show you something."

And Jenny wants to sing. Those are the words one uses for a liaison, aren't they?

Zeke's arm doesn't leave hers. "I've met people like her in the wild, but never that direct, you know? Just when I forget why I go to protests and yell about assholes, one of them comes out to say hi! Mostly it's someone I meet at a party or the bar or something, like a guy you think is all right, but then he starts telling you how Satan has forces everywhere."

Jenny tries to keep up with what he's saying. "People are very fond of demons. It's convenient to be bedeviled."

"It is?"

"Yes! You can blame anything you like on devils."

Zeke chuckles. "You're right. That is convenient. If I ever meet a demon, I'll thank her for all her hard work."

Jenny, who has been called a demon more than once in her long life, feels a warmth gather inside her. She nods quickly, recognizing they have been drawn closer together than ever.

"Want to go to a movie?" Zeke's energy is infectious. "There's one playing at the Brattle in, like, an hour. We can relax. Maybe not meet any weirdos working out their issues at strangers?"

"The Brattle," she repeats, wondering how remote this place is exactly, how secluded and quiet.

"It's a theater, yeah. Right around the corner."

She imagines the darkness of a playhouse, rows of empty seats. She smiles. "Yes."

"Cool, cool. I'll pay this time."

She takes his hand like yesterday. It's awkward to initiate such contact again, but she feels his hand instantly relax in hers. When she looks down to admire his knuckles, she sees hers now have a green blush.

It's not enough to make her panic that she's about to assume her previous hue, not yet, but if she's going to eat him, it should happen today.

They stop at a crosswalk. He looks both ways before continuing onward.

"You usually walk without thinking of anyone else." She leans close enough to let her breath run along his neck, hoping it's seductive. "I like that about you."

"Oh, I don't care about cars when it's just me."

"Why not?"

"I just don't." When she looks up at his smile, it's false. Pasted. He's lying.

It makes Jenny want to fold herself up and slide into his pocket. She can change her skin, teeth, and hair, but her shape? No, she can't change that. She must remain the ungainly girl clinging to him on the way to the movie theater. She can't be there to understand all his private pains. When she cracks his head open, the things over which he secretly despairs will remain unknown to her.

There's a line of people who stand outside the theater door. Not too many, she assures herself. It's fine.

But inside, there are even more people, crammed against a booth selling food. Zeke vanishes to buy tickets. In the tight space, she smells cooking grease and stale sweat, hot butter, the remnants of marijuana and tobacco smoke, fried sugar, beer, mildew in the carpet, and breath laced with garlic, laughter, spit, and heat. It's a haze, a swamp of humanness in which she is drowning. It feels very obvious to her that she is not one of them. Can't they sense it, too?

She wishes she had bitten the human, eaten her and all her hate. It would have been a relief to take that inside of her, hide it in the caverns of herself. Also, it would stave off the green blush on her hands.

Zeke returns holding small rectangular slips of ripped paper. "Hungry?"

She hesitates, feeling dizzy because Ralph's remains have not been enough, but then shakes her head.

They ascend the stairs and enter a room that roils with humanity. Jenny tries to breathe through her mouth as she and Zeke walk up and down the aisle, looking for a pair of empty seats nested together. Meanwhile, everyone is talking. Screaming. She's so busy trying not to smell them, trying not to be annoyed, that she can't control how she hears them. This is like the nickelodeons in the evening, crammed with drunkards and delinquent children. She expects a brawl to break out at any moment because some man insulted another's woman.

The only seats left are near the screen.

Perhaps the woman who snapped at them on the street has followed them inside. Maybe one of these giggling strangers will turn, eyes bright, and call her a monster, too. A demon.

Jenny squeezes Zeke's hand. She's ashamed her fingers are slick with sweat, but his are also warm and slightly damp. He runs his thumb along her knuckles.

She turns to look at him, but his eyes are fastened on the heavy curtains at the front of the room. He doesn't look afraid. No, he's as placid as the surface of a pond.

The curtains pull back on what she assumed was a stage, but it's a screen. The crowd roars with delight, like they've never seen one before. The room darkens, and the movie ignites in front of them. Words crawl across it too fast for her to read.

"It's called a Trash Bash!" Zeke has to shout to her above the din. "So the movie's supposed to be kind of bad, right? Usually something that people saw at a handful of drive-ins in the seventies or that went straight to video in the eighties. And everyone laughs at it."

He doesn't laugh. Neither does she. They watch everyone else do that for them, squawking and pointing as a man in a lizard suit swims through crystal clear shallow water. Jenny watches bubbles come out of a green mask and rise from a gap beneath his chin. It is too peculiar, too much of a costume to be like her, but it makes her wonder if someone might turn and see a resemblance.

A pinkish boy in the row in front of them yells, "More like *Creature from the Garbage Lagoon*, right?"

Next to him, a sallow woman glares and smacks him. Jenny jumps, as if she's been smacked herself.

Jenny misses watching films at the house with Clyde and Faun nearby. They weren't always quiet, especially when they bickered, but she knew what the films were about and what was happening. She wishes they were nearby now.

Zeke touches his pocket suddenly. Stands. He holds up his phone, that damned instrument. "Ugh. I'm so sorry," he whispers in her ear. "I have to take this!" And he jumps up and leaves her in the theater.

Jenny stares at the screen, where the man in the green mask watches a woman through a window. She's in a bra. The audience is a chorus of boos and whistles and laughter. Do they enjoy it? Despise it? The woman is fine, but the crowd has made Jenny ill.

If they saw her, really saw her, creature and woman both, would they also boo and laugh? Or would they simply tear her apart? She imagines becoming the entertainment instead of the film. Like Faun and the suited men she remembers and clearly fears, Jenny suspects the humans around her would be very interested in seeing her insides. And when they see she doesn't die right away, how long would their violence continue?

Jenny is surrounded on all sides. To bite someone now would end poorly for her. She stands up stiffly and leaves.

Through the door where Zeke left, Jenny finds an alley. Based on the smell of the building next door, they are near a restaurant. He's there, propped up against a brick wall, shoulders hunched forward. He looks miserable, tears in his eyes. His phone is nowhere in sight.

Jenny feels nauseous in a way she wasn't in the theater. She is scared for him, she realizes. "Zeke?"

He looks up at her, startled. Then he smiles, slowly, embarrassed, and holds up his hands in surrender. "I swear, I haven't had a panic attack since I was a kid! That woman messed me up more than I thought, you know? I've met people like her before who hang around campus, trying to pick a fight." He takes his glasses off, wiping his eyes. "I keep waiting for her to jump out at me in the theater."

Jenny steps forward. Before she can say, "Yes, me too," he continues on.

"What's she going to do, anyway?" He laughs in scorn at himself and it's an ugly sound. "It's stupid, isn't it?"

"No! It's not stupid." Jenny takes hold of his arm. It's warm under her touch, and for a moment his scent overwhelms her. She's drunk on it. "I don't like humans very much."

He puts his glasses back on, and his look has that same drunkenness to it. "Me neither."

She takes his chin and cups it. He smells wonderful, all vanilla and that damn coffee. He smells like Zeke and he smells good. His lips, when she brushes them, kiss her back, and they taste the way light feels. They are plush and soft and *meat*, and this reminds her of hunger. But when she opens her mouth, he presses his tongue inside, and she aches. He does, indeed, taste very good.

Briefly, she leans her head too far to the right and grinds her nose against his glasses. She jumps back, terrified she has ruined it. But then he laughs and, relieved, so does she. They kiss again and Zeke's tongue slides along hers, finding her teeth, seeking her edges out wherever she might try to hide them.

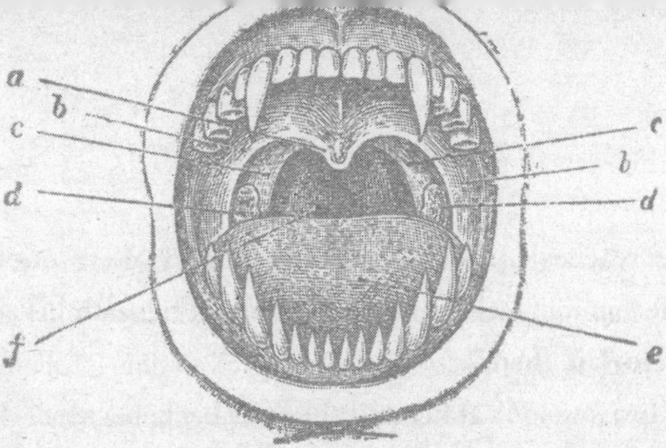

Chapter Fourteen

MOUTH

When she pulls back, his eyes are sleepy and his glasses pleasantly fogged. "My place?"

Jenny's confused for a moment, her head humming. She has to remember how English works before she can respond. "Oh. Yes. I want to go there with you. It would be better." Private, she hopes, so as to devour him with success. She holds his hand more tightly, squeezing in a couple of quick pulses.

His glasses magnify the sweetness of his eyes as his mouth curves. "Yeah. Come on." He pulls, and like a wolf pretending to be a lamb, she follows.

She feels her heart melt into her stomach. No—she tries to refocus. "Will anyone else be there?"

"I have a roommate, Amir, but his boyfriend has his own apartment, so they're usually there. I have a friend who sometimes shows up without telling anyone, but he clears out quick enough if the door's locked." The tips of his ears are flushed.

She reaches up and grazes her fingers along one earlobe, and she can just feel the heat of the blood beneath his skin. "We should lock it, then."

He turns to look at her and she jerks back, because what if she overstepped? But he smiles and brushes the side of her face down to her chin.

When she tilts her head up toward his, they kiss again.

And the world is electric, radiating out from under her skin, as if she's a jellyfish with a long, glorious veil of tentacles. She feels dizzy and hot all over.

His house is on a hill and built on a slant. Its neighbors are, too.

Zeke fumbles out his keys and fits one in the lock. Then he stops. "Hold on. Wait. Ha! I actually am getting a call." He pulls out his phone and shows her inside. Then he cradles it to his chin and says, "Lupe! Hi! Listen. Not a great time. Are you . . . ?" He doesn't finish the question. "Oh yeah? Really?"

Jenny hears a tinny, fluted voice emanating from the bottom of the rectangle. It's a girl sound. Hoping he won't be long, she leaves him speaking in the doorway.

The front room of his apartment is dark. There are framed posters on the walls. One has a giant woman in white crouching over traffic and holding a car. It reads ATTACK OF THE 50 FT. WOMAN. She's very much a woman but she's also wrong. Gorgeous and cruel, she towers over the humans who run between her feet. Monstrous.

"No, no." Zeke wrinkles his brow as he pins the phone between his cheek and shoulder. He begins to turn on each lamp, illuminating the white paint puckered along the ceiling.

"Yeah, but if she's going to be at the party, I don't think it's a good idea I'm there, too."

On the shelf is a stone mermaid. Jenny frowns at it, reaches forward, and picks it up. It's heavy, roughly made, a woman with a potbelly and a curling tail.

She nearly drops it when she hears Zeke laugh. "Lupe, it was barely a date, but what if she's there, too, and it's awkward?" He laughs again, this time more strained. "Look, I'll try to go, but I can't promise anything. Okay? Yeah?"

Jenny feels a stab of jealousy. It's unbecoming, she decides, but she can't pretend it away. She wants Zeke to be hers and hers alone.

When he puts the phone down, Zeke practically grovels. "I'm so sorry! My sister calls, and I think, 'Oh God, an emergency,' but it's usually not. Maybe never. She was just calling me about this party at her place."

Jenny does not want to talk about a party at anyone's place. She does not want to be festive and jovial and watch him besotted with past paramours; she wants him besotted with her, right now.

When she looks at him, his face has new color in it. She can feel the heat radiating from his body. Shame, she realizes, but only because she knows the feeling well.

She holds up the mermaid. "What's this?"

"That?" He stops himself from talking about any more parties or other women. Instead, he looks sheepish. "I made that a long time ago."

She puts it back down on the shelf.

Zeke lurches forward to move it back to its original place. His fingers graze it reverently.

Jenny's eyes drift away from the lurid bright colors to a black book on a shelf. It has *Zeke* written with an unsteady hand in red paint on the spine.

"Oh God," he says as soon as her fingers graze it. "Anything but that."

Jenny goes very still, arm outstretched. She feels like a hunting dog asked to heel. There was a time she could never imagine being any human's dog, much less a man's, but here she is, utterly still and her eyes turned wide and questioning toward him.

"No, no." He laughs and waves his hand. He flushes prettily. "You can look. It's a lot of junk, mostly ideas that never came together. One day, I realized I didn't want to write academic papers anymore, I just wanted to make a whole new society. I should have sat down and written a sci-fi novel. See?" He takes the book and flips it open.

Zeke shows her pages of dense words, forests that aren't legible to her at all. Tracks of letters run wild and dissolve into drawings. She sees women with the legs of squid, the mouths of vipers, the eyes of deer, locks of hair like writhing snakes, and of course breasts, some comically rounded, others pendulous, and a few that are boyishly flat, nipples on small hills of skin. The sketchy face in the center reminds her of Zeke, though a polished and far more boring variation where he wears no spectacles, his jaw is narrow, and his eyes point in the same direction. But it must be him, because she recognizes the way he looks when he walks into the paths of oncoming vehicles, mindlessly confident, pleasantly cognizant of the danger and enjoying the risk. Here he's awash in a much more exciting sea, but rather than traffic, he is lost in a whirl of violent, beautiful monsters.

"Lovely," she says, running her finger absently down the off-white page and its dried ink.

Zeke clears his throat. "Thank you." Beneath the magnifying lenses of his glasses, his brown eyes remind her of wet earth on a humid summer day, when one's only hope of staying cool is hiding in the mud until the sun recedes.

Her lip curls as she looks right back. "You're lovely, too," she says.

Now she watches his pupils blow up into dark spots. He exhales in a jagged breath. "Well, you're beautiful."

Jenny grins and feels her breath speed up. She has not been called beautiful in a very long time, not since the huntress who, along with being swift and practical with a knife, possessed many honeyed words that she dispensed with ease. What a thrill to be in the presence of a young man who can both see what's obvious and articulate it just for her pleasure. "I am, aren't I?"

He smiles, eyes crinkling. "And so modest."

What would it be like to hold him down and pluck out each eyelash one at a time? He would yell and twist beneath her, trying to pry her off him. She supposes she would have to straddle him. That thought makes her heart jolt and redouble its thumps.

While she stares at his mammalian hair, he seems to be looking into her face. He reaches out and touches her, thumb lingering on her chin, the edge of his clipped fingernail grazing her lip.

She opens her mouth. "Kiss me again."

It's an invitation he seems to want to accept, first pressing his thumb to her lips, but he goes still. A tremor runs between them. He does not move forward.

She darts her tongue out to lick his finger as she holds his gaze. It does not taste of meat, peculiarly, just sweat and soap.

A gasp bumps its way out of his chest.

"Hungry," she says, her breath sliding past his human skin.

His eyebrows push together. "I don't have much in the house right now." His confession leaves him looking pained. "Cereal, mostly. Maybe some rice and beans? We could order takeout?" He withdraws from her.

Jenny catches his hand and presses it to her jaw once again, this time with more firmness. "I'm hungry to have you."

Now he seems to light up from within. He leans forward, wrapping an arm around her low back, and presses his mouth to hers.

The relief of breathing smoothly and into the gasping lips of another warm creature is instant. It causes her to shiver and her sex to tighten between her thighs.

When Zeke pushes his tongue into her again, Jenny thinks muzzily of the insides of animals. Warm, pulsing, wet with life, meat running along her own tongue.

She explores the shape and smoothness of his teeth and thinks, with excitement, about when she can strike. Now, with his mouth hot along hers, can she bite him? Later, while they rut, can she somehow summon the power to let her true teeth grow once again and feast as he bucks into her? She imagines his arterial blood splattering her face and bathing the both of them in a gory baptism.

An embarrassing noise escapes her mouth at the thought, a soft mewl she associates with cats in heat. She pulls back and covers her lips.

He's panting, and he has a sort of dazed smile, like a pilgrim who has at last reached his temple of worship. She examines his face critically until the curve of his bowed mouth goes slack. "We don't have to go fast. If you don't want to, anyway. I mean, I like fast, but, like, I can also do slow? Or between fast and slow?"

She's deeply enchanted with his fluster, so it disturbs Jenny when he pulls farther away. She wants to taste his tongue again. So she closes the inches between them until their pelvises meet.

She looks him in the eye and shrugs off one of the sleeves of her jacket, then the other. Beneath is what Faun called a tank top. A strap slithers down her shoulder and reveals the nipple on one of her breasts.

Zeke's jaw drops. Then he inhales as if he can smell the perfume of her, the scent of the cold, grimy water that makes her skin clammy and cool, the dirt and weeds that used to weave themselves into her hair when she wasn't paying attention for years at a time. She pretends he can see all of her, whether she's covered in the blood of prey or wearing the scent of humans.

And instead of running and yelling, or firing an arrow into her chest and collapsing one of her lungs, he takes her hand and kisses it. His lips graze one knuckle at a time.

She takes his head in her hands and presses a kiss to his forehead.

In turn, he palms her bare breast and brushes her nipple. It's sensitive. She whines. "Yes."

Zeke, encouraged, pinches it.

She moans.

Jenny can hear him swallow. "Let's go upstairs," he says.

"Yes." She presses another kiss to his open mouth.

He pulls her up the stairs, which are wooden and creak with their steps. It sounds like they are many, a whole cavalcade of lovers in a creaking race. They pass a closed door with yellow tape strung over it that reads CAUTION ("That's Amir's," Zeke says) and then another door that's slightly ajar and appears to have a long curtain like a veil inside it ("That's the bathroom").

Zeke's room is a soft, sweet blue. It reminds her of the volcanic baths she's encountered in northern countries, the steaming, beautiful water rich with silica that turn it a milky hue. To the side, there's a desk, but rather than a sheaf of paper and an inkwell, there are more books sitting on top of one another. Posters line the walls, advertising *Phantom of the Paradise* and *Twins of Evil*. The latter reads "Which is the virgin? Which is the vampire?" This is a little confusing, as Jenny's knowledge of vampires is limited to stories where bloated corpses spread disease rather than sex.

He follows her gaze. "I like monster movies. Have you seen these?"

"No," she says honestly. "You can tell me about them later," she adds, less honestly.

He presses both hands over his heart in a motion she recognizes as a mocking swoon. "Ah, the movie lovers' dream! A hot date watching your favorite films, hopefully while not on her phone."

Jenny cackles. "I don't have one."

"Oh, that's perfect. For me, anyway." He flashes his teeth. "I'd love to know why you don't have one."

"It's not important." She touches the hem of his shirt. "You should take this off."

He pulls it over his head immediately, which is deeply pleasing. She helps him.

Then she slides out of her pants—more of an undignified wriggle—and watches with interest as he slides out of his. His stomach, a little softer than the rest of him, is lovely. His hips have small divots above his pelvis. His sex, nested in black curls, is hard and flushed.

Jenny rolls down her underwear and kicks them behind her. She watches him inch backward to the bed. She helps by pushing him the rest of the way down.

He shakes as she climbs onto his lap. His skin, a soft and lovely thing that she wants to lick and probe, has a golden haze in the low light of the room. Her fingers run down his face, brushing his thick lips. She opens her own mouth as she stares at his. She wants him. Not inside her mouth so she might digest him, but inside her body. Jenny grinds against him and bucks her hips.

Later, she thinks. I'll eat him later.

He presses a hand to her waist. She can feel the callouses on his thumbs, the softness of the rest of his fingertips like butter on her skin. He takes a great inhale and moans. "Fuck, I want you." He looks up at her. Grins. "You're gorgeous."

"Yes." She's perverse for wanting this rotting creature, this beautiful man who will one day grow slow, then brain-addled, then dead, then dust, when she is still whole, and vibrant with life. It's sick to want him as any kind of partner.

But Zeke looks up at her, his hair mussed. "God." He looks at her sex and presses his thumb to her netherlips. He slides his fingers down, and then, in a swift stab, upward.

She feels them in the slime slickness of her, thrusting, and so she rides his fingers.

"I want to taste you," he whispers, all earnestness. "Please. Let me."

Jenny is sure he does not mean more kissing. She imagines lying down, legs spread, as he kneels before her as if in supplication, finding the most vulnerable part of her body.

She moves, levering herself off him.

He catches her hips. "Instead of you on your back, could you, uh . . . ?" He licks his lips, and she can see a sheen of spit on them for a moment before he begins to pant again. "Could you be on top?"

She's confused. "What?"

"You would, like, be on top of my face? Like straddling my mouth."

She feels a thump of distress. "Would you suffocate?" She's chilled. Is that what he wants? Like this?

He throws his head back and lets laughter rip out of his throat. She feels his stomach vibrate beneath her. When he looks up again, it's with an obscene, delighted smile. "That's a hell of a way to go. But no." He coaches her up his torso, his neck and the beautiful bobbing of his throat, and then, his hands on her hips, he balances her over his face. "Just press down. Gently."

Jenny, fascinated, eases down on top of his mouth.

Again, she's struck by the softness of his lips. His tongue, to her delight, twists against her clitoris. It's a shock to have someone touching such an intimate part of her again. In the intervening years since a huntress stole her heart, in both a poetic and physical sense, she has grown used to taking care of it herself.

He takes one of her hands and threads their fingers together. Then the other.

She puts her weight on those hands because otherwise, she is terrified she will crush this man's head like an egg. It would be a difficult thing to do, but she feels so precarious, she's sure she'll hurt him before she's ready to.

His tongue presses inside her and she groans. The pleasure radiates outward, rising from her nethers in a gauzy dream. Her forearms and thighs dot themselves in gooseflesh. Sweat slides down her brow.

Jenny bows her head forward, but he keeps her from falling too far. She still wants to devour him, but here he is, devouring her instead, with intimacy and care.

Like remembering a long-dead language, something opens up in her mind. An unused corridor.

She sees now, with rising horror, that she doesn't want him to die. She just wants him.

At that thought, her perception flares, and she can feel the blood in his fingers as she squeezes them, his pulse, and the sigh of his sweat-slick skin against hers. A bubble in her chest bursts. She gasps.

His lips pull away from her and he gently presses her thigh to the side so he can free himself. Jenny dismounts, out of breath. When she sees Zeke wipe his mouth with the back of his hand, she shivers. She pulls her knees under her chin, as if making herself small will undo her pleasure and the guilt that now twists her guts into greasy knots.

And Zeke smiles at her. His mouth looks swollen. "Damn."

"Yes," she responds immediately, because what if she stays silent and he asks her to leave? She doesn't want to go. "Very damn."

He laughs and then crawls toward her, still flushed, his prick bobbing between his legs. "Hey. Want to keep going?"

He's still human—she can smell the rot of him, all the things that make him mortal and aging—and he should still be livestock to her, yes. Absolutely. She also wants him to live as long as a human can live. Longer still, so that she won't have to go looking for companionship elsewhere, someone who is interesting and kind and doesn't scream when she comes near. "Yes," she says thickly.

Zeke's eyes widen. His cock is still hard, but his face looks more unsettled than amorous. "You're crying," he says.

And she opens her mouth to tell him no, her face is just scrunched up, that's not the same as crying, but tears spill from her rapidly blinking eyes and trace streams down her cheeks, her jaw. It makes her face feel uncomfortably wet and hideous.

"Oh no," Zeke says. "It's okay. Let's stop for a second, all right?" He puts his hands on hers with terrible gentleness.

Jenny bows her head and weeps. In her chest is a broken dam. A very broken dam. (Very dam.) She was not lonely until now, she thinks, or at least she didn't realize she was. Thousands of years skulking under the water, watching humans with curious eyes, laughing at their pain, not letting them climb inside and twine around her heart like duckweed.

"What's wrong?" He runs his thumbs in circles over her wrists. He gives her a hesitant smile. "I didn't realize I was that bad!"

"You're going to die," she says, because it's true and because she can't think how else to explain the paroxysms of misery. "And I'll be all alone."

He stills.

"You have to die because you're human," she says, hoping to clarify. His face is blurred through the tears laminating her eyes.

Zeke releases her hands. The mattress dips as he slowly stands before walking to the bedside table, looking like a hunted rabbit.

Jenny wipes her eyes. When she looks up, Zeke is holding a small, blunt stick. He pushes the edge open with his thumb and it unfolds into a blade. He touches the point to her throat. She feels the sharp edge dimple her skin. His face is carefully blank. "I'm not dying today."

Chapter Fifteen

VEINS

Zeke having a knife makes sense to her, in a bone-deep way. He's a human, and humans make and own knives.

He's a naked man at his bedside table, glistening with sweat, yes, but he also looks like a child who wandered into her bower, ripe for drowning and disemboweling. But she knows he isn't a child and she knows, now, that she doesn't want to kill him.

She keeps her eyes on his as she slides off the bed and stands before him.

"Don't come any closer." A small smile lingers on his face, but his eyes are wild with panic. Excitement. Terror.

Jenny raises her hands. "If you want to cut me with your knife, Zeke, you may do so," she says gently, equitably.

His mouth becomes pinched and small. "What?"

She grins at him, lets her arm snap forward, and grabs his hand. He remains stock-still as she pries his fingers from the knife. This is done in the space of a breath from his tender human lungs.

Jenny holds the knife up. "This is what happens when you cut me." She skids the edge of the knife down the center of her chest, right where her heart is. She doesn't press deep, but somehow that makes it sting more. The porcine skin parts and she pulls back a flap, like a page being turned in a book, revealing the wet, frog-slick green beneath. She presses it back to her flesh and it begins to knit together. "There."

Zeke stares. "You're her. You really are the one who jumped me."

She is hurt he didn't say it sooner, but she is also euphoric. "Have you always known it was me? Why didn't you run when I came to you?"

Slowly, he opens his hands, palms upward. "I wanted to be sure. I played along." His Adam's apple bobs. "And I wanted . . . I was curious . . . But also. I just—" He stops himself. "Okay. Breathe." He does just that. "Even if you could hurt me, even if you *did* hurt me, I needed to know you were real. I needed you to be real." His eyes focus on her and drift to another poster on the wall beside them, an image populated by humans in monstrous costumes. "I needed something besides this world to be real."

"'This world'?"

"When I was a kid, I always thought the world would be bigger, but adulthood is just TV pundits scaring your parents, studying something you don't love like you used to, and getting a job so you don't die. And all I can think is, 'That's it?'" He laughs without humor. "But you. You're something else. I don't care if you're a vampire, an alien, or even if you're, I don't know, a performance artist with amazing special effects makeup. You're proof there's more out there than this." He motions around his room.

"You didn't turn away when I came for you." Her heart leaps. She's special to him, in all the unlikeliness of that. She looks down at the knife. "But you have not surrendered to me."

He hesitates. "If surrender means you're going to kill me, because humans have to die or something, no."

"I'm not going to kill you."

"You said humans must die, right?"

"I meant that you wither and die over time. I do not."

"What?"

"You must be jealous of me." She flips the knife onto the bed. "I'm taken with you, though I will most certainly outlive you." She cups his chin in her hands and tilts his head, gently, toward hers. Beneath her fingers, his pulse races. It's very important that he kiss her again, but he doesn't move to do so.

Now his eyebrows meet. "I'm interested in what you are. I want to know you, as long as you don't want to strangle me."

"But are you jealous of what I am?"

Zeke hesitates. "I don't think so. No."

"But I'm immortal."

He winces. "That's awful."

Jenny feels shock run through her. She releases his face and stumbles. Why wouldn't a human want to be a forever thing? Why would he be content to live a life where his fellows will only leave him or be devoured by worms?

He takes one of her hands in his. Then, with a deep breath, he presses his lips to her knuckles, not so much a loving touch but a polite bump of pillowed flesh against fingers that have swum through rivers three thousand years dry, have touched the bows of boats long moldering beneath the waves, and have wrapped around countless throats of humans who stumbled across her.

"Could you wait here a second?"

Jenny exhales a sigh and nods.

He walks through the door and down the hall to the washroom. She can see it's tiled in yellow and white, the color of dandelions both young and old. He seals himself inside and she wonders if he'll come back out.

He's not envious of her immortality? She can't stand it. What in the world is the point, then, in being a creature among humans? She admires their cleverness, of course, and their facility with music. But their respect, their fealty, their awareness that she is more significant than they—she needs that. Because, otherwise, why has she stayed both in the human world and separate from humans for all these years? What has been the purpose of insinuating herself here? Has she stayed because she wants to be near them? They named her Jenny Greenteeth, after all, and she let them do it. Now it's what she calls herself.

Jenny looks at the bed, still warm with Zeke's body heat, blankets mussed with their scrambled, half-done lovemaking. She can't bear to touch it. Instead, she leans her head against the wall. She closes her eyes and feels how cool it is against her skin. She can hear water rushing in the pipes. It may be a trickle compared to the roar of waves and the babbling of rivers, but it grounds her. It echoes with the same primordial song that ran through the train station for years, the hollowness of the place between.

There's an entrance to the waterways nearby.

Immediately, she's hit with an idea.

She hears the gush of the faucet and knows he's standing on the tile in the middle of the bathroom. She runs to the door and pushes it open.

"Hey!" He squawks and covers himself, as if they weren't just rutting. "I'm almost finished!" He removes his hands and their Puritan hovering to set down a bar of soap.

"I have to show you something," she announces.

He remains alarmed. "Do your people usually charge into bathrooms when folks aren't done?"

"My people are gone." She probes the corners of the bathroom as she looks for where the soft place might be. Water moves and flows and so do the soft places. She can show Zeke! Then he'll see what a loss it is for him to be human and for her to be so much more. "I don't know what they would do with indoor bathrooms. All my sisters were killed a long time ago."

"What? How?"

"Humans, mostly. Storms. But mostly humans and their spears."

Zeke stares at her, mouth open. "That's awful!"

"It happened." When he continues to gawk, she adds, "Yes, it was very awful. It was also a long time ago."

"But spears! I'm so sorry."

"They're quicker than knives." She gives him a small, pointed smile.

He has the decency to blush. "Ah. Well." He pauses and tilts his head toward the tub. "Wait. What are you doing?"

"I promise this is important." She walks until her shin brushes the white bathtub. She frowns down at it and then grins. She can feel that it's different than the sink or even the toilet. "This will work just fine. An excellent basin! I'll show you!" She crouches and manipulates the handle. When there's no jet of water, she tries to twist the spout.

"Hold on. It will break." Zeke sits next to her. He twists the handle one way and then the other, until a waterfall begins. Out of the corner of her eye, she sees his face isn't annoyed. One of his eyebrows has climbed up high over his spectacles. He's still curious and that thought warms her.

Jenny watches the water begin to swirl around the drain. "Do you have a stopper?"

Zeke shakes his head. "The plug works like this." He pushes a small silver spoke inward. "Voilà!" he says, waving his hand, and indeed, the water is no longer draining away. Another innovative piece of human design!

She grins. "Good. Now we wait to get in."

"What, are we taking a bath?"

"No, we're making an entrance." Jenny watches the water fill and then climb along the sides of the tub. She runs her fingers over the surface. "But we should both fit in first, like we're bathing."

His face darkens. "I've tried the sexy-bathing thing before. It was ages ago, and it was with an ex, but, like, listen, it's not as sexy as people think it is, especially if you don't have a hot tub. Or if your roommates come home and there's just the one bathroom and suddenly they're banging on the door."

"This will do for our purposes. It won't take long." She grants him a beatific smile and reaches forward to stroke his cheek.

His eyes go unfocused and his lashes flutter closed. "That feels good," he murmurs.

She pulls him into her arms. As she nuzzles the side of his neck, she cards his hair.

"Did you cast a love spell on me?" His breath is hot in her ear.

"No." She shivers. "I'm no witch. If you want me, it's because you simply do."

His fingers run along the soft hairs at the nape of her neck.

And they stay like that.

When she finally looks up, she sees the tub is almost filled to the brim. She rushes to turn it off, remembering how he manipulated the dial and the handle.

"You catch on quick."

"That's one of the reasons I have survived so long." It's not entirely true, she suspects, as she thinks she is also long-lived because of luck. Serendipity continues to keep her alive. Jenny pushes that thought away, instead focusing on her fingers trailing blue light along the water. It bleeds out like India ink over the surface. She turns to him with a cutting smile. "Want to see the other reason?"

His jaw is slack, and every muscle he has stands tense beneath his skin. "What the hell?"

All she cares about is that he doesn't run. "Come here. I promise I'll bring you back." She holds out her hand.

Zeke hesitates. Then, slowly, terrified, fascinated, he touches his fingertips to her dry palm. The water shifts and laps at them both. He trusts her, however hesitantly.

She grips him. Her gills blossom open and he jolts.

Jenny falls into the tub and takes him with her. His arms flail out and, as they leave, she hears the faucet running once again.

The bottom of the tub blooms open, a blue flower that pulls them down. Water rolls sweetly over her skin as they join the brightness of the waterway. She missed this! She didn't realize how much! It's different from rain, from sweat, from a bathtub, from everything. It's the ocean behind the oceans, and it holds her.

Zeke kicks out. His legs beat hard, twisting left and right. He snaps his head back and forth, too, obscuring his face with bubbles.

Jenny hadn't thought to tell him to take in breath. She thought it was a natural thing one thought to do, but then, she has gills, however they may be obscured, and he doesn't. Which means he's drowning.

Idiot, she thinks, and with it, a pang of deep affection for him.

Her heel brushes against a soft space, a vein of waterway ore running beneath her. Jenny pulls them both down into it.

The surface of this new body of water is easy to find because the sun is out. Thank all the bright, little souls of her sisters, all the beasts that claw between the stars.

Zeke speeds past and breaches the surface before she does. Below, all she can see are his feet. His legs scissor together up and out, and then begin to tread water as he spins, looking for her.

She obliges by rising quickly and bursting into the open air alongside him.

He embraces her immediately, which is delightful, and his salt-touched skin is slick against hers. "Jenny!" Then he takes her shoulders and puts the length of his arms between them. "What was that? What is this?"

She furrows her brow and motions around them, splashing as she does. "Don't you like it? We traveled."

Rivulets run down his face and glasses. He bursts into laughter. "Of course we did! Yes! This is insane! And amazing, but Jesus." He squeezes her hand. His joy is an infection that leaps from him to her. He kisses her mouth, the smell of the equatorial heat in her throat and the scent of his blood in her nose.

It's with horror that she admits to herself, yes, she still wants to eat him. That puts a dark blush to the sun's haze.

She hears the hiss of water on the nearby surf.

"Let's swim over there." Jenny points toward a land mass bristling with palm trees and outcroppings of blue-black rock. The sand looks hot, soft, and as white as coral. She slides away from his hands—his fingers, their grip—and cuts through the ocean.

Zeke splashes after her. Yes, the difference between her and humans seems obvious here in her element. He moves slowly, clumsily. She can hear him gasp for air with his tender body.

Her feet find the sandbar. Then she walks to the shore. She wrings out her hair as she walks, suspecting she displays her hindquarters to her advantage. When she twists to see if Zeke has reached their destination yet, however, she sees him still bobbing a ways off, like driftwood.

Jenny sits and waits. He kicks fine and paddles all right, but his hands might as well be kitten paws. Zeke has no innate sense for the movement of the waves. He doesn't understand the ocean's undulations. Does he know they're in a body of water bigger than a creek?

He makes it to shore and gasps out, "Where are we?" So perhaps he doesn't.

"The Atlantic. I think."

Zeke narrows his eyes at her and gives a strange half smile. He thinks that she thinks he's stupid, which, yes, is perhaps unfair.

"Martinique, I suppose." She squints at the distant rocks and sees trees pushing out toward the sun. "Maybe Grenada. Or Guadeloupe. The one that sounds like your sister's name."

His eyebrows climb his forehead. "You have a good memory."

"It's a necessity for me to remember certain things."

"How do you remember all the places you go to?"

"I don't." She points to her head. "They're all here, somewhere, but I'm very good at hiding things from myself."

He gives a short, brief laugh. "Aren't we all?"

"It's a necessity for me to be observant." She thinks of her inability to understand so many human things, the wall that will always exist between her and that world. "As observant as I can be," she amends.

He sits down beside her, wincing at the heat of the sand. He spreads his hairy legs wide apart. "I don't see any houses nearby. Did you do that on purpose?"

"I don't control the waterways. I just follow them."

"It's nice and private. Beautiful." He looks out at the water and grins. It ripples and murmurs, green beneath the sky.

And she looks at him, at his wide smile and healed-up nose, and says, "Yes. Beautiful." She leans over and touches her shoulder to his.

The current that runs between them is warm. His ears heat up and he turns to her. "Nothing to do here. I bet we can figure something out, though."

She notes his length. It's flushed and growing hard. The way it resembles a rosy mushroom makes her smile, too. She wraps her hand around it and he lets out a shuddering sigh.

While she moves along his shaft, she watches his face, a changing landscape. Pinched eyebrows create valleys that, with a hitch of his body, go as smooth as dried, newly formed volcanic rock.

He gasps and his warm seed jets across her knuckles.

She lifts it to her face and smells it. Briny, she thinks.

He breathes hard. "That was . . . thank you." He's flushed and wonderful.

She examines his ejaculate with curiosity. She glances over at him.

Jenny wants to kiss him and then, playfully, bite him, and then bite him again, not so playfully. The thing she smelled that night when she first wanted to devour him was familiarity, desire running like hot oil from a lantern, spilling and burning her with incandescent want. She can resist eating him because she wants to speak to him, but the idea of simply talking without expectation of either coitus or consumption is so terrifying, she would rather have to clean up his viscera.

Her voice is soft. "Where. Um, where are you from?" She can't meet his eyes, so she instead licks his ejaculate from her fingers. It tastes of squid.

His breathing evens out. "What's that?"

"Tell me about you."

He snorts. "God, I like you."

Now her face heats. "Why?"

"Because this is happening"—here, he motions to the water, and then back to her, as if she created it and did not simply pull them there—"and you ask something so normal like that." He wears a small smile. "My parents raised me out in Iowa before they decided to split. I thought I wanted to do politics when I grew up, but these days, I mostly want to nap. Or quit and restart the monster blog I had as a kid. What about you?"

"Me?" She's still figuring out what he's just said.

"Yeah. I mean, were you ever a child? What was it like?"

"I was part of a brood. I had many sisters. Our mother raised us in a green-scummed pool and, later, swamps." Jenny rubs her arm. "She showed us the waterways and taught us about the land and the stars. She taught us how to hunt and eat. Then she left us."

He nods, considering, and lies back on the sand, elbows propping him up. He looks drowsy. "When was this?"

"Long ago. I didn't think much about how years worked, then, unless it meant it was too cold to find something to eat."

He laughs. "So it was like at the dawn of time?"

She doesn't know what that is. "I know that when I finally saw men, they had spears and small boats, but nothing like the ships that came later. Eventually, the humans began to gather together in villages that grew ports and markets and statues. And I realized, in time, they all made long, complex sounds at one another, and these sounds were words for things."

He whistles. "Wow."

She blushes.

"And you're nearly invincible?" Zeke's eyes have a shine in them like Jenny's the most precious thing in the world.

Slowly, she shakes her head. "No. I get hurt." She shows him where she cut the skin from her body back in his bedroom. The tissue has already smoothed into an uninterrupted surface. "I just haven't died yet."

His smile is so wide, his eyes bright. "Do you know how great this is? How impossible?" Yet his face holds no disbelief. He seems sweet and pleased. "Why are you in Boston?"

Jenny shrugs. "The empty train stations. The people who sing sea shanties and the ones who came over knowing the name of Jenny Greeneeth."

"'Jenny Greenteeth.'" His voice is a whisper. "I used to hope so damn hard for people out there who lived forever. Secret vampire covens and Greek gods who still walked around."

She's startled. What would anything like that have to do with her?

"But you're real. Thank you for that. Whatever else, thank you for being someone who turned out to exist."

She doesn't understand what he means. He looks on her now like she's a thing from the stars even though she came into being in the seas here, and it's a strange moment. She has been feared and she has been given offerings, but she's never been praised for doing nothing at all. For just being.

It fills her with joy, but that joy is mingled with terror. She has been seen. He wants to know her more intimately than anyone else.

Zeke fills the silence between them. "I wasn't coordinated at sports or good with people as a kid, so I decided I had to be smart. I tried to learn to do translation. My Spanish is bad, but I thought I could do it like my dad does. Then I realized I barely get by with English. For Hebrew, I know two words, and one of them is 'fork.' You probably know more than a couple languages, right?"

She nods and taps her forehead. "They're all here."

"I'm jealous. Can you switch between them?"

Jenny rubs her arm, feeling shy. "Not easily. They're all stored away in different parts of me."

"That's amazing. When I realized I didn't have my dad's ability with language, I tried to play chess but never won a game. So I did the biggest nerdy thing I could do. I read. Do you read?"

She can't think of a place to keep books in her abode where they wouldn't immediately become waterlogged. Pages stuck together, growing soggy. "Not as much as I would like."

He nods like he understands. "Me neither. I wish I did it more now. It was the thing to do when my parents went nuclear." He laughs uncomfortably. "Sorry. You don't want to hear about this."

Jenny does, but she's having trouble following. She seizes on the last strange word. "What's 'nuclear'?"

He turns to her, startled. He looks like he's aching from the inside out. "Oh. I guess you wouldn't have a reason to know that. It's sort of an explosion?"

"Nuclear," she repeats. "Like the center of a thing?"

Now his mouth drops. "Yeah! Like nucleus!"

"Or nucula." She holds up her thumb and forefinger, now clean, just far enough apart that she could be holding an acorn. "Like a nut."

"Is that Latin?" He grins and his eyes seem to shine adoration.

His excitement! Like wine, like beer! She puffs out her chest and lets the memories click into place, conjures to mind the smell of the cities, the libraries and their scrolls, the building where they were kept that sat by the bank of a river. If she wasn't seen, she could sit and read for hours. From that moment in time, she says, "Scire quod sciendum."

"What did you say?"

"'Knowledge which is worth learning,'" she says. "I don't know all Latin, as I don't know all English. I find what I need and keep it."

"What else do you know? Or, well, keep?"

She speaks to him in French, then Korean, Persian, and a language of a people long gone whose name she never learned. "I've been listening to English for years beneath Boston." She thinks again. "When you said, 'nuclear,' did you mean like The Bomb?"

"More like a metaphor with that in there, sort of. What do you know about nuclear bombs?"

"I know women whispered to each other about it and men laughed with strained voices. I know they were afraid. I could smell their fear."

"People are scared bombs like that can end the world."

She laughs bitterly. "Everyone thinks the world will end. All the time. Always."

"But what if one day they're right?"

She thinks about this. "I suppose one day they will be."

Zeke, unaccountably, takes her hand. He doesn't kiss it or guide it back to his member. Instead, he holds it, carefully, and gives it a squeeze. Just a single pulse. "I guess that's right. Would it be better for everything to end at once?"

She realizes he's melancholy. "Everything dies one day."

"Not you, though."

Jenny squeezes his hand back. "Not yet."

Zeke sighs. "We live longer these days, at least."

Jenny shrugs. Of the things she's paid attention to over the years, this hasn't been one of them. "Living two hundred years still isn't very long."

He shakes his head. "You know humans who've lived for two hundred years?"

"Isn't that how long you live?"

Zeke howls with laughter. "One hundred if we're lucky. Usually closer to seventy or eighty."

She jerks in horror but doesn't let him go. "That's all?"

He laughs again, like she's telling a joke.

"But that's not long at all!" She feels a tremor growing inside her and stills it. "You'll be gone soon."

"In, like, fifty or sixty years?" He clicks his tongue. "I'll tell you what I told Lupe when she came crying to me when we were kids. She had just learned people die. 'That's a long time from now.'"

But it isn't. Jenny knew humans didn't live long, but to think Zeke is here now and will be gone in a handful of decades, if he isn't mashed by a vehicle or drowned or devoured by a bear or felled by sickness? It's too much. Her eyes sting. "I'll keep you safe," she whispers, and knows it's an empty promise.

The smile he turns to her is ignorant of the nature of death, its definite end, its gruesome and humiliating truths. "I appreciate that," he says to her like she's a child. "I think I'm okay with dying one day."

"I've watched many humans die. None of them like it very much."

"More humans like me?" He raises an eyebrow.

"I haven't spent my time with them the way I have with you."

"No kissing?" He winks.

"A few times." She's wistful. "Mostly, I've drowned them."

He laughs hard. "Oh yeah?"

She's grave as she clutches his hand more tightly. "This is why you must believe me when I tell you how terrible death is. I've inflicted it myself."

Now Zeke's beautiful eyes, with their flecks of copper, go wide. His body is now tight as a bowstring. "You're serious?"

She's startled. "Of course."

"Well, of course you've killed people in self-defense! I pulled a knife on you and everything." Zeke attempts a smile but it won't hold. She can smell the sweat prickling under his armpits.

"Defending myself is important. Other times, I've killed them because they were lost and I was hungry. There have been too many to count."

Though she anticipates the slackness of his jaw, how impressed he is with her abilities to kill and not be killed over the centuries, she's surprised to see the color draining from his face. She hears the thudding speed of his heart. Then he laughs uncomfortably. "It must have been a long time since you've done that."

She knits her brow. "No. I killed a woman a couple days ago. I've been eating a man whose parts are in the fridge. When I do, I can grow a different shade of skin and walk among you."

His eyes are remarkably round. "When you attacked me," he says slowly, "I thought you were confused."

"You disrupted my slumber." She's now bashful. "But I decided I wanted to know you better. Now I barely want to kill you at all." She waits for him to thank her again.

He doesn't. The silence stretches between them. He stares at her and she waits for him to speak.

Finally, she talks first. "A vampire is a creature that's supposed to drink blood and devour humans, yes?"

"I— Yes?"

She opens her hands beneath her face, as if to reveal herself to him. "Didn't you say you wanted to know something like one?"

Zeke's throat works for a moment without making a sound. "I want many things."

"And you can have them." She eyes his full mouth. When can she kiss him again?

"Just because I want things doesn't mean I should have them."

And that, Jenny thinks, is the most baffling thing he's said yet.

"Where are your clothes?" says a deep voice from behind them.

Jenny twists to see the voice's owner, a lean man with dark skin and a wrinkled forehead. He wears a shirt with an open collar and has his hands in his pockets. Something about him is like a soldier patrolling the shore, looking down on those he encounters with suspicion and curiosity.

Zeke covers his manhood, stands, turns, and runs into the water. He begins to swim out to sea, perhaps looking for the waterway gate that will return him home.

The man shrugs. "Better go after your man, then. If you have a boat, get on it and go away. Best not to come back afterward. This is a private place."

Jenny isn't sure if he's her "my man" anymore. He might have been for a few moments, but those moments seem to have evaporated.

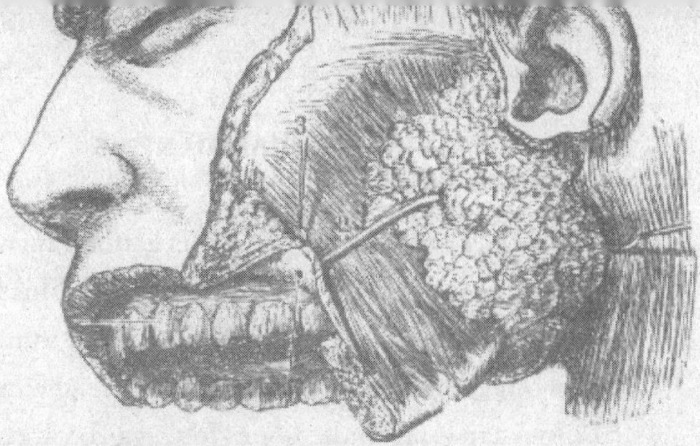

Chapter Sixteen

CHEEK

Zeke desperately treads water, trying to keep away from her. "Take me home."

"Then breathe deep." She presses her lips together, takes his hand—which is stiff, colder, doesn't move when she squeezes—and pulls him down with her.

The strip of electric blue is a burning chasm. When she shuts her eyes against the light, it leaves white flashes beneath her eyelids.

They swim to the surface in another ocean, this one hot and salty, like waking up in a still, cooked soup. When they reach the air, Zeke winces at the sun. "It feels brighter," he says without looking at her. "Where are we?"

"Italy," she says, though in truth, maybe it's Greece or Turkey or Syria or Egypt. She touches Zeke's shoulder and points to the shore. "That's where I crawled on land after a storm and a man shouted, 'I knew it! Men first gestated in the mouths of fish!'" Her translation from Greek—ancient and in a dialect not spoken here for a long time—is halting. It conveys none of the man's ecstasy as he laughed and spread his broad, tanned arms to the sky, calling her "nymph" and raining down joyous words that, when she heard them, seemed well deserved. She looks to Zeke in the hopes his regard will revive to similar heights of euphoria.

She can barely hear his words over the lapping of the waves. He looks pained as he stares down at his treading legs. "Did you kill him after that?"

Jenny is brought up short. "Not him."

Zeke looks at her, dripping and miserable.

"I don't kill everyone all the time," she emphasizes.

Yet still he shrugs away from her touch. It couldn't have hurt worse if he had struck her.

She pulls them both back down to the waterways.

Off the coast of an island in the Pacific, thick with green. She can't forget the smell of moss, the generations of turtles burrowing into the sand.

"This is where I first learned the moon was a rock hanging in the sky and not just a disk pocked with divots made to float." She smiles as she points at the shore, self-conscious.

"Sorry?" Zeke fights to keep his head above the water. Drops cling to his spectacles and he tries to wipe them away, serving only to make them more opaque as he splashes about.

"A fisherwoman told me while she was prying open clams," Jenny continues on anyway. "She and her people knew the moon was round by how it turned throughout the seasons. They knew and named the craters on its face. I never thought to look so closely before then! She is someone else I didn't kill," she adds, hoping to win back his favor.

But all Zeke says between breaths is "I think we're getting even farther away."

"We'll get there," says Jenny with confidence she doesn't feel.

He puffs with exertion as he pumps his legs. "You can just take me as close as you can—Canada or Jersey or wherever! I can find clothes maybe, and then get some money. I can take the bus back!"

Her pride smarts, but he offers his hand once again when they rise up out of the water near, according to signs on the horizon, the city of Dakar. She hears the hum of fishing boats and vehicles farther inland like a threat. He looks moodily at the unfamiliar landscape. If only he would instead look at the swaying trees and be close to her, as he was before she spoke about devouring human flesh. She opens her mouth to ask him if he can do this, but Zeke saves her from this humiliation by speaking first.

"Whenever I get back, we need to talk," he says.

She pulls him down and they next break the surface in a small pond in the north, probably England, perhaps Scotland based on the hills. He looks increasingly flustered. Nervous.

Their next jump is colder, much colder. Zeke yelps in real pain, as if he's been stabbed. The water has ice in it and an Arctic breath. Jenny hates it, too, but she hates it even more as she sees Zeke's face fold in on itself, turning a ghastly red, like he's burning alive. She opens up the waterway as quickly as she can.

Eventually, she feels the cool porcelain of the bathtub under her hands.

They both sit up. Zeke gives a great, shuddering sigh. He rubs warmth back into his arms and hands and looks around with wide eyes. He seems startled.

At once, Jenny understands why he's surprised. When they left, they must have knocked the tap back on, and during all this time, water has spilled over the side of the tub. It splashes over the tiles like a tide pool free from barnacles and crabs. Someone knocks very hard at the door, so hard that it shakes in its frame.

"Zeke!" a man yells. "The ceiling's leaking over the kitchen! Did you slip while taking a shower or something? You're not dead, right?" A heavy pause that stretches taut. "Zeke?"

"Yeah, I'm here." Zeke's face is like a brick wall. He lifts his spectacles to wipe his dripping hair out of his eyes, reaches over her as if she isn't there at all, and shuts off the faucet.

Jenny is hurt by this, reduced to a ghost when she has tried so hard to show herself to her best advantage.

Zeke stands, wobbling. Water sluices down legs that appear stiff with cold. His feet splash along the floor as he trudges forward to take one of the linens hanging from the wall, wrapping and tucking it around his waist. Then he leaves the other on the top of the toilet seat.

She realizes then that it's for her, she's supposed to take it, and that he would rather leave it on a waste receptacle than touch her again.

Jenny feels cold, despair oozing in her belly.

The man on the other side of the door says, "I think Mira can probably get some guys over here to fix it if the toilet's backed up? I don't care, really. It's fine. But we should handle it now."

"Amir, it was just the tub." Zeke opens the door so that Jenny can see the golden sliver of the hallway light. "We're both really sorry about this. If Mira wants payment or something for damages, I got this."

"'Both'? You're both sorry?" The man looks through that opening and it's enough for him and Jenny to see each other. She sees copper-brown skin, a tuft of beard, and dark, dense curly hair wavering over an eye like a deer's. His dark brow arches when he sees Jenny. "Oh. Hey. Sorry." He covers that eye and turns away. "I didn't mean to interrupt! It's just the kitchen, man. That's all. And, okay, the hallway a bit."

Jenny is reminded how strange humans can be in regards to nudity. One of many things she dislikes. She stands, heavily, and wraps the linen around herself. It's a thick material that immediately soaks up the lovely sheen of wetness on her skin, leaving her uncomfortably dry. How is it that humans are both so prudish and so clever?

Zeke speaks gently to Amir. "It's fine. We're done. Sorry we made a mess."

That's twice he's said that they are both "sorry," and Jenny doesn't like that very much at all. She wasn't here when the tub overflowed! And she certainly isn't going to tell Zeke she's sorry for eating when she's hungry either, she decides. "Why would I be sorry?" she asks.

Zeke turns on her. His chin is high and his eyes, like his chest and throat, have a gleam of water. "You should go."

Jenny feels her insides sink.

The other man peeks at Zeke through his fingers. "You're going to let her dress before she leaves, right, man?" He cracks a smile that looks like it hurts his face.

Jenny can neither stand being dismissed nor being pitied. "I'll dress in my clothes and leave and you won't see me again," she announces.

"All right." The ease of Zeke's acceptance seems to rip free a new, stinging layer of skin from her body.

Jenny strides out of the bathroom as stately as any empress whose face has been printed on a coin, as proud as any actress on the stage. Amir dutifully steps aside, eyes averted. She finds her clothes where she left them, in Zeke's bedroom, entangled with his.

While she pulls on her trousers, she hears his voice. They're not even talking about her, but their house and landlord. She is as insubstantial as air to them. Good, she thinks as her eyes burn. Her skin crawls when she considers the casual way Zeke estimated that the rest of his life could be measured in a few decades—a few years, really! And no one will be kind enough to eat him when he dies. His little life will be a waste.

She descends the creaking stairs, toes on her shoes at the door, and walks out into the chill sunshine. She curls her lip and gives the sun a snarl.

All at once, the day falls on her like a great weight. She is exhausted from the anticipation of cornering Zeke, their quick and lovely coupling, and the many leaps she took inside the waterways with a mortal beside her.

And, yes, perhaps the fact he has outright refused her. She deigned to share herself with him, and all was well and fine until she told him what she eats! He was the one who ruined it, she insists. Horrible, little, human man.

All the houses look the same as she heads home. But there it is, and there's the woman, Sister Mary Catherine Charles, just standing there, in a brown, wide-shouldered coat, a dark handbag, and thick boots, frowning at the door. When Jenny comes up, the nun turns and gives her a warm smile. "Oh! Hello again."

Jenny glowers at her.

"I'm so sorry to bother you," she says. "I just keep thinking about Ralph. Have you seen him?"

Once upon a time, this woman was in love with the man Jenny killed. He must have loved her back. It makes her sick and jealous and bitter. "No."

"Well, I'll give you my number." The woman pulls out a piece of paper. "When he comes back, you can call me."

"He's not coming back."

She pauses. "That's a possibility, but based on what he's done in the past, well. He turns up."

Jenny is tired of pretending to be human, of the blunt little teeth she grew, of being something she's not. She wants to hurt someone, and she wants to do it now. "I killed him."

The nun looks at her.

"I cut him up." Jenny waits for the woman to scream. "Once in a while, I eat a little more of him."

There's still a remnant of a smile on the woman's face, but her eyes seem unfocused, confused. "Sorry?"

It's Zeke all over again, looking at her with wonder and surprise when he saw her the first time.

Jenny opens her mouth and yells without words. She leaps on the woman, hands hitting her round shoulders, and bites into her soft, sweet face. Her cheek is a fibrous, screaming apple.

Even Jenny's unsharpened teeth know how to bite. The first hot sluice of blood hits her tongue and it's delicious and salty. Too salty. Tears are falling down Jenny's face, too, angry streams that obscure her vision.

She doesn't see Sister Mary Catherine Charles raise her little fists to hit her. The punches, on any other day, would be ineffectual. Embarrassing. Jenny would answer them with an easy fluidity. The nun with the rounded bite mark beneath her eye, leaking red down her chin and neck, would already be meat.

But Jenny falls back. She's crying too hard to focus, to find her strength, to make her prey a meal.

The woman slides the straps of her handbag down her arm and swings it. The purse hits Jenny in the stomach, driving the breath from her ridiculous lungs and making her gills flare.

Though Sister Charles wheezes hard, she doesn't scream. She looks at Jenny with wide, terrified eyes and doesn't see anyone worthy of compassion, much less an umbrella. She turns and runs.

Jenny's despair grows deeper, more painful. She sinks to the ground, finding air again as she sits. She wipes tears and snot and the nun's blood from her mouth.

This is what you are, she tells herself, sitting there in the awful sunlight, dry and alone.

Soon, she hears the wail of sirens, sees vehicles that wash the streets in red and blue discordant lights. They park at the front of the house.

Jenny hears the clack of hooves and turns just as Faun takes her hand in a viselike grip. "Come on," she says through gritted teeth. "They're going to see us." She hooks their elbows together and does an about-face.

Jenny squeezes Faun's hand back because it's comforting in its solidity, its sureness, even if Faun's pulse hammers hard. Keeping away from hunters looking to capture her is something she's done innumerable times before. She falls into step with her in gratitude.

"Walk as slow as you can. We're just two simple, stupid, mortal women," Faun says. "We have nothing to do with that house."

They stroll down one street together, turn, move slowly down another, and casually cross to a third street that hooks oddly into yet another road. The flash of lights becomes distant, no more threatening than a mote in one's eye. Jenny's tears are gone but she can still taste them in her throat.

Faun's jaw is set. "Someone ratted us out, sweets."

"It was me. I was in the waterways." Jenny smells the sex on her own skin, masked by salt water and scummed over by sweat. "When I came back, I tried to eat a nun."

"A what?"

Jenny feels her face grow hot. "A nun. She got away."

Faun grows angry. "Where did you get a nun?"

"I didn't get her from anywhere! She knew the man."

"What man?"

"Ralph McGish!" When Jenny still sees Faun is uncomprehending, she says, "The one we killed!"

"Oh! Gods. Him." When she sighs, her nose flares. "And then she told the authorities, I see. How nice." Faun's voice drips with acid. "You're very bad at hiding, aren't you? You're bad at fighting and passing for human. How in the world have you not died many times over?"

Jenny straightens. Faun's insults make her sulky, petulant. "I don't want to pretend to be human anymore."

"Know what? That's fine. I couldn't care if I tried." Faun's mouth is a lemon-sour pucker. "We just have to hide again. Get out of town. At least you can help us with both of those."

The waterways, Jenny realizes. "Today?"

"If you could, sweets. We went back to the tunnel and there was yellow tape up. They're gonna tear it down or renovate the station. Clyde and I saw it with our own eyes."

Jenny aches. Her home! She hasn't even gotten the chance to say goodbye. "Are you certain?"

"Something's happening there." Faun clucks her tongue. "We have to get to the nexus soon."

"I can't." She thinks of Zeke and her exhaustion from herding them from one gate to another. If she weren't running from officers, she would be settling down for a good sleep. "I need rest."

Faun glares. "And we need a roof over our heads and a place to stay where no one would think murderers would be and not to be arrested and experimented on and tortured." She is lost to her memories now.

Shame bubbles inside Jenny. "I didn't think when I attacked the nun. This wasn't what I meant to happen."

Her goat-legged companion shows her teeth. "You didn't think."

"I have instincts, and they grow so great sometimes, they overwhelm me." Softly, Jenny adds, "Please."

"Please?"

"Please understand," says Jenny.

Faun is chilly and silent for a while. The afternoon is grim.

Then Faun says, "It's supposed to rain tonight. I'm all right with being soaked but it's not comfortable, is it? We have to find someplace."

Faun said "we." Jenny feels a terrible relief. She sees they're walking again toward the mansion where she peeled off her skin.

She can see Clyde, standing tall at the gates. He looks sad, distant. "There you are."

"Came back here when you saw the cops, huh?" Faun gives him a poke and a half smile.

Clyde returns neither. He doesn't look interested in being playful. "You murdered the owner of that apartment, didn't you?"

Faun cackles before Jenny can answer. "Like you didn't suspect! You didn't actually believe me, did you?"

Fury crumples Clyde's features and he points at Jenny. "This woman right here? She didn't promise to be my partner in this." He drops his hand and it trembles. "She just has access to what we need. But you, Faun, keeping things like this from me? Killing an innocent?"

"Oh, innocent, my ass! You should have heard what he yelled at us! I know, I know—" She waves away Clyde as he tries to interrupt. "'You shouldn't kill humans for insulting you.' They've killed our sort for a lot less!"

Jenny's gut tightens. She remembers her sisters on the ends of spears. She can no longer remember their faces.

Mother, she thinks again, and swallows down the thought.

Faun and Clyde ignore her in order to better argue with each other. They assume parts they've no doubt rehearsed before. Their shouts spiral into mentions of hogging a mattress in an abandoned hat shop and the time someone locked someone else in the back of a vehicle called a "Ford Thunderbird." They speak of a fire that demolished all their things and they can't agree who started it. Jenny crouches on the ground near them, waiting for them to stop, and thinks that if the Algonquin were right about the thunderbird existing in the sky, then perhaps the underwater panther they speak of exists, too, and she simply hasn't run into her yet.

Does Zeke believe those creatures exist? What does he think of them? Would he speak to them as he spoke to her? Would he want to see them, too?

Jenny scratches her wrist as she tries to be patient. She feels the top layer of her skin flake away before she looks down and confirms, yes, there are patches of green peeking out beneath the pink. "I have to sleep," she announces. "And I have to eat." She shows them her arm.

Clyde's warm brown glare is ice. "A minute, please."

A minute stretches into an hour. Green spirals down Jenny's arm like she's twined it with duckweed crowding the surface of a pond, but it's her own skin peeking out at her. It teases. It reminds her that she can wear any skin she wants, but what's underneath will never be far away.

She daydreams. What if she had reassured Zeke she really wouldn't eat him? Her eyelids grow heavy and, the same way she finds the gates into the waterways, she reaches out and falls into sleep. Clyde's and Faun's mutterings could be the chattering of a river.

Rain patters down on her head and she wakes, peering through a fog. The rain grows denser, more insistent, and she catches a tress of her hair in her hand, sees how some strands have gone green. She's always thought it was beautiful, but in this moment, it seems like the color of pus, like an infection leaking out of her.

Clyde touches her shoulder gently. "You're awake? Good. If you still want to come with us, if you still want to open the door, I know where we can go for now." Clyde's words are hard as flint but his shoulders slope downward, defeated. He turns and leaves before she replies.

Jenny gets up on wobbling feet and clambers after him and Faun. When she reaches them, she stumbles and then rights herself. "When I'm better rested, I'll take you," she says.

Clyde immediately turns to her. "No more delays?"

Jenny shakes her head. "No. Just let me rest a little more, and I'll take you both. I don't need to be in the city anymore."

He exhales. "Me neither. I don't need to be near any more cities for a long time." There are raindrops on his lashes and the smallest smile on his mouth. Then it's gone, his lips smooth once more.

"Are we going back to Zoe's?" Faun stands at the gate, shielding her eyes from the downpour. "Because the tunnel is full of workmen now."

Clyde doesn't look at her, still angry. He just walks and lets them follow along the wet, slick sidewalk.

Faun *tsks*. "You're trusting. It's just your nature." She touches his back with a soothing hand. "It's nothing to be ashamed of."

Clyde pulls away from her and marches forward. Jenny can see the way his jaw is set. He's been lied to and, knowing Faun, it's probably not the first time. "I trust foolishly. It's plenty to be ashamed of when I keep trusting the same people over and over again. I don't need any more deaths near me."

"We're forever creatures living in a world of mortals," Faun says. "We're surrounded by the dead, aren't we?"

"You think so little of them because their lives are short." Clyde curls his lip. "You're as bad as any creature that turned into an animal to copulate with women, crawled up a mountain, and called himself a god."

Faun is indignant. "You leave my forefathers out of this."

And they're off, snapping and sniping at each other once more.

Jenny pulls the cuffs of her sleeves down over the fractures of green on her skin.

In the diner, her hair and clothes dripping on the floor, Jenny doubts she'll get much rest, but as Clyde and Faun settle into the booth stuck to the wall, as they all squeeze into seats that squeak beneath their respective persons, she folds her arms on the table and finds they make a nice pillow. She rests her chin on them and watches a woman—the waitress—and thinks that she ought to harvest someone like her to stave off her green skin.

But her eyes wrinkle at the corners like Zeke's. And when she comes to the table to give them all coffee, she mentions leaving soon to pick up a child at something called "fencing." "They have little swords!" she says in delight.

Jenny closes her eyes. They're damp again. She opens them once more when she wakes to Faun shaking her shoulder. "Are you ready to take us? Or do you need more rest?"

She looks at them both blurrily, coming more fully awake to burnt coffee, grease, and the sickly sweet ooze of soap. She thinks of Zeke again and she is even more exhausted. "Please. A little more."

When she turns, she sees the inside of the restaurant is dark. The man, Rashid, wipes the counter with a cloth and suds. He then looks at them meaningfully.

"We can't stay here, can we?" Jenny deflates.

"I have one more place." Clyde slides out of the booth and stands. "Come on."

The clouds suggest the rain will begin again soon. She can smell it.

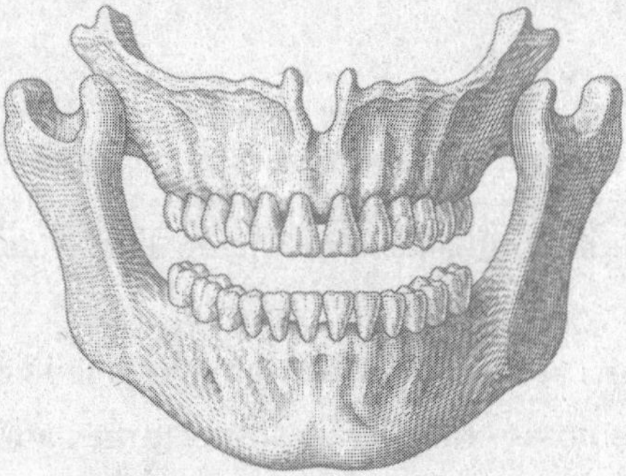

Chapter Seventeen

JAW

"That looks like an old factory." Faun seems doubtful.

"Because it is." Clyde moves stiffly through the hazy dusk light. "A bunch of people moved in."

"Oh? They turned it into one of those apartment buildings?" Faun squints at the structure.

"No. They just moved in."

"Ha! I remember when people could do that without the police showing up. Just a rival family. Good old days, you know?" She looks at Clyde hopefully.

He walks on.

Jenny shuffles behind Faun, rubbing her eyes. She can smell the wharf, beer bottles rolling in nearly empty bottles, urine-splashed pavement. She hears the sea lap the docks. Jenny leans in to whisper to Faun, "We should have told Clyde when we killed the man."

"He would have liked it even less if we had." Faun scowls at her. "I guarantee it. He's never liked more than a little bit of the truth at a time. I doubt you would, either."

"I like hearing truths just fine." Jenny likes it more than Zeke did, anyway.

Faun laughs at her. "You do, huh? No one likes the truth, I promise." It sounds cruel. Jenny suspects they are not quite the close friends she thought they were. How well does she know Faun, anyway?

They near the giant building, which reminds Jenny of a mill made obscenely large. The air is spiced, threaded with incense, hashish, and cheroot.

A small woman throws open a red door. Her orange hair is in a long, loose braid and her face is gold and freckled. She runs up to Jenny and hugs her tightly around the middle. She smells of cloves and the fresh, pumping blood right in her veins. "Hello!" she cries sweetly. "You're so beautiful!" She kisses Jenny on the cheek.

Under her sleeve, a strip of Jenny's skin peels beneath the young woman's affectionate embrace. It stings.

Jenny hisses in pain, and the woman releases her. "Sorry! Won't touch again!" Then she seems to forget Jenny's existence and runs up to welcome Faun, who shrinks down even smaller at her touch. Then she hugs Clyde, who good-naturedly pats her head.

"Good to see you're well," he says. "Sorry to say I forgot your name."

"I forgot yours, too! You're . . . Clark?"

"Clyde."

"Welcome back, Clyde! We'll have dinner ready soon. It's pancakes and bacon."

Clyde's eyes are melted tenderness. "All right, all right. Thanks for letting us just drop in. Sorry to impose."

"Everyone's imposing all the time here!" She laughs. "'Impose!' That's so British." She pulls Clyde and, by some invisible gravity, Faun and Jenny through the doorway with its peeling paint.

On the other side, the floor is cement and the walls are cinder blocks covered in a looping, amorphous painted design that flows into itself like water. Lights that Jenny's only seen from creatures in the deep sea and at Christmas line the ceiling, staining everything an ethereal blue and a hot, violent red. The cold floor is covered in woven brown rugs and coats shed like snakeskins. From a loud, clanging room that appears to be the kitchen, the smell of fried meat rises, along with burning sage.

A dark young woman and her pale companion are curled up tightly around each other on a couch. On the squat table in front of them are plates with fluffy, whipped eggs that they happily put into each other's mouths. A sallow man with grimy thick spectacles laughs and, balancing a plate of his own, tries to sit on top of them. They unwind their legs and kick him fondly.

Jenny is either in a den of mystics or opium. Perhaps both.

The orange-haired woman turns to her. "Do you like our place?"

"Yes." Jenny's fatigue makes her think anywhere that's warm is welcoming.

"She needs a place to sleep." Clyde sits on a faded yellow sofa with its stuffed innards hanging out from its pillows. Faun sits beside him, though not close. Her hands are folded in her lap.

"I have a place." The orange-haired girl holds her hand out to Jenny, having forgotten her oath not to touch her again. Jenny sees that her nails are bitten down to the quick, and woven, beaded bracelets clatter together on her wrists. On her dirty knuckles is embedded ink, individual blue stars and a lopsided daisy.

The girl's hands are the same color as Zeke's but far more slender. Jenny takes one hesitantly, and when she looks up at the girl, she's met with a dimpled smile.

"Be good!" Clyde shouts after Jenny. "I mean it!"

Jenny allows herself to be pulled to another, heavier door made of metal. Behind it are stairs scaled with rust. As they mount them, Jenny's knees begin to quake. She feels faint.

"You okay?" The girl tilts her head.

"I expended myself too much today."

"Coming down?" The girl nods with understanding. "Been there, yeah. I usually have a glass of water and then I'm fine. Don't worry. Does pot help you?"

Jenny has never once been helped out by crockery in the entire span of her existence. "No."

"Aw, damn. I don't really have anything else. Just a bed."

"Yes. Bed. Good." Jenny watches the girl brush her braid from one shoulder to the other, revealing a freckled cheek, plump and soft. She's reminded of how she bit the nun's face.

Jenny punches the guilt down into her gut.

"You look sort of sick."

"I don't get sick." Jenny sees the girl through a haze now. She might as well be sleepwalking. "You're like Zeke when he's kind," she says as she's steered down the hallway (hallow way, yes, but that's no longer something she needs to know, a cliff face of knowledge that's crumbled down into the sea of time). "He's angry at me. He thinks the way I survive is wrong."

"Zeke? Ugh. Don't let haters get you down." The girl is magnanimous. She pushes open another door, this one painted green. Someone broke a mirror and glued the pieces of it to the front, so that Jenny sees her face a dozen different times at strange angles. The tiny Jennys who stare back at her are pallid, the pink meat along their eyes waxing green. She thinks of her sisters and her chest seems to eat itself, so she takes her memory of them, folds it up, and hides it from herself once more.

Inside the room, the girl points to a dark gray chair trimmed with lace.

"We got that off the side of the road. No bedbugs! We checked. There's a beanbag chair, too, but that's where I've been sleeping." From her pocket, she takes a thin stick, paper wrapped around tobacco, and a small metal box. She runs her thumb over a wheel at the top of the box and it produces a flame. The end of her cigarette burns as red as the inside of a cherry.

Jenny sits on the chair to test its softness. She runs her hand along it and thinks how it has the same color as the Atlantic in the morning, as her own true skin in curtained light. What does Zeke's skin look like before dawn? she wonders. She supposes she'll never know.

She wakes alone to the pulse of drums. Jenny is convinced, before she opens her eyes, that she's been unlucky enough to end up in a bog on a battlefield. One band of soldiers calls to another with sounds that hum right through her body, rattling the teeth in her head.

But no, she's still in the same room the girl showed her to, though she and the smell of her cigarette are gone. The window is no longer full of sunset but suffused with blue light that becomes green, then blue again. It would feel like the deep sea if music wasn't spilling up from the floor.

Jenny jumps to her feet. Have the police come again? Where are Faun and Clyde?

Her muscles are awake. She is ready to leave Boston for good, at least until part of it has been subsumed by the sea. She's done with this confusing city and Zeke's human judgment and his human smallness and his beautiful, strange eyes.

She looks down at her hands. They're ribbed with waving stripes of green.

Her nose smells human meat and its sour sweat. She turns her head as the door opens, revealing a man with a red beard and knit hat. His eyes are wide and blue as she vaults over the chair and grabs his shoulders. In his gloved hands, he clutches a glass pipe, like an unlucky peasant with a crucifix.

She releases the man. He coughs. "I wasn't going to do nothing." His face is moon-pocked with scars. "I shouldn't have gone and scared you. Lupe told me a girl was up here and not to scare her, so you know, all on me. I'm real sorry."

"Good." Jenny stands. The name Lupe is familiar to her but she can't place it. "In recompense, give me your gloves."

"What?"

"I want your gloves."

"You're crazy." His face twists. "You need them?"

Jenny obliges and shows him her hands, spreading them open like starfish so he can see the webbing that's begun to grow back. "Yes."

The man squawks. "Jesus Christ! Are you sick?"

"No," she tells him honestly.

"Cool. Right. Awesome." He quickly peels off his gloves and tosses them at her. "Here!"

They land at her feet, a small offering, which seems appropriate. She decides to give this stranger her gratitude. "Thank you."

It's satisfying to watch him sprint away. She then hears him shout, "She's got something! Stay the fuck away from her," which is less satisfying.

And who should arrive on the floor as he flees but Clyde? He glances at the man as he runs down the hall. Then he sighs and turns back to Jenny. "I told you to be good."

"I was." She stoops to pick up the gloves and pull them over her hands. "I didn't kill him. In fact, I haven't killed anyone today."

When he speaks, his voice is soft. "How often do you eat people when you're on your own?"

She considers telling him "Only when they get in the way," but supposes that's not an answer he would like to hear. Zeke certainly wouldn't. "I don't like to kill and just leave the body. That's much worse."

Clyde scrubs his eyes with the back of his hand. "I know the natures of those like us. If you had explained it to me in the first place, I would have understood."

She frowns. "Faun said you wouldn't have." Jenny suspects she has trusted her too much.

"Oh, I would have yelled." He shrugs. "But I would have come to understand I couldn't fully understand."

She rolls this over in her mind. "I spend a lot of time knowing I'll never understand certain things, either."

He sighs through his nose. "I just want to leave."

"Me too. And now that I'm rested, I can take you." In her mind, she says goodbye to the drowned train station, the beautiful scum in the dark, and the way the water held her, both in blurry-eyed wakefulness and silent dreams. Jenny knows she has lingered too long among humans, because she has become nostalgic. Once she frees herself of the yoke of human contact, she'll be joyful again. Lonely, yes, but blissfully unaware of pain and a sense of inferiority, because she has shoved them into a different corner of her mind.

Clyde gives her a small, flat smile. "Let's get Faun and go."

They traverse the stairs, which are now full of people, laughter, and music. Clyde squeezes between partially clothed bodies and Jenny follows. As the red sign marked EXIT bleeds through the thick air, Jenny thinks of a dense coral reef. Instead of fish swimming through anemone, she's swimming alongside excitable humans hugging, screaming, and waving phones that glow and pick out their faces in eerie light. They drink from bright red cups and laugh.

The music thumps like a heart, like they are wandering the innards of a whale.

There's a moment where a tall, full-bosomed woman with a shiny white suit blocks Clyde from Jenny's line of sight. When the woman moves away, he's gone.

Instead of feeling lost, however, she knows she's safe in the press of people. It will be a relief to leave humans, of course, but when she's by herself, there is little music, less dancing. She wants it all a little longer.

For a strange moment, someone takes her hand, his human smell cloaked in smoke. She can see the wink of lights bouncing off his glasses, like a pair of will-o'-the-wisp affixed in the comforting heat of a bog. She squints at his face.

And her heart sinks because the hand and spectacles belong to a stranger, a smiling man with a sharp chin and elf locks. He has yellow paint spattered over his jaw and cheek. He slides a glowing bracelet onto her wrist, winks, and retreats back into the crowd.

Jenny finds it in herself to smile as she fingers the bracelet. It's the sort of detritus she sees moving along the bottoms of rivers and the slimy mud of lakes. Here she sees its purpose is decorative, a thing that exists merely for momentary pleasure.

Clyde reaches out and grazes her shoulder with his hand. "Exit's this way!" he shouts.

She follows again, this time keeping her head down.

"I love this song!" says a girl without any hair.

"I love you, too!" says her companion.

"What?" the bald girl replies.

"What?"

Another couple is locked in a heated exchange, their fury as noxious as sulfur. "No, it's gross," a man in a silk shirt yells at a man without any shirt at all.

"It's literally cartoon characters with lollipop heads and bowling ball eyes. They're not real."

"You're just mad I'm right!"

A boy with different-colored eyes shouts among the throng, "My shoe strap broke! Has anyone seen my shoe?"

Behind a black curtain, Jenny can see three humans writhing against one another. A hand bathed in red light strokes a soft, rounded hip cupped in shadow. Someone laughs sweetly and another gasps.

Clyde looks at her and says, "If you see Faun," and the rest of his words are immediately swallowed up. Clyde can't outyell a woman strumming an enormous lute plugged into the wall, so he leans toward her. "Let's go outside and see if she's smoking!"

The difference between the inside of the factory and the stillness of the cool night outside shocks Jenny. How strange it is to remember absence of sound is also loud.

Several party guests stand beside the wall, producing smoke like chimneys. Tobacco and marijuana perfume the air and dissipate with the wind blowing off the wharf.

It's only as she gets closer that Jenny sees one of the people there is Faun. She smokes the stub of a cigar, puffing with more pleasure than Jenny has yet seen her take in anything else. "She's an honest girl, more than anything," Faun is saying. "I think she's got a different set of brains than yours."

"'Yours' like 'mine'? Or 'yours' like 'humans'?" The man's voice sends a shock through Jenny, a terrible jellyfish sting that aches like a brand, but all over.

"Humans." Faun shows him a flat smile with a brown tooth. "People like us don't survive unless we're different than you lot."

"Can you tell me more about that?" he asks her.

"No. I wouldn't have spoken to someone like you at all if you hadn't begged." Faun blows a pair of smoke rings.

"I didn't really beg."

"You did. I hate humans, as a rule."

"I see."

Jenny hangs back by the doorway, barely concealing herself. If Zeke could hear heartbeats as she does, he would look up and know her, but he doesn't. Clyde stands with Jenny, letting the shadows obscure them.

"You're lucky I break my own rules all the time," Faun continues. "And my friend, Clyde? He read that stuff you used to write about. The words on people like us. He said you almost got it right."

Zeke conceals a small, proud grin. Jenny wants, in that moment, to tackle him and sob into his chest. She also wants to bite into his mouth, slick red oozing down their chins. Kiss him. Take his member in her hand. Make him weep at her feet, apologizing.

The orange-haired girl with them is the same one who let Jenny sleep in her room. She no longer has a cigarette but puffs on a small piece of metal that lights up and produces a cloud that smells like molasses. "At long last, Zeke, you found your monsters."

He turns to her and shakes his head, desperately. "Why are you so casual about this?"

"I don't know. Big brother calls me, says he thinks he found a fish woman but he's not sure." The girl, Jenny realizes, would have the same nose as Zeke's if hers, too, had been broken at one point and healed a little crookedly. "Tía Milagros believes in Amazonian monsters. If it's good enough for both of you, it's good enough for me, I guess."

Zeke sighs. "And you're also high."

Lupe giggles. "That, too. Everything's a little easier when it's foggy. Loosen up and take some yourself, robot boy."

He knocks his shoulder against hers, an affectionate bump. With an actor's inflection, he says, "Negative! This body is fully human! I am most certainly made of meat."

Lupe looks revolted. "I don't want to hear about your meat."

Zeke laughs.

"There's no honor in being fully human." Faun taps the ash of the cigar onto the ground. She pauses to smooth her skirt with her free hand, making sure her goat legs are concealed. Then she looks over and sees Jenny and Clyde. "You should ply Jenny with questions instead of me. Hallo there, sweets!" Faun nods to her.

Zeke turns toward her, eyes wide, mouth parted. He's as beautiful in the streetlamps of the evening as he was naked on the beach earlier. She can see his throat bob as he looks at her.

Jenny straightens and lifts her chin high. "What do you want to ask me?" She strides over and Clyde tries to take her arm.

"Really?" Clyde says through clenched teeth. "What happened to leaving?"

Zeke clears his throat. "Does it differentiate between salt or still water? What about naturally occurring bodies versus sewers?" He speaks in a rush.

Jenny stares.

"The, um. The thing we went through? The waterways?" Zeke flushes, his lovely blood pushing against his lovely skin.

Jenny feels herself warm, too.

Lupe giggles again as Faun rolls her eyes.

Clyde appears crestfallen. "You took him before you took us?" It's somehow worse than the disapproval over the body in the fridge.

Jenny feels sick because she has disappointed these friends of hers. Shame courses through her and she clenches her jaw. "I will take you and Faun now." She says this as airily as she can, but it comes out as a croak.

"Finally!" Faun drops the cigar and flattens it with her obscured hoof.

Zeke's eyebrows meet. "Take them where?'

Jenny sticks her chin out, proud. "Where I took you."

He blinks rapidly and reaches out his hands, as if to take hers. "Can we talk when you get back?"

Jenny promised herself she would leave and doesn't want to give him more of herself than she already has. "I don't think so."

Zeke is clearly brought up short. "Oh."

"You'll become angry again," she murmurs. "I'll tell you everything I've done and all my hungers and you'll make me leave."

"I needed a moment. Or two. Or an hour." His mouth becomes a line and he looks away. "It's still sinking in. This is all new to me."

It's a relief that Jenny doesn't have to meet his eyes. "It's better I don't come back."

Zeke's jaw works, but he doesn't open his mouth.

"Damn." Lupe looks thoughtful. "And he came here to warn you and everything."

"Warn me?"

"A woman says she was attacked, by, well . . ." Zeke looks at her with meaning. There's a softness to those eyes of his. "Another woman who bit her cheek. The police sent out a warning, which was picked up by the campus police. I got an email about it. You're, um. A suspect at large."

Jenny is overwhelmed with the fact he still hasn't run away. Why did he want to find her?

Then she becomes distracted by the smell of rain. The clouds above are readying themselves to burst. It's the most beautiful scent, Jenny finds, though she's sensed it hundreds of thousands of times before.

"I know you can protect yourself." Zeke looks apologetic. "But the police are the police, you know?"

Clyde looks toward Faun. "Do you think they've gone to the house and found the body?"

"The what?" Lupe squints at them. In that moment, she looks more like Zeke than ever before. "Did you say 'the body'?"

Faun gives an indignant grunt. "Clyde, if you had been there, you would have wanted to shove him in the fridge yourself."

But Jenny feels embarrassed even though Faun does not. "I needed to eat."

The sirens begin. First, they sound small and distant. As they grow near, Jenny sees a daisy chain of red and blue lights stretching across the road. More vehicles than before.

Clouds roll in over the bay.

"How do we do this?" Clyde asks quickly. "Run into the water?"

The rain begins suddenly with a sweeping hush. It feels like a thousand small kisses where it touches Jenny's skin. She spreads her arms. "Today, the water comes to us."

Raindrops glow from the inside out, brighter than her bracelet could ever be. They are the tiniest jewels. Where they touch—Jenny, Faun, Clyde, and, yes, Zeke—the light slides and clings to their skin. Each of them except for Lupe is absorbed, and as everyone falls into the waterways piece by piece, Zeke says, "I should hold my breath, right?"

Jenny doesn't answer. Her mind is with the raindrops, which become as clear as glass once they hit the pavement.

She watches Lupe grow damp but, by Jenny's own will, untouched by the light. Lupe squawks as she watches pieces of her brother and his new companions dissolve into the air. Her scream is one of horror and delight, amazement and terror, and it's the last thing Jenny hears before she is swept away.

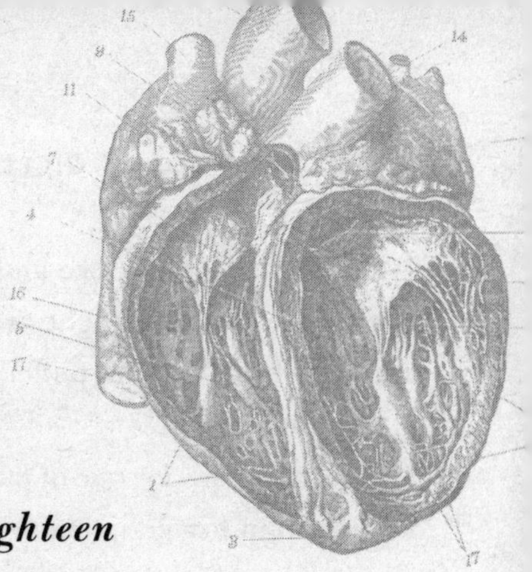

Chapter Eighteen

HEART

In the waterways, it feels like they are caught in a net of neon algae. Jenny's gills open more fully. She looks through the twists of blue-green light and searches first for Zeke because the water might be getting into those human lungs of his. Oh, why only have one set of breathing apparatuses? Wouldn't it be better if he had gills, too?

She sees Faun first, floating in the water, loops of her white hair rising and circling her brown face. Bubbles leap from between her lips and her skirt balloons up, revealing her furry legs. She begins to windmill her arms, looking for a surface to breach.

Beyond her is Clyde. As uncomfortable as Faun looks, he looks at peace. A soul in his element, a duck returned to water. He is home in a way that Jenny recognizes. His eyes are ink dark and his smile—gods, she's seen him smile before with humans, but now? It's transcendent.

He is home.

Good, she thinks. One must learn to exist beyond humans.

Then she sees Zeke and her heart sputters and stops. His eyes are squeezed tight as he presses his glasses against his nose. His cheeks are puffed out. He kicks now, spins, and fails to right himself.

Jenny grabs for one of the fluttering streams of light. It slides away from her grasp, an eel. No—less substantial than even an eel. She reaches for another tendril of light and it arcs right over her head.

Her clothes weigh too much, she thinks. She sheds the jacket and her shoes. She reaches again.

Faun is alarmed, and Zeke is running out of breath.

She finds his hand and laces her fingers with his. His grip is firm, reliable, and more intimate than she can articulate. She is his anchor, though he continues to thrash. Bubbles pour out of his mouth and rise up across his nose, his forehead, his hair. Briefly, it looks as if his head is touched with snowflakes.

Another blue strand of light ripples past them and Jenny seizes it. The water boils around her hand. It feels like she's touched a hot poker. She opens her mouth to yowl, but nothing comes out.

Jenny keeps her hand locked with Zeke's and hooks her leg around Faun's hoofed foot. She looks for Clyde and there he is, swimming past them and away. He kicks toward a completely different ribbon of light.

Clyde glances back at her with his sweet, dark eyes and they glitter with a larger, more sprawling story of himself than she can know. He also spares a glance to Faun, whose eyes are wide and staring. He shakes his head at her, slowly.

Then Clyde seizes his own bolt of blue light. He slides through it, a door into elsewhere.

And Jenny has to go through her own jagged entryway before it descends into the darkness like a water snake.

Jenny, Zeke, and Faun emerge into muggy, humid air. They don't even have to claw for the surface; they're already there. Jenny smells swamp before she sees it. She shakes her head to dislodge water from her ears. The last of her pink skin flakes away.

Vines like looping, tangled intestines are knotted along the surface of the cool green water. Misshapen yellow flowers bristle like hedgehog quills along alien plants that stand up straight and grow as white as tubers. The sky is gray and flat, without any edges or definition to the clouds, unyielding as stone.

The sun looks small and wrong.

Faun sits in algae. Her wet curls hang limp to her shoulders. She coughs and green slime falls out from between her lips. With a shaky hand, she wipes her mouth. "He really did it. He said he was going to find his skin. I thought he was going to take me with him after all! Idiot. What does he think will happen when he finds her?"

"Are you all right?" Jenny asks.

"No." Faun snarls, wounded in her heart. "Leave me alone. Clyde did. Why don't you?"

Jenny feels the sting of that rejection, Faun's bitterness hot and new, and withdraws to look for Zeke.

He's right beside her, which is where he ought to be. He's also face down, like a floating corpse.

She shoots forward and pulls him up only to find his face and glasses bright green. His mouth slackens immediately, but instead of saying something, it just remains open.

Jenny pulls him into a sitting position. She scrubs his glasses to see if his eyes are moving. They are not. His lids are mostly shut, except for a slice of eyeball, the iris dark as the sea, the pupil a black half-moon. He isn't breathing. They were in the waterways too long.

She panics and shakes him. "I decided not to eat you," she babbles. "You're not allowed to die. Please, please don't die." Her voice cracks at the end.

Faun trudges over, announcing her presence with a great sigh and the splash of water that clings to her furry haunches. Her skirt is gone. "Hold on." She leans over Zeke, and Jenny is filled with the fear that Faun will help in the way she did with the other man, but no. This time, they are working together to preserve a man's life, not take it.

Faun tilts Zeke's scum-slopped head to the side and slaps his back several times.

She and Jenny wait. Silence.

Jenny hits his back, too, hammering it like a door.

Zeke's body shudders from the inside out and he coughs up algae. "What?" he croaks. He focuses on Jenny and bursts out laughing, revealing his teeth have been stained green. "You look so worried!"

Jenny takes his shoulders in her hands and presses her forehead to his. Her breath rattles through her, all terror that hasn't yet been cleared away by relief.

"Don't want to eat me anymore, right?" His breath against her mouth. "Is that what you said?"

Jenny laughs but it comes out a sob. "I do, but I don't."

He inhales and holds her back. "I'm sorry about earlier. I didn't know how to react. That's why I wanted to find you." He fights to reclaim his breath, swallowing air. "You're really not like any kind of human I'm used to. This is hard."

He apologized! Jenny hunches her shoulders inward, as if pinching her ears with them will lessen the ache inside her. "It would be easier between us if we were just predator and prey."

Zeke's eyes crinkle. "But it would be less fun. And I wouldn't get to know you."

Jenny feels her face heat.

"Are we in Louisiana?" Faun asks loudly. "The Amazon? The sun looks white. Is this fog?"

Jenny looks past Zeke's face and notices, yes, the sun even sits wrong in the sky. She's only ever known Earth, and to her knowledge, the waterways have only ever looped her in and around it. There's a subtle uncanniness to the sky, a closeness to it that would make more sense on a different world. "That's not the sun," she says finally.

"How can you tell?" Zeke's mouth twists.

Faun sniffs. "You're young. We're older than you. You'll have to trust we know, sweets."

He opens his mouth, glances at her hairy goat legs and backward knees, and closes it again. "Oh. Right," he says.

She preens. "I like a man who knows when to be quiet."

Zeke frowns at her and focuses on cleaning his glasses.

The silt beneath the water moves. Jenny has the sense that they are standing on a giant fish burrowed beneath the mud. It rolls over. The three of them fall against one another to find surer footing.

"What is it to not kill a man. What is a man but a thing already dying." A great, dark velvet voice erupts all around them. Zeke claps his hands over his ears and Faun looks about, wild. "They, the daughters, each to each, into their mouths, the bitter cruelty. Flavors the tongue. Love tinged by it."

Jenny is full of fear. "Hello?" she asks the trees. They sway in a wind. No—the trees tremble, like hairs on the back of a neck. Bristling. There is no wind, but now that she listens, the swamp has its own set of lungs. Gills. It breathes, contracting and expanding. The heat has a smell to it, she realizes, like sour breath, maybe like the inside of your mouth after you wake from sleep.

"Hello here? No. Hello there." The swamp echoes with that raw, dark voice, flowing like the way people speak in dreams. Jenny's dreams, anyway. "Hell. Oh. Low down there. Low down you are, here."

Zeke, who has acclimated himself to the sound, looks up toward that ball of sun. "Are you up there or below us?"

"All up. All down." The sun blinks, a great eye that cloaks the world in darkness and then brightens it again. The fog breaks.

There are other, smaller suns. Wait! They're eyes. A spattering of wet, luminous eyes. "All everywhere at the same time. Daughter, I am here."

Jenny stumbles. She stares at the cascade of eyes, down at the green waters, the tangle of vines like entrails. The smell is not just the dense air. No, it's familiar. It's the smell of her old life, discarded long ago. "Mother?" she rasps.

"Little thing. My own." Out of the fog comes a mouth, a green wound that opens into a great cave of teeth. "You said, told me, said, 'Mother, something happened today or it didn't happen,' and that you were hungry and wanted to eat a man. Then you stopped."

Jenny is elated. "Yes. I had to stop! I didn't want to kill him." Her eyes slide to Zeke's, which are round.

"Your mom?" he mouths, pointing to the water below.

Jenny nods happily.

The swamp of her mother rumbles. "You stopped talking, and I waited for more and you said nothing. I slept and dreamed again. Was there not more to say, to tell, to give? I heard you. Always hear you."

"Mother, where have you been?" Jenny whispers.

"Here," says her mother. "The passages, the places in between that no one can access but you. I am a bubble of air floating along the waterways. Daughter, I've been here, keeping my own counsel."

Jenny's chest seems to collapse in on itself. When she places her hand over her heart, what a surprise to find it's still whole. "Did I know that once and forget? Did you tell me?"

"I get confused between then and now," Mother says. "I know I'm telling you now. Perhaps I forgot then because I thought now had already gone. Time is all at once, and I don't have the right mind to see it the way you do, the way humans do."

"I'm not human."

"You are like them, more than I, a thing who feeds on their refuse, on them. You are more like a human than I am. You even have a human name—Jinny, right?"

She clears her throat. "Jenny."

"Yes. Rusalka. Meg. Daughter. One of many, one and only. Of course, you hesitate to eat one of them."

When Jenny glances at Zeke again, his mouth has a small, disbelieving smile on it. "You told your mom about me?"

A grin threatens to break over Jenny's face now. She wants to laugh. She folds her lips over her teeth to suppress it. The warmth between them grows sweeter than the muggy swamp.

Faun sloshes, kicking the water. "You really control the nexus?" she yells at the swamp. "Keeping it all to yourself? I've been looking for you, you old bitch!"

The swamp doesn't move, but it stands at attention, seems to face Faun. The many eyes of Mother look to the diminutive form of the goat woman. Her head, or rather the giant thing that holds her many eyes and the cut of her mouth, tilts. "I guide. I see. I listen. When I want to, I talk. I crawled out from between the stars to your world and am beholden to no one on it."

There's a flash of fear across Faun's face, but she sets her shoulders back, thrusts her chin out, and says, "You could do much more. The man I was with? We almost gave up on finding a way into the damn water tunnels you have. He just wanted his skin back, and I just wanted to help him."

"I like my tunnels, my glorious veins, the byways of my heart that move from one body of water to the next. I am happy where I am and doing what I do and speaking when I wish," says Mother to Faun. "Are you not happy?"

"Of course not!" There's a sheen of wetness on Faun's eyes and a crack in her voice. "Do you think I love wandering the same blue-green-brown globe and seeing the same shit, year after year, one century to another?"

Jenny surprises herself by reaching out a comforting hand, but she is shrugged away. Faun is caught up in her misery.

"People die and leave me every time. It's what they've always done on this dirt ball. So no, you great monster." She sneers. "I am not happy."

Mother seems to exhale. "Why move in just one world? There are many thousands, millions more, sliding in and out of existence."

Faun's silver eyebrows climb her forehead. "There are what?"

"Worlds?" Zeke looks lit up from the inside out.

"Star strewn, wet, desert, bright, dead. All manner of worlds." Mother is helpful but she is also taunting. "Goat woman, do you wish to see them, new and glittering?"

Faun hesitates. Then she lets out a laugh. "Fine. Why not?"

All at once, Jenny sees what will happen before it does. A memory surfaces from the depths of her mind, one where a human man stumbled across Mother when she lived on Earth. The man spit on Mother and then relieved himself in her waters. Jenny and her sisters offered to be kind, to eat him, but Mother was quicker.

She is quick now. The vine creeps up Faun's furry flank, a thin green worm that wraps itself around her waist. It squeezes tight. Faun looks down too late, reaches to break the vine from her middle, but oh, another extends from the water and binds her arm.

She struggles.

"Is your mother doing that?" Zeke asks softly.

Jenny grabs his hand, afraid he'll be taken, too. "Mother, I don't think Faun knows what she's asked." She feels nauseous. Stopping Mother would be like stopping the tide.

Mother's laugh is terrible. "It's easier, sweeter, better to travel without a body."

Faun mule-kicks. "You can't kill me!"

"I'm not. You will receive a new body in time," says Mother. "Perhaps in some millions of years."

And Faun, to Jenny's shock, goes slack. "I never have to see humans again?"

"Not those humans, never, though one day, you may polyp your own."

Faun laughs, unhinged and savage. "Good! Free at last!" There is a distant look in her eyes, a note of despair though she smiles one of her puckish, goaty smiles. "Could be fun!" A vine sinks directly into Faun's arm. Instead of blood, a gold ichor flows down her skin. She grunts.

"Only for a moment will it hurt. Or a year. I forget," says Mother.

Another vine sinks into Faun's body. Her eyes roll back so that only the whites are showing. "Ah! The stars!" She giggles and it turns into laughter. "They're spreading! It's like being drunk again but I'm— I've become—!" Her skin begins to burn away. Its grilled-meat smell fills the swamp.

Jenny reaches to cover Zeke's eyes. He stops her green hand before it can touch his face. He glances at her, just once, and shakes his head. "Let me see. I need to."

It's the same mettle she saw in Zeke the night he looked on her and said her name.

Great stripes of living, roiling muscle are revealed beneath Faun's charred skin. She gasps in a silent scream as the vines cut into bone. Steam rises up and curls her hair further. She is laughing as her body is stripped from itself, now just a head in twisting vines that seep between her human ribs and goat-bone legs. Then the vines pull her down into the water with a great, steaming splash, the soup of Mother churning with a new morsel. Faun scream-laughs with her lidless eyes, burbles as she's submerged. She sounds like a woman galloping away on a horse, shrieking with laughter as her voice becomes small.

When the bubbles stop, Zeke looks toward Jenny with a face drained of blood. He puts his hands on his knees and dry heaves. She presses a hand to his shoulder as he does and she feels his body shake. Finally, he clasps that hand and says, "We should go."

"Mother," Jenny says to the swamp. "I'm so pleased to see you again, but we"—she clears her throat—"there was a friend we had who was with us. Clyde? He should know that Faun has moved on. Can you take us to him?"

"Faun?" says Mother.

Jenny looks down at the waters. "The woman you took?"

"Yes, of course, Jinny."

"Jenny," Jenny corrects her, gently but firmly. Mother is powerful but not always discerning.

But Mother is also warm and full of cheer. "You must come visit, come see, come talk to me soon." The water beneath them shines an iridescent blue. Before they're pulled down, Jenny hears Zeke take a deep breath as he holds her hand. He is catching on to her world as she has had to understand his. She fills with pride.

Chapter Nineteen

THROAT

In the neon-blue water, Zeke doesn't flail. He just holds on to her. She swims through the undefined space in the direction that feels the most right, the safest, the quickest way from Mother. Zeke kicks his ridiculous human legs. Yet she feels an affection for that wobbly, strange body of his, its mortal peculiarity. She is shocked to realize she admires him for it.

He said he would likely be alive for a few more decades. She takes that dreadful fact, folds it away, into a cavern in her brain.

The blue light recedes as they arrive in bleak water. There's a white lamp blazing down at them through the surface, and Jenny kicks her way toward it.

It turns out to be the moon high above them.

When she breaches with Zeke, he gasps, says, "God," and continues to hold her hand. It feels sweet, a blessing.

"Zeke," she begins as she floats on the ink-dark waves.

He breathes out a jagged breath as he splashes. "The shore," he manages with water sluicing into and out of his mouth. "Shore first."

Jenny holds him close as she kicks to the sand. He joins her in peculiar, clumsy strokes. She's grateful that his lovemaking is much better than his swimming.

Once on the sand, she finds the night air humid.

Zeke's face is picked out by the moon, then sliced with acidic orange light from a nearby parking lot. He takes the bottom of his shirt and wrings it out. She can see his smile in the darkness. "That really was your mother?"

"It was."

"Huh. You going to be like her one day?"

She chews her lip. "I don't know. I think Faun will be."

Zeke becomes solemn. "I'm sorry about your friend. She seemed . . ." He hesitates. "Nice?"

"Faun? She wasn't." Jenny sighs. "I'll miss her." It hurts, but she takes the memory of Faun, folds it tenderly, and puts it away as best as she can. The absence is already dreadful.

Jenny clears her throat. At times like these, she has learned from observing humans that one must fall back on the custom of "manners," a practice that largely centers on speaking on matters in such a way that obscures embarrassment. "My mother is very traditional."

Zeke falters. "Whose tradition?"

"Her own. Or her star-crawling brethren."

"Oh. Like aliens?"

"Their lives are measured in eons. Mother has consumed Faun, yes, but the essence of her will likely live into the next epoch. Her consciousness, like Mother's, can now splinter across worlds."

Zeke laughs, sounding slightly panicked. "My condolences. Or my congratulations. Or both, I guess." He looks toward the black water.

Silence sits between them as they stand on the shore. He grazes her fingers with his as a breeze picks up and turns the night cooler.

Zeke leans into it. "Do you think this is the Atlantic?"

"Sometimes I know, sometimes I don't," Jenny admits. "It's all water in the end, whatever name it's given."

"The names change over time?"

"Always." Jenny takes a shaky breath. "Are you going to leave me?"

"What?" He stares at her. "I tried that. I really did. But I needed to find you again. I went to Lupe just to talk, but there you were. I shouldn't be surprised, because Boston really is small." Zeke stares out at the dark waves. "I have a lot of questions and too much curiosity. I don't think I'll like most of the answers you give me, such as you, well, eating people."

She deflates. "Yes. I do that."

"That's not going to change, is it?" His mouth still has something like a smile on it, but emptier.

Jenny looks at his face. Even now, his full cheeks, glistening with salt water, make her hungry. "No. It won't change at all."

He exhales and wipes his forehead with the back of his hand. "I thought so. Are you cold?"

She shakes her head. "You must be."

"Not yet. I'd like a towel, I guess. Everything's wet." He tries to wring out his shirt again but there's not enough water. Without shifting his tone, he says, "What do people say when they find out you're going to eat them?"

"They scream when they die, whether I'm the one doing it or not."

"You don't always kill them?"

"Sometimes I just pick over what's left. Like a carrion crow, I feast on offal. Bodies on battlefields near lakes. The drowned." She swallows. "Children who lost their way and fell. I leave what I can't eat, like the bones."

A silence passes between them. "You really are good at being honest."

"Humans are just more practiced at lying than I am."

"We are. The center where I work at the university, they bring in a lot of people and a lot of them are liars. They all have power in government or want to have it. Some use that power better than others."

Jenny feels the threads of understanding that connect them. "My mother was the first example I had of power."

Zeke nods in agreement. "A lot of power."

"Both benign and dreadful."

She can see the admiration in his eyes and the fear that fills them, too. "I want to know you better," he says.

"Yes." Jenny lets out a breath she didn't realize she was holding. "I do, too."

A scream splits the air. Jenny snaps her head toward it. Under the parking lot lights is a pair of humans, standing close, illuminated as if on a stage.

One of them is Clyde. His face seems drained, gray. He's shed his patchy clothes except for his trousers. Water droplets cling to his tight, dark curls.

There's a woman with him.

Like Faun, she's small, but her long hair is a washed-out yellow. Her skin is an over-scrubbed pink. Beneath her neck, she dresses all in dappled brown. She yells at Clyde, shaking her gloved fists.

"What? Who are they?" Zeke takes off his glasses, cleans the lenses with his thumbs, and puts them back on. "Is that that guy? Clyde, right? The one Faun said read my blog?"

Jenny's nostrils flare. The breeze brings his scent to her. "He smells the same," she says.

Zeke glances at her. "You can smell people? Wait, never mind. Do you know the woman he's with?"

They watch her push him. He flinches, as if the fact she's pushed him is worse than any physical pain she could inflict.

"I've never seen her before." Jenny walks toward them.

Zeke follows. "Is she in a wetsuit?"

Understanding dawns on her. The tight oiliness of it clinging to her body, the way her teeth flash as she speaks, and her wide, fearful eyes. "No. It's a sealskin."

"Made from seals?" Zeke asks.

"Just one. I think she took it from him long ago." She points toward Clyde. Then she breaks into a run across the sand, kicking it up like dust as she goes.

She hears Zeke murmur, "Fuck," and he pants as he tries to catch up with her.

Jenny arrives at the edge of the lamplight. It's so similar to the hue of the home she made at the train station, but distant. Strange. Clyde is the first to look her way. He does so slowly and without a smile. "Hello again, Jenny."

The young woman with him snaps her gaze to Jenny. "Who's this, then?" She speaks with an Irish lilt. "You come for me but you have a woman, too? Right bastard!" She holds her hand up to strike him. It's sheathed in sealskin.

Clyde lowers his eyes, dark brown lashes bronze in the light. "Elspeth, please," he begins.

"You gave me your skin fair and square!" She's bawling. "You can't just find me all these years later and demand it back!"

"You asked to borrow it for an afternoon," he says softly. "I remember. I waited. I thought you had gotten lost."

"You're telling me I would get lost in the waters where I grew up?" Elspeth's face grows red in indignation. "I walked with my mother there when I was a wee thing. I fished in it with my father. How dare you, Clyde? How dare you!"

"You stole my skin." His eyes have a glassy quality. Tears sit there but don't fall.

Elspeth lapses into silence. She seems furious, but Jenny, having walked among humans these last few weeks, thinks she can also see shame.

"You took it from me." Clyde stops abruptly, breathes deep, and tries again. "You betrayed me all those years ago."

"Accusing me of stealing! Lord." She throws her yellow hair over one of her shoulders. "How dare you."

"But you did."

"I'm your wife! You share things with your wife."

"You're human," Jenny interrupts. "And you took his skin."

Elspeth turns the force of her hatred on Jenny. "What business is this of yours, whore?"

"No, my name's Jenny." She straightens her back. "You shouldn't steal from people, especially him, because he's helped me a lot. And separating someone old like us from the water? It's cruel."

Clyde shuts his eyes tight. "It's hurt, Elspeth. So many years like this. It's been awful. This is hell. It was made so much worse when I realized you did it on purpose."

"Of course I did!" Elspeth cries. "What woman wouldn't take immortality for her own? I've outlived every neighbor I've hated and outlasted all my enemies. Would you deny me a world with new medicines and buildings that touch the sky? Who wouldn't trick a god out of their power?"

Zeke comes up behind Jenny. He seems to have heard the whole thing because he says, once he's caught his breath, "I wouldn't."

"Who in hell are you?" Elspeth rears up in all her height, which is not much. The sealskin draws tight over her diminutive chest and narrow shoulders. On her feet are flippers.

"Zeke," he says, a little nervous. "I'm a graduate student at Harvard."

"A Yankee?" Elspeth laughs, showing her small white teeth. "I know for a fact that you don't much recognize a marriage between me and this man. It ain't his sealskin you got a problem with but his human one!" She points at Clyde.

Zeke looks baffled. "What? Is this, like, about interracial marriage or something?"

"Inter-what?" Elspeth's peevish now. "I'm saying I had a right to take this man's skin."

"Because you're human?" Zeke sours.

"And he isn't!" Elspeth looks satisfied.

Clyde presses a hand to his chest. "I loved you," he says. "I still love you. I must. It wouldn't hurt so terribly if I didn't." Tears roll down his face.

Jenny smells the salt, and something inside her burns with anger. She growls. "Give him back his skin."

"You going to force it off me?" Elspeth radiates an anger Faun could never touch.

"Yes." Jenny leans close and shows her teeth. The sharp ones poke out of her gums, growing over the blunt human incisors and molars. She has a shark's mouth, the beginnings of a double row of teeth.

Elspeth's eyes widen. "Jenny Greenteeth." It's reverent. "Oh, I've been hearing about you since I was a child. My grandmother said you'd snatch me if I wandered off too far on my own. If you're as bad as they say, what care you whose skin is whose? Why bother yourself with petty grievances?"

"I told you," Jenny says. "I like Clyde."

"I'm not threatening his life," Elspeth says. "He'll keep living. I just will, too."

Jenny looks to Clyde, waiting for him to take the skin himself. He doesn't move. He is immobilized by love, she thinks. Years have passed and his adoration of her has not yet dimmed. He is trying to move but he needs help.

"It's his nature you're taking from him," Jenny says. "Give it back."

"Make me, Jenny Greenteeth." Elspeth squares her shoulders and raises her fists. She's corded with muscle. "If you refuse to be the witchy woman of the deep, I'm more than happy to take up the mantle."

Jenny jumps on her.

Elspeth twists away. She trips her up, sending Jenny flat to the cement.

Quickly, Jenny flips onto her back and kicks upward. She hits Elspeth's stomach and hears the breath leave her in a dreadful *whoosh*. When she stumbles, Jenny takes the opportunity to kick her feet out from under her.

Elspeth is struggling for breath as Jenny tackles her.

But using the waterways, visiting Mother, has made Jenny weak. When Elspeth regains her breath, she also gains enough strength to get on top of Jenny. She wraps her hands around her throat.

Jenny's gills open as she struggles to breathe with her lungs. But Elspeth has covered those up, too. She can't breathe at all. Jenny's insides are on fire.

"Elspeth!" Clyde calls. "For goodness' sake! Stop it!"

It's so much easier to hunt humans underwater, Jenny thinks as her vision darkens. She has spent years telling herself how much stronger she is than every single human, but the dreadful truth is she's a bottom-feeder.

Zeke pulls Elspeth into a chokehold. She shrieks, turns, and tries to bite him, but oh, her teeth aren't sharp. Yet when she bites Zeke on his hands, he jerks but doesn't let go.

Jenny smells his blood. Just a drop.

She feels hunger tinged with horror. He isn't allowed to die, and yet if he does, there's nothing she can do to change it.

In a rage, Jenny pushes Elspeth off her. She strikes her face once, twice, and then begins to bite. There's far more blood in the air now. The meat in Jenny's mouth is stringy but also very good.

Elspeth breaks Zeke's hold with desperate, clawing fingers lubricated with her own blood.

Jenny gets up, trying to pull breath down through her bruised throat, and takes Zeke into her arms. He holds her but looks past her. When she follows his stony gaze, she sees Clyde. He's taken advantage of the fray and has ripped the rest of the sealskin from Elspeth's body. He holds it like an oil slick stretched between his hands. His face twists in agony and then grows placid.

Elspeth hisses, red weeping from her gashes. "Don't you dare take it."

Clyde looks up at her. "I still love you. Just not enough." And the skin begins to melt into a liquid. It is no longer a faulty cloak but a true skin with its owner. It crawls along his hands, up his arms, along his chest, his neck, down over his thighs, legs, and feet. "I need to be away from humans for a while." His voice has a deep, new resonance to it as he becomes his own creature.

Elspeth's body tenses to spring forward and Jenny grabs her shoulders. She holds her in place as Elspeth gives a soft cry, weak and kittenish. Her skin slackens, growing as soft as an old woman's. Jenny watches age spots bloom like flowers. Great blue veins thicken and push closer to the surface.

Where Faun had gasped and writhed in pain as her body was devoured, Elspeth becomes sedate. She shrinks inward, seeming to collapse into herself. She becomes smaller, thinner.

Clyde, however, is resplendent. He stands tall as the sealskin encases his body. His eyes turn to inky pools. He looks from the parking lot to the beach. Then he is on all fours, forearms bending into flippers. His back legs fuse, and the shadow of his body becomes a humped outline against the lightening sky.

A seal jumps into the water. He swims into the sea quickly. He's no longer human enough to look back.

Elspeth lets out a long, ragged breath that curdles into a death rattle. Her hair is still yellow when she goes light in Jenny's grasp. When Jenny lets go, a tiny old woman falls to the asphalt, defenseless, lovely, and very dead.

"God." Zeke is covered in sweat. "What in the world?"

"Clyde took his skin back."

He stares at the wrinkled, naked body of the little woman. "She's like a baby bird. Before they get the feathers, you know? When they fall out of their nests."

Jenny's stomach tightens. "Yes." She swallows as she stares at Zeke. "She looks like meat."

Zeke blinks rapidly. "You're hungry, right?"

Jenny feels a stab of guilt. "Very hungry."

He holds the hand that Elspeth bit. "I understand."

"I know you don't want to see—"

"No," he says. "I meant it. I understand."

Jenny is all gratitude. "You can turn away."

He doesn't. His shoulders are handsomely angled, not slumped but firm and stubborn. She loves that he's so near even as she knows how he strains to look.

Jenny bends down, takes hold of what was once Elspeth's arm, and begins to tear it with both sets of her teeth, old and new. She eats. The man she adores watches.

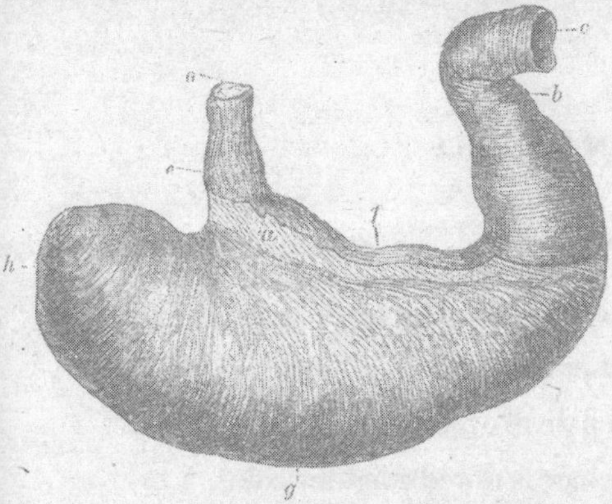

Chapter Twenty

HUNGER

In the middle of her meal, Jenny hears Zeke leave. The sand blunts his footsteps, but she hears the silence where his breathing was. She feels tears prick at her eyes again as she continues eating. Blood sticks to her lips and gristle hugs her chin. Clyde, Faun, and now Zeke—she's alone again.

She tries not to think about this long, sad life. Years stretch behind her and perhaps even more stretch out in front of her. The world continues and so does she. Maybe one day it will all end, the sun will burn out and the Earth will go cold, and even then she'll go on.

There's nothing left but stained bones and inedible vitals when the sun rises. Her stomach hurts with its own weight. Jenny gathers the remains as tears run from her eyes and she walks toward the sea. She hugs them to her chest before releasing them to the waves. They fall into the tide, eddy briefly, and disappear.

She pauses, takes off her clothes, and peels the green from her skin. It hurts—it always hurts—but it feels better than Zeke's absence. It's easier if people think a naked woman is swimming in the water rather than a naked monster. Her teeth are still sharp but she doesn't remove them. Let them stay.

Her skin is Elspeth's now, a pale phantom that burned away in the morning light like fog. Her hair is tinted a lighter color.

The wind picks up. Then she smells him.

Excitedly, she glances down the sand. Zeke sits on the beach watching the sunrise. He has a bundle with him.

Her heart leaps. Jenny's so happy, she runs toward him. When she remembers the offal spread across her face, she pauses to dip her hands in salt water and hurriedly scrub herself.

She reaches him.

"I found clothes for us." He nods toward the pack—a shopping bag wrapped around cloth. "If you want them," he adds.

"I do!" she says immediately, and pulls the bag apart. She pauses to look at him. "Thank you."

Zeke doesn't move as he stares out toward the distance. "My credit card was waterlogged, but it worked. Can't say the same for my phone, but it's like my apartment. The damage can be fixed. I got some new stuff from a store nearby, too. Turns out we're in Maine. Maybe two or so hours from Boston. Small world, you know?"

Jenny doesn't know but she smiles and pulls on a dress that's electric blue, with smiling green fish printed on the front. Her nipples press against the smooth, strange cloth and she laughs. "It's like the waterways!"

Zeke shivers. "Yeah. I thought so, too. It felt like you." His smile is so sweet.

Carefully, nervously, she sits down next to him.

"You're always hungry for humans, right?" He swallows.

"Usually."

He nods slowly. Then realization breaks over his face. "You literally are what you eat! That's why you look more like the woman with the sealskin. That's why the muffin made you break out!"

Jenny's toes delve into the cool sand. "Human flesh is best for me. If I eat a piece of garlic, I grow white and peel. If I eat a pig, I get white hairs all over my body."

He chuckles. "You'd look cute like that."

She lights up.

"With your hair and skin different—yeah. I don't think the cops will spend a lot of time looking for you anyway, but now they'll look through you."

"Yes. Now I don't have to murder any officers." Jenny knows that when you murder police, they send more. She takes his hand and is relieved he lets her.

"Not today, I guess." Zeke has a small frown. "Have you always wanted to eat me?"

She hides her eyes. When she removes her hand, he's still there, but now he's looking at her. Waiting. Patient. "Yes. I want to do that now. I also don't want to."

"Yeah?" He pulls his mouth into a twisted half smile. "Think I taste bad?"

She has to exercise her jaw before she can push the words out of her throat. "Because I like you a lot. And I want to stay with you."

The tide hisses and fills the quiet.

As soft as the water on the sand, he says, "Yeah. I like you, too."

A smile spreads across her face.

His eyebrows rise. "Your teeth change, too?"

Jenny swats a hand over her mouth. How frustrating to be self-conscious about her body! What a thing to be around humans. She has absorbed so many of their habits!

Zeke reaches forward and touches her wrist. She lets him pry her hand from her jaw. He tilts his head from one side to the other as he examines her sharp teeth. "Beautiful," he murmurs. "Amazing." Jenny realizes he's looking at her fingers. Did he see her remove the green layer of skin? He traces the webbing between her thumb and forefinger.

Jenny shivers.

"I want to ask questions about where you've been, what you've seen, for as long as you'll answer them." His eyes meet hers. "But why in the world would you have any interest in me? I'm, like, what, a talking cake to you?"

She brushes her hand across his cheek. It's so warm. "I just like you."

He smirks. "Oh, did I seduce you with my natural charm?"

"And your eyes." She tries on the same smile. "And the fact you do look tasty."

Zeke exhales. "What if you get so hungry, you decide you really do want to eat me one day?"

"Ezekiel Fuego-Eckstein," she enunciates. "As long as you live, I'll honor your heart and body with the best of intentions. And when your life passes from your body, I can honor you once again by—" She hesitates.

"Eating my remains," he finishes. He closes his eyes and she realizes he's thinking about it. When she's sure he will be like that for hours, he opens them again. "All right."

She chokes on the air. "You're certain?"

"No. But I want you, you want me, and if that means your version of forever is devouring me when I'm gone, okay."

"In many years! You may change your mind," she says quickly. "A long, long time from now!"

Zeke's face goes wicked. "Or next year, if I get into a terrible accident involving a runaway tiger—"

"No!" She laughs but she feels a great, terrible sadness.

"—or if my thesis kills me—"

"I will fight it for you," she says, wondering if a thesis is a land animal or from the water. Is it as nasty as Elspeth was?

Now he looks at her sadly. "I know one thing, and it's that you're going to outlive me. When I go, take the parts with me you can keep, all the words that leave good things in your memories. All the particles of my body you can carry in your own flesh."

Jenny puts aside her desire to cry. Folds it up with every other piece of her life she keeps inside herself. Instead, she kisses him, warm and sweet, as the Atlantic murmurs nearby.

They curl up and move together, Zeke laughing as sand sticks to his thighs. It scratches Jenny and she doesn't care. She lifts her dress and mounts him. When she presses against him, he gives a great, shuddering sigh. They kiss and he gives her a gentle bite that makes her bark out a laugh.

They stay together like that for a long time. When they pull apart, she feels briefly empty. Sweat clings to their skin and the morning sun warms them.

Zeke asks, "Do you think your friend's okay?"

"Clyde? I think he needs to be on his own for a while."

"Are you going to find him? Tell him what happened to the satyr woman?"

"When he's ready, he'll find the waterways. He'll find me. I'll tell him." She swallows. "And if he wants to know more, we'll find my mother again."

"I hope you find her easily. That place was. Well." He rubs his arm. "I don't think that was our world."

"No. It was all her own, I think." She looks to him. "If you want to see her again, we can ask."

"I go where you go, Jenny."

"Good. What do you want to do?"

"I think I'm hungry?"

They leave the beach and cross the parking lot. Soon, he spots a diner near a bus station where he can sit and eat. She watches him, holds his hand beneath the table as the shore sighs nearby. He leans over to kiss her. Then they are still, sitting in that moment so that it feels long, permanent. All things will return to the sea one day. Eventually, so will she.

But not yet.

THE END

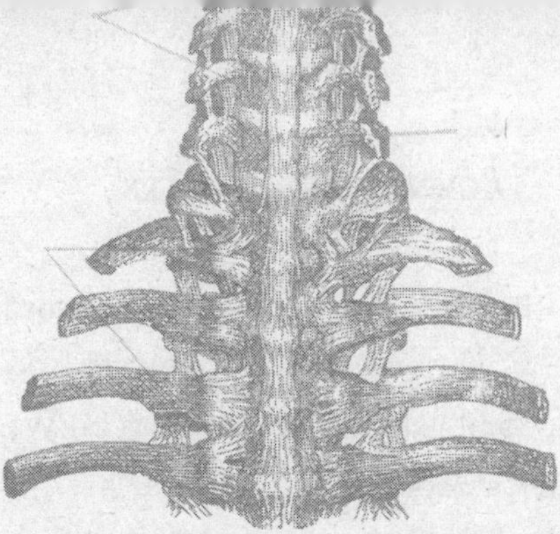

ACKNOWLEDGMENTS

I want to begin with thanking my enthusiastic, savvy, and inexhaustible literary agent, Jenna Satterthwaite. Thank you for plucking this book out of your query pile and deciding to fight for it. I'm so happy you're in my corner.

To my editor, Kimberly Laws, working with you is a joy. Thank you for your thoughtful words and help in bringing this book to life. I appreciate the hard work of the entire Gallery team, particularly Jamie Selzer, Kelli McAdams, Julia Jacintho, and Jennifer Bergstrom.

I have nothing but endless gratitude to the members of B-Spec, a writing group that has helped shape my work and given me so much happiness. This includes Lyndsay Ely, Kyle W. Kerr, Jess Barber, Lauren Barrett, Kat Black, Elizabeth (E.A.) Brenner, Andrea Martinez Corbin, Clare Fitzgerald, Victoria Sandbrook Flynn, Julia Gilstein, Stacy Gordon, Michael Hilborn, Eric Mulder, Jay O'Connell, Caleb Slowinski, Emily Strong, Caitlin Walsh, Rae Zakuta, and others who have come and gone over the years. Special shout-out to Tristam Chad Chadwick III (aka Trip), our resident party ghost who I'm sure is deeply disappointed whenever we go to bed on time or fail to drink to excess.

Thank you, Cambridge SF Workshop (CSFW), for helping to make me a better, sharper writer.

My gratitude to the Boston Horror Society for helping me find and see fictional horror, the Boston chapter of the Democratic Socialists of America for helping me stand up to the real thing, and the Studying Up Book Club for helping me better understand it.

RIP Zoe's Diner, a staple of Harvard Square whose closure officially dates this novel to pre-2024. Thank you for the inspiration.

To the Clarion Writing Workshop (UCSD) Class of 2011, I was on a path away from writing and y'all pulled me back to the beauty and satisfaction of it.

Special thanks to Sarah Caughey for being my writing partner while finishing her master's degree. I always welcome your company, not to mention the many meals you have made for us over the years. The whiskey is always good, too! May David Bowie always look down and smile upon you.

April Grant, thank you for being a fellow monster enthusiast and early reader. Your artistic accomplishments, like you, are wonderful. Nathan Comstock, your excitement for this novel came at a time I really needed it. Arrin Kaplan, Cat Scully, and Steve Berman, thank you for encouraging me not to give up on it.

Mom and Dad, you're my bedrock. To my brother, Richard, thank you for always calling.

I want to thank many friends, family members, colleagues, and comrades I've known, but I think everyone will understand that I'll end by thanking Brisbane, a charming cat and a terrible writing assistant. Never change. I'm so happy I adopted you after I had to say goodbye to a previous feline companion, Lionel. Thank you to cats everywhere for making life better and more hilarious.

ABOUT THE AUTHOR

Gillian Daniels's poetry and short fiction have appeared in Nightmare Magazine, Strange Horizons, and Beneath Ceaseless Skies, among more than thirty other publications. She was born in Des Moines, Iowa, grew up in Greater Cleveland, Ohio, and she now writes, works, and haunts the streets in the Boston area of Massachusetts. She also makes comics and zines, searches out little-known horror and indie movies, and definitely wants to see pictures of your cat. This is her first novel.